THE KING

A. RIVERS

To Kate and Caroline
For helping me make this story what it is.

Prologue - 7 years earlier

Willow

Was this what a broken heart felt like? This strange, splitting sensation in my chest?

Tears streamed down my cheeks as I perched on the edge of my father's desk, barely able to see the familiar row of vintage guns through my blurred vision.

I was an idiot. Such a monumental idiot.

I should have known better than to think a guy like Emmett had really been interested in me, but I'd been flattered by his attention and gone along with it.

So naïve.

Now, all I wanted was a hug from my dad, but according to his personal assistant, Sonia, he was in a meeting. She'd ushered me into his office and told me I could wait for him here. I think she hadn't wanted to deal with my tears. Especially not where I could disturb the employees. My father ran a security company with dozens of staff who were too busy protecting others to have time for a teenage girl's hysterics.

I wouldn't want them to see me like this anyway. It was far too humiliating.

The door swung open, and I jolted in surprise.

"Can I have a word with you, Frank? It's about the Walton account." The man looked up, and his smooth voice broke off when he realized it wasn't my dad sitting at the desk. "Oh, Willow. Hello. I was just looking for your father."

I stared at him, momentarily unable to speak. Ronan King, the hottest man in the universe, had always had that effect on me. He had thick brown hair, a strong nose, and a delicious five o'clock shadow Emmett and the other high school boys could only dream of. Something fizzed in my stomach, and tingles spread over my skin. But then the sensation soured when I remembered that I was sitting on the edge of Dad's desk with puffy eyes and mascara-stained cheeks. This seriously could not get any worse.

I hunched inward. "Hi."

He glanced at the door then back at me, probably wondering whether to leave. "I should…" He trailed off as fresh tears sprang to my eyes. "Are you okay?"

I shook my head, my face burning with embarrassment. I'd been intrigued by Ronan ever since he'd come to work for Dad when he was fresh out of college five years ago, and this wasn't the way I wanted him to see me.

He took a reluctant step into the office. "Can I, uh, get you a glass of water?"

"Yes, please." At least it would give me something to focus on other than him.

He left the room, and I stared at the row of guns while I waited for him to come back.

Remington, Winchester, Savage, Smith & Wesson.

I knew them by heart and could shoot better than most of the guys my age. But I could also hold my own on a ballroom floor. My socialite mother may have died years ago, but she'd made sure I was equipped for the life she'd dreamed of me having.

When Ronan returned, he passed me a glass of water. "Are you okay here by yourself?"

"Yes," I muttered, not making eye contact. "Thanks for the water."

"No problem." He moved toward the door.

"Ronan," I started, but I couldn't think of what to say. "Never mind. Sorry."

My shoulders slumped. I hated him seeing what a mess I was, but I also didn't want to be alone.

He turned back to me. His expression was patient, but I could tell he was uncomfortable. "Something is clearly bothering you." He paced over to the plush sofa in front of the window. Chicago sprawled behind him through the glass. "Want to talk about it?"

"Not really."

"Do you want to talk about the weather, then? Because I don't feel like I can leave you alone when you're so upset. I had a quick look for your dad while I was out there, but he's in a meeting."

"I know. Sonia already told me."

"So." He cocked his head. "The sunshine is great today, isn't it?"

Despite myself, I laughed. I doubted Ronan ever got outside the office during daylight hours. Dad was always saying what a reliable worker he was—something that annoyed my brother, Tom, who held a similar position at Lennox Securities, to no end.

"It's nice," I agreed. We sat in silence for a few moments, then I sighed, realizing he wasn't going anywhere. "It's nothing serious," I told him. "You don't have to worry."

His eyebrows drew together. "If it's enough to make you cry, then it matters. But you don't have to tell me. I'll keep you company until Frank finishes with his meeting."

I huffed. "You don't need to do that. It's just boy trouble."

A flicker of something flashed through his gaze—probably regret at being stuck discussing boys with his boss's daughter. "I'm sorry to hear that."

It wasn't much of a response, but now that I'd started talking, more words seemed to spill out of me. "I overheard my prom date saying he wouldn't have asked me to go with him if I wasn't from a rich family." I rolled my eyes as though it didn't hurt. "I don't know why it surprised me. I should have known someone like him wouldn't be interested in someone like me."

Ronan scoffed. "He sounds like an asshole."

My mouth dropped open. I hadn't really expected him to say anything, let alone that.

"The number in your father's bank account shouldn't matter," he continued. "It's what's in your heart that counts, and from what I can tell, yours is too kind to waste on someone like that."

The organ in question sped up, and my palms were clammy. "Uh, thanks?"

He shot me a look. "If the guy can't see your value, then you should ditch him. Go back out there and find someone who deserves you."

My lower lip quivered. "But prom is tomorrow."

He shrugged. "If you can't find anyone who'll treat you right, then go with your best girlfriend. You have one of those, right?"

I nodded, my thoughts wandering to Sage Nichols. She was going with the guy who ran the audiovisual booth for the drama club and who worshipped the ground she walked on. They'd gladly have me as a third wheel. In fact, I didn't think I'd even look for another date—although I'd definitely kick Emmett to the curb.

I wiped away the remnants of my tears and gazed at

Ronan. His thoughtful words had just set the new standard for men in my life, and I wasn't sure any high school boy could live up to them.

"Willow." The sound of my father's voice drew my attention to the doorway.

"Hi, Dad."

He scanned my face, his forehead furrowing with concern. "What's wrong, sweetheart?"

"Just some school stuff." I glanced at Ronan. "I'm actually feeling much better about it now."

Dad smiled. "I'm glad to hear it. Why don't you come here and give your old man a hug anyway?"

I happily threw myself into his strong embrace. He smelled faintly of cigarettes—a habit he'd never managed to kick—and his shoulders were broad enough to carry the weight of my world. Ronan may have been the subject of my unrequited crush, but Dad would always be the most important man in my life.

ONE

Present Day

WILLOW

I peeked through the slit between the door and frame.

Still no sign of him.

He'd left his office five minutes ago, but I wanted to make sure he was well and truly gone for the night before I ventured out of my hiding place.

I adjusted my position among the mops and vacuum cleaners, wishing there were somewhere I could sit. I'd been standing for hours. Still, I could continue for several more if I needed to because this cupboard had a prime view of Ronan King's office on the top floor of the building that housed his company, King's Security. The cupboard also had a clear line of sight up and down the well-lit but now empty corridor.

I needed to move soon, though. I'd stolen a cleaner's outfit and snuck in during work hours, but the real cleaning staff would arrive soon, and I couldn't risk them finding me here and reporting me.

I wondered what the penalty would be for trespassing. I probably should have looked that up before now. But considering the stakes—saving my family's company—it was worth the risk.

Something tickled my nostril and I swiped at it, fighting the urge to sneeze.

It tickled again.

I sucked in a breath.

Don't sneeze, don't sneeze, don't sneeze.

I sneezed.

The sound echoed in the tiny space, and I froze, my heart galloping in my chest. What if someone had heard? The office floor seemed deserted, but that didn't mean it actually was. I counted under my breath as the seconds passed. Nothing stirred. When I reached thirty, I decided I was safe.

I eased the door open and tiptoed into the hall. There was nobody in sight. Still, I didn't relax. That would have been a mistake. Instead, I hurried toward Ronan's office. It was locked. Entrance could only be granted by inputting a number into a keypad. Fortunately, I'd seen the passcode earlier and typed it now, releasing a sharp breath when the door clicked open without an alarm going off. I had no doubt I was being recorded, but as long as I was able to get in and out before building security arrived, then I didn't care. I was confident the office was dim enough that seeing the details of my face would be near impossible.

I switched on the flashlight app on my phone and went straight to the heavy oak desk. With the aid of the extra illumination, I scanned the surface. It was mostly clear.

I pulled open a drawer and sifted through the papers inside. Invoices and records. I made a sound of exasperation in the back of my throat. Ronan was up to something. He'd been sniffing around Lennox Securities for weeks— contacting minor shareholders and asking questions that made me nervous. I was afraid he was working toward a hostile takeover. I needed to know for sure.

I glanced at his computer. There was a single monitor with cords connected to a laptop. Maybe what I needed was on the computer, but I hoped not because I hadn't managed to decipher his password during my earlier spying.

I checked another drawer and came up empty. My eyes traveled back to the computer.

Couldn't hurt to try.

I touched a glove-clad finger to the mousepad and the screen lit up, requesting a password to access the desktop. There was pretty much no chance I'd be able to guess correctly, but I might as well take a shot. I clicked into the box and entered his birthday, which I remembered because of my crazy infatuation with him when I was younger.

It didn't work. Of course not.

I tried a couple of other options in quick succession but stopped when a warning popped up, advising that I'd be locked out of the system after one more failed attempt.

Abandoning the computer, I opened the bottom drawer and dropped to my knees to look inside. It was while I was on the floor, the desk obscuring my view through the office door, that I heard footsteps rapidly approaching.

My blood turned to ice. I dove for cover beneath the desk, only realizing when I got there that I'd left the drawer open. I inched forward and started sliding it shut but stopped when an ominous click sounded in the silent room. I recognized that click. Whoever had entered had a gun. I was in trouble.

"Come out with your hands up."

I closed my eyes as relief washed over me. I knew that voice. Ronan had come back. I was reasonably sure he wouldn't shoot me, but I didn't move. Perhaps if I was quiet, he'd think he'd been imagining things. It was nearly dark in here. There was a chance he wouldn't see me or notice the open drawer.

"I know I locked the door," he said, his tone arch. "And my computer is wired to alert me if someone tampers with it. Either you come out, or I'll come to you. Your choice."

I pressed my fists to my forehead and bit back a curse. He'd caught me. What would happen now? Would he call the police? He wouldn't take kindly to me being here, that was for sure.

I weighed my options. I could stay here and wait for him to drag me out, or I could do as he said and maintain a sliver of dignity.

Pride won out. Lennoxes did not quiver in the corner, no matter how many odds were stacked against them.

I shuffled out from beneath the desk and scrambled to my feet with as much grace as I could muster. I tossed my head back and met his furious gaze. But the sight of a handgun pointed at my chest made me falter. He wouldn't use it on me, would he? No matter how much he hated anyone with the last name Lennox these days, he wouldn't shoot an unarmed woman.

The clench in my gut wasn't only fear though. However angry he might be, Ronan was a fine specimen of a man. If he'd been appealing at twenty-eight, he was magnificent at thirty-five. Pure masculine beauty with luscious hair, unfathomable eyes, and his sleeves rolled up to reveal the tattoos on one forearm that usually remained hidden beneath his suit.

He frowned at my uniform. "You're not the cleaner."

I contemplated saying I was filling in for the night, but he wouldn't believe me. "I'm not," I agreed.

"Do you have a weapon?" he asked.

"No." I let my hands fall to my sides so he could see I was no threat to him. At least, not physically.

He lowered the gun. "Who do you work for? Start talking."

I blinked. My lips parted.

He didn't recognize me.

I'd just assumed he'd know me on sight, but he had no idea. The irony was glorious. I'd spent years dreaming of him, whereas he may as well never have seen me before today. If I weren't so scared, I'd have been pissed.

"Ronan, it's me. Willow." At his blank look, I continued, "Willow Lennox."

His eyes widened, and he raked his gaze over me from head to toe. "Willow? Shit. You look different in that getup."

I winced. Given the situation, I had more pressing concerns than how unflattering the uniform was, but I still had a fleeting moment of regret that it was our first time speaking in years and he was seeing me at my worst.

His eyes narrowed. "What the hell are you doing here? And don't tell me you're cleaning because I won't buy it for a second."

I took a deep breath and stood my ground even though my pulse had ratcheted up so much that I could hear it in my ears. "You're planning something with Lennox Securities, and I want to know what."

RONAN

She had guts; I'd give her that. Not many people would have been brave enough to stare me down the way she was. I wondered how it was possible that this feisty woman could be the same sophisticated socialite I'd seen with Tom at charity galas and high-society events. But despite the outfit, I could tell her slender body curved in all the right places, and her moss-green eyes glimmered with emotion.

She may have looked different than she had at those events, but not necessarily worse. This version of Willow Lennox felt real in a way that her untouchable princess façade never could. Whenever I saw her in public, she held herself distant, as though her mind were someplace else. Now she was very much in the moment.

"So you thought you'd break into my office to find out?" I kept my tone light, not letting on how much it had thrown me to find her here. I couldn't afford anything going wrong when I was so close to wresting control of Lennox Securities from Tom—a man who didn't deserve his father's legacy.

"Yes, I did." She maintained eye contact. "Clearly, I didn't think it all the way through, but the idea was solid. So, are you going to tell me?"

I laughed at her sheer audacity. It impressed the hell out of me. I remembered her as a sweet girl. A little spoiled, but good-natured. It seemed I wasn't the only one who'd changed.

"I think you already know what I'm planning."

She deflated. "A hostile takeover."

I hated the pang her dejection caused in my chest. Beautiful or not, I couldn't let myself feel anything for her. There wasn't a female less suited to me in all of Chicago. "You won't find any evidence of that in here."

"Of course not." She pursed her lips. "I should have realized you'd have everything on an encrypted cloud server or something along those lines. But I'm still not sure how you plan to go about it. Even if you managed to buy *all* of the shares not in the Lennox family, you'd still have less than half of the company."

I didn't react to her statement, although it was interesting to know she was unaware her brother had sold some of his shares. "Did Tom send you?"

Tom now headed up Lennox Securities, which had

been on a slippery downward spiral since he'd inherited the business after Frank passed away six years ago. Meanwhile, King's Security, which I'd established soon after leaving Lennox Securities, had been steadily on the rise. The two companies dealt with similar corporate clients, but King's Security also offered bodyguard services and cyber security solutions that Lennox Securities did not.

When she didn't reply, I took it as a silent affirmation and gestured to one of the chairs. "Sit."

She crossed her arms. "No, thank you. I'd rather stand."

"Suit yourself."

I strode past her and dropped onto my executive chair. The faint scent of vanilla tickled my nostrils. From her perfume or body lotion? I suddenly regretted my choice to move. It had been a power play, but I hadn't counted on how her nearness would affect me.

"Are you going to call the police?" she asked, backing away a couple of steps and glancing at the door. She didn't try to run. She must have known it was pointless.

I considered the question. The idea had a certain appeal. Ever since Tom had fired me shortly after Frank's death, there wasn't much I liked more than getting under his skin. He'd be distraught if his precious sister were arrested. But it would be wrong of me to make Willow pay for her brother's actions. Yes, she'd broken the law, but she'd done it out of loyalty to her family, and I respected that. I also couldn't help admiring her backbone in standing up to me, and her cleverness in managing to get inside my office in the first place.

"I don't think I will," I said finally. "But I have you on camera, and I'll be showing your photograph to the guards at the door. If you come anywhere near here again, I'll send the recording to the police."

She gasped. "You're blackmailing me?"

I hid a grin behind my hand. "I'm giving you a good reason not to break any more laws."

Her teeth sank into her lower lip. I wanted to tell her to stop. That her flesh was too tender to abuse like that, but I kept my mouth shut.

"Fine," she snapped, her eyes sparking with temper. "I'll stay away. You've told me all I need to know anyway."

"We're in agreement then. I'll escort you out of the building."

"Don't you trust me?" she demanded.

"Not a bit."

To my surprise, she fell silent. Her gaze lowered to her shoes. "Look, Ronan, Lennox Securities is all we have left of Dad. I know Tom made things difficult for you after Dad's death, but coming after the company isn't right. Tom isn't the only one you'd be hurting. Think of the employees."

"If something such as a takeover were to happen, I'm sure they'd be taken care of." Contrary to what she believed, I'd given it some thought. I'd even looked into the employees closely enough to know she held a marketing and communications position within the firm.

Her eyes shone with what I feared were tears. "Lennox Securities should be run by a Lennox."

Please don't cry.

I sent up a prayer to the universe. Women's tears weren't something I'd ever been comfortable with. Especially not when the woman in question was stunningly beautiful and more loyal to the Lennox name than her brother deserved.

"This isn't personal," I told her.

"Yes, it is." She sighed. "The company is the mark that Dad left on Chicago, and that means something to me. You're trying to erase the last piece of him I have left."

Her words were a punch in the gut. I shot to my feet,

my jaw clenched in anger. "Why would I want to do that? Your father was the only man who ever believed in me. Your brother is the one harming Frank's reputation. In my hands, the company could become the success it used to be."

"It could still be successful if not for you stealing our clients," she retorted.

"Stealing them?" I snorted in disbelief. "They come looking for me when Tom lets them down."

"You're unbelievable." She shook her head. "I should never have come here." She started toward the exit. I followed close behind. "You seriously don't have to walk me out. I'm leaving."

"Consider it me being a gentleman." Even if that were far from the truth. If Willow thought there was something in this building she could use to save Lennox Securities, I had no doubt she would.

I accompanied her to the elevator. She huffed in displeasure as I got into the box with her and pushed the button for the ground floor.

"You're not how I remember," she said as we moved downward.

"Neither are you," I replied. "How are you getting home?"

She rolled her eyes. "Seriously? I broke into your office and you're worried about making sure I get home safely?"

I shrugged. "Dangers of the job."

"I'm walking."

"Oh?" I'd never have imagined the Lennox princess walking anywhere. "Is your place nearby?"

Her gaze skittered away. "Not too far."

My eyes narrowed. I didn't like the way she'd answered. "I'll have my driver take you home."

"Absolutely not. You're being ridiculous."

I counted to five in my head and wondered what I'd

done to deserve being stuck with this stubborn woman, even if it were temporary. "Accept the ride. Consider it me making sure you don't come back."

I could tell from the glint in her eye that she wanted to push me. "How do I know your driver isn't going to stuff me in the trunk?"

"I guess you'll have to trust me."

"Ha." But she didn't argue again. I dialed my personal driver's number and summoned him. "You're so used to getting your own way."

"Willow," I warned, and I could see all the smartass replies she wanted to make flash through her mind, but she wisely stayed quiet.

The elevator reached the ground floor, and we disembarked. I escorted her to the street, where my car was idling by the curb, and watched to make sure she got inside before returning to the office. As I did, I smiled to myself. Willow Lennox was unexpected, and I liked it.

Chapter Two

WILLOW

I scowled as the driver escorted me into my apartment building. "This really isn't necessary."

Although I didn't mind it as much as I should have because I had the strangest sensation that someone was watching me as we'd gotten out of the car. The back of my neck prickled, and a jitter ran down my spine.

But I was being paranoid. Nobody was there.

And now the driver would be able to report back on my living situation to Ronan. It was the kind of intel my brother's enemy would no doubt love to have.

Willow Lennox, reduced to living in the kind of apartment her father would have hated to see her in.

Not that there was anything wrong with it. In fact, I was proud to pay for it using my own hard-earned money. But it had nothing on the penthouse where we'd lived when Dad had been alive. Unfortunately, Tom had gotten his hands on my trust fund after Dad had passed, and while I'd had enough left to get through college, there wasn't anything remaining for a better home.

"I was instructed to see you safely inside, and that

means all the way to your apartment." The driver puffed as we ascended the stairs. My place was on the third floor, and while there was an elevator, I usually took the stairs because it made me feel less guilty about not having a gym membership.

"Nobody is going to mug me in here," I assured him as we strode up the corridor. I stopped outside my apartment and withdrew a key from my purse. "I'm here safely."

He gave me a look that said he wouldn't leave until I was shut inside. Despite myself, I admired the man's dedication to doing exactly as his boss had ordered. Loyalty could be a rare commodity.

I let myself in and locked the apartment door behind me, relieved to escape that sense of being watched.

"Willow!" Sage appeared from her bedroom, her hip-length chestnut-brown hair swaying as she hurried over to scoop me into an embrace. "I've been sending you positive energy through meditation. How did it go?"

I sat with her on the sofa and told her everything, starting with my attempt to find what I needed in Ronan's desk and ending with his driver escorting me home.

"He was different from how I remember him," I told her. "He pretty much admitted what he has planned and didn't seem to care at all about the damage it might do. He made me so angry."

"It's been years," she reminded me. "People change. Especially when they've gone through as much as he has."

"Still." I shivered. "It's hard to process that the man I spent years half in love with is the one who's trying to tear my family legacy apart." I buried my face in my palms. "What am I going to do?"

Her hand smoothed up and down my back. "Perhaps it wouldn't be such a bad thing if he took over," she said gently. "You could pursue your art full time."

I released something that could have been either a

laugh or a sob. "I'm not good enough to be a proper artist. I like to play with watercolors, but I'm nothing special. I'd be broke in no time."

Painting was a pipe dream. A beautiful one, but unrealistic. I was no better at art than any other rich girl who'd had private tutoring.

"I don't think so." Sage touched a fingertip to my forehead—the part she liked to call the third eye despite the fact she knew it freaked me out to envision another eyeball there. "You don't have enough faith in yourself."

"It doesn't matter anyway. Saving Lennox Securities is what's important. Protecting my dad's memory and keeping the family together. At least, what's left of it."

"Willow, do you think—"

My phone rang, cutting her off, and I was grateful for the distraction, right up until I saw who it was.

Tom.

"Don't answer," Sage urged. "Let him stew for a bit. He takes it for granted that you'll put yourself on the line to fix his problems when he won't risk his own neck to do it."

But I answered the call. Tom might have been troubled, but he was my only family, and that meant something.

"Did you find anything?" he demanded, sounding as though he was teetering on the edge of panic.

"No, but—"

He sighed loudly. "Did you at least get in and out without anyone seeing you?"

"Um, about that."

"What happened?"

"He caught me."

"Shit. Did he call the cops?"

"No, thank God. But he didn't deny he's planning a takeover."

Tom groaned. "Hell. I was afraid of that."

"Me, too. What now?" I asked. "Is there something we can do to stop him? Surely there's no way he can be successful since you have a majority share."

"We don't know what else King has up his sleeve," he said. "He wouldn't make a move on our minor shareholders without something solid. Don't worry, I'm putting steps in place to protect us."

"What kind of steps?" I needed specifics. Tom was good at making promises that didn't pan out.

"I can't tell you, but I will soon."

"Uh-huh. I hope you know what you're doing."

"I've got this."

His words didn't make me feel any better. "See you tomorrow?"

"Yeah." His tone was brusque. "See you then."

The call ended, and I couldn't help but shiver. Tom and his schemes made me nervous. I could only hope he wouldn't do more harm than good.

Sage took my hand. "I'm going to do the forgiveness practice tonight, and you should too. I don't want you bottling up all those negative emotions from dealing with Ronan and Tom."

"Maybe I will."

I doubted it.

Sage had shown me how to do the practice, which was supposed to cleanse your emotional wounds, but sometimes I'd rather stick a Band-Aid on the problem and pretend it wasn't there.

Chapter Three

My encounter with Willow Lennox was fresh in my mind when I met with my two business partners in one of King's Security's conference rooms the following day.

"What's going on?" Kade Campbell asked as he dropped his massive frame onto a chair that looked ridiculously small by comparison. Even sitting, he was taller than some people and twice as broad across the shoulders.

"King had an unexpected guest," Zeke said with a sly smile. Ezekiel Watts, the head of our cyber operations, always knew things five minutes before anyone else. He'd probably been aware of Willow shortly after I was.

Kade's brows rose. "Trouble?"

"Possibly," Zeke mused. "Certainly intriguing."

I sat opposite the two men and looked at each in turn. "Willow Lennox broke into my office last night."

Kade jolted. "Tom Lennox's sister?"

"Yes. She was looking for evidence that we're intending to take over their company."

Zeke laughed. "She didn't find it, of course."

"She didn't," I confirmed. "But the cat's out of the bag anyway."

Zeke shrugged. "Not the end of the world. With the way things are going, Tom won't be able to stop us no matter how much forewarning he has."

"I've never met Willow," Kade said. "But I've heard she's really something."

"If you like the ice queen type," Zeke replied derisively.

I internally disagreed. From what I'd seen of her last night, Willow was anything but cold. Perhaps she wore her untouchable princess persona as protection.

"Whatever she is, it doesn't change anything." Kade crossed his arms over his chest, his biceps bulging in ways that mine never would. While I was no slouch, Kade could be The Rock's lovechild with Arnold Schwarzenegger.

"No, it doesn't." I couldn't let myself regret the fact she was going to be collateral damage.

Zeke cleared his throat. "Actually, maybe it could. I have an idea if you'd like to hear it."

I nodded, always interested to know what was going on in his devious mind. "Go on."

"First, tell me more about the girl. I looked her up after she left, so I have the basics."

I suspected he knew far more than the basics. Zeke's version of "looking someone up" was a greater invasion of privacy than a police background check. Kade and I exchanged glances. "What do you know?"

"She's twenty-five," he replied. "Works for the family company. Has a degree in fine arts, with a preference for painting. Lives with Sage Nichols, a yoga instructor and online lifestyle influencer."

Kade scoffed, not a fan of anything even remotely woo-woo.

"But what is she like?" Zeke asked, leaning forward.

"As a person, I mean. She comes across as very distant, but that perception isn't consistent with a woman who'd sneak into your office to go through your private files." He fell silent, and both men gave me their full attention.

"Yesterday was the first time I've spoken to her in years," I told them. "She was a sweet kid." I hesitated, remembering the time I'd encountered her in her father's office, in tears because of her idiot prom date. "Frank doted on her, but she wasn't selfish."

"By all accounts, not a bad person," Zeke said. "With a rap sheet purer than a nun's. Not so much as a parking ticket."

"What's your point?" Kade demanded. He knew this was going somewhere, as did I, but neither of us was sure where. That was the trouble with Zeke. You never knew what was coming until he wanted you to.

"We should employ her."

My jaw dropped. "Are you crazy? No, it's not happening. Even if, for some insane reason, we wanted her here, she'd never agree to it."

Zeke held up a hand. "Slow down for a moment and just think it through." He rubbed his knuckles along his scruffy jaw. "How much would it kill Tom to know his sister worked for you?"

Kade groaned. "He's finally lost his last fucking marble."

Zeke had a point though. I wanted Tom to regret everything he'd ever done or said to me, and for someone with a lot of pride, knowing his own blood had defected to the other side would be a bitter pill to swallow.

Kade's eyes widened as I considered the idea. "You can't be taking this seriously. You'd use the poor girl to settle a score?"

Put like that, I didn't like the sound of it, but I had to admit, the idea appealed more than it should have. It was ruthless. Manipulative. And Tom Lennox wouldn't be able to do a thing about it.

"It's not the worst idea you've ever had," I said to Zeke. "But why would she agree to work for us? She's completely loyal to Lennox Securities."

Zeke raised a brow. "So use that against her. Tell her you'll consider stopping the takeover if she works for you for, say, a month."

There was just one problem with that. "I have no intention of stopping the takeover. I don't want to see Tom run Frank's company into the ground, and that's exactly what will happen if he keeps on the way he is now."

"So don't," Zeke countered. "Just tell her you'll think about it and take the chance to torment him a bit."

The possibility tempted me. Not only because of what it would do to Tom but because I liked Willow. She intrigued me, and I wanted to see more of her. I admired her spirit and respected her loyalty to her family legacy. But if Frank Lennox had taught me anything, it was the importance of honor in business. I couldn't lie to her.

"No," I decided. "If I do this, and at the end of a month she can't see how much better off her family's company would be in my hands, then I'll go after Tom another way. He's up to his neck in something shady, I'm sure of it. We just need to find evidence."

Kade looked at the ceiling and muttered something under his breath. My old friend had never been good at subterfuge. He preferred a full-frontal assault with none of the sneaky stuff that Zeke excelled at. "I don't want any innocent bystanders to be hurt," he said. "That includes the sister. I'll stand with you, but the moment that girl gets caught in the crossfire, I'm out."

I nodded. "I respect that."

Zeke stood and slipped his hands into the pockets of his faded black jeans. Although he was a genius by any scale, he looked more like a rock star who'd lost his way to a concert. The moment he'd been officially cleared from duty, he'd gotten full-body tattoos and several piercings, so there was no way he could ever blend into a crowd again. It meant we couldn't use him in the field because he was so recognizable, but it also meant his former employer couldn't snatch him back because his appearance would be a liability. They preferred their operatives to be nondescript.

"I'll get my guys digging into Tom," Zeke said. "Meanwhile, you think about how we want to play this. Willow may have useful information."

"She might." I'd already had that thought.

Kade rolled his shoulders back, his forehead creased with worry. "You two are asking for trouble."

Chapter Four

Willow

"Just. Like. That." I shifted a piece of text on our latest advertising campaign and smiled. "Perfect."

Lennox Securities needed more customers. Many of the ones who'd been loyal for years were slowly defecting to King's Security, and we weren't plugging the gaps fast enough. Managing the company's communications didn't always keep me busy, so I'd taken to working on marketing campaigns during quiet periods. My phone vibrated, and the strains of Vivaldi broke the silence. I frowned when I didn't recognize the number but answered the call.

"Hello, Willow." It was a woman's voice. "This is Fiona from King's Security. I'm Ronan King's assistant."

"Oh?" My heart gave a little leap. "How did you get this number?"

"I assumed you'd given it to us."

"No, I definitely did not."

Fiona sighed. "In that case, I have my suspicions but I really can't say anything. Confidentiality, you understand."

No, I didn't. Had they obtained my details illegally? Or perhaps they'd just asked someone I knew? It wasn't as though my number was a state secret, but I guarded it more closely than the average person might.

"Why are you calling?" Ronan and I hadn't exactly ended our encounter on good terms.

"Mr. King would like to arrange a meeting with you as soon as possible. Can you come over now?"

"Huh." Perhaps my words had gotten through to him. Or maybe he'd changed his mind and decided to hand me over to the police after all. If he'd been the one breaking into my office, I'd probably have called 911 within the first twenty seconds, regardless of anything he might have said. "Do you know what it's about?"

"I don't, sorry." She sounded genuinely apologetic, so I couldn't be annoyed at her. "I was asked to contact you. That's as much as I know."

With what Ronan had on me, I couldn't afford to turn him down in case he retaliated. My frustration grew. I felt so powerless. "Fine, I'll be there, but I'm at work so I'll have to let my boss know first."

I reported directly to Tom, which I didn't think was appropriate, but he'd claimed a Lennox shouldn't sit beneath anyone other than another Lennox. I had a feeling Dad might have agreed with him, so I went along with it.

"When you arrive, tell them to show you through to me, and if Ronan is busy then we'll slot you in as soon as he's free. Do you know where we're located?"

"Yes." My cheeks flamed as I realized this must be the woman I'd seen at the desk outside Ronan's office yesterday. I also remembered what he'd said about making sure it wouldn't happen again. "Um, does security know I'm coming?"

"Mr. King has given orders for them to let you through." Her tone was amused. "You won't have any problems. See you soon."

I hung up and stared into space for a moment, trying

to get my thoughts in order. Was this summons a positive sign or a negative one?

I stood and made my way down the corridor to Tom's office, where I rapped softly on the door before entering.

"Oh sorry." I came up short at the sight of an elegantly dressed older man sprawled in a chair opposite my brother. Adrian Petrov. One of my dad's former business rivals, whom Tom seemed to be working with a lot lately. Rich as sin and creepy to boot. "I didn't realize you had company."

Was it too late to back out? Petrov made my skin crawl.

"Willow." Petrov rose to his feet and extended a hand. I placed mine in his, expecting a handshake, but his damp lips touched my skin. I itched to snatch my hand back. When he finally released me, I didn't dare wipe my hand on my skirt. Something told me that wouldn't go over well. "You look especially lovely today."

I glanced down at myself. Blue skirt, white blouse, and all the important bits covered. Nothing about the outfit warranted the lecherous gleam in his eye. "Thank you."

I did not want to be polite to him, but his firm sent us clients when they didn't have the capacity to handle their cases, so we owed him.

"Adrian, please," Petrov said.

I glanced at Tom, who watched the exchange with interest. "Can I speak to you for a moment?"

Tom ran a hand through his ruffled gold hair—a motion that had caused dozens of women over Chicago to swoon—and nodded. "Excuse us for a minute, Adrian."

Tom stood, his rangy frame rising to a height somewhere over six feet, and strode around the desk. He cupped my elbow and guided me out of the office, closing the door behind him.

"What is it?"

"Ronan King's assistant just called," I said. "He wants me over there ASAP."

Tom frowned. "Asshole. He's playing power games. Making a Lennox run around after him because he has leverage on you."

"Yeah, well, it's not as though I can argue with him. I'll be gone for a while, but hopefully not too long."

"Thanks for letting me know." He glanced at his Rolex. "I want to know what's happening as soon as you get back."

I nodded. "You will."

"Perhaps he's interested in you," he mused, almost to himself. "He always wanted things he couldn't have."

I could hardly rein in my disbelief. No way was that what this was about.

I opened my mouth—to say what, I didn't know—but closed it again. It wouldn't matter what I said. Once Tom had a crazy idea in his head, he wouldn't hear sense.

"Be back soon." My cheeks burned as I left him and headed for the stairwell.

By the time I'd made it down to the street, I had my embarrassment back under control. Being a Lennox meant knowing how to compartmentalize and always putting on a good face.

I took a cab to the building that housed King's Security, rode the elevator to the top, and eyeballed the security guard on my way past.

He stared me down.

I approached the receptionist and told her Fiona was expecting me.

She nodded briskly. "Hold on a moment." She dialed an extension on her phone and had a brief conversation. "She'll be here in a few minutes. Please wait over there." She gestured to a sofa.

I sat and crossed one leg over the other. I hadn't taken the time to look around when I'd been here last night, but now I studied my surroundings at leisure. Not a single mark marred the tile floor. The receptionist's desk was in perfect order—a far cry from the messy state of affairs at Lennox Securities. Art hung on the walls, and I could tell from the signatures in the bottom corners how expensive each piece must have been. I would have liked to look at them more closely, but I worried the security guard wouldn't tolerate me poking around, so I didn't budge from my position.

Before long, a statuesque redhead appeared in a doorway to the side of the reception desk. She scanned the room, and her gaze alighted on me. Some of the tension in my neck vanished. With a warm smile and a dusting of freckles, she was the kind of person who instantly put me at ease.

"Willow?" she asked.

"Yes, that's me." I stood and offered her a hand. "You must be Fiona."

"Lovely to meet you." She tilted her head toward the door. "Come right through. Good timing. Mr. King just finished a phone call, so I'll show you to his office."

I followed her down a lushly carpeted hall, past a number of rooms with glorious views over the city. Unconsciously, my shoulders hunched. This place was so much nicer than what I'd grown accustomed to since I started working for my family firm. I'd grown up around wealth, but our family money was long gone, and we'd had to downsize. We also passed the cleaning closet I'd hidden in, and I tried not to look at it.

By the time we paused outside an office labeled Ronan King, CEO, I felt well and truly out of my element. Being here during the daytime, when the place was alive with energy, felt different from my previous illicit visit. I was very conscious of the fact I didn't belong.

Fiona knocked and stuck her head around the door. "Willow is here for you, Mr. King."

"Show her in." His voice was smooth and rich but didn't give away his mood.

I entered the office and Fiona slipped away, closing the door behind herself. I looked around, better able to take in the details that I'd missed last night. The wall opposite the door was entirely glass, and the view beyond it was even more spectacular during the day than it had been at night. To the left, Ronan's desk faced out into the room, and to the right, a narrow table extended along the wall with a couple of chairs tucked beneath it—presumably for visitors.

I wandered to the glass wall and gazed out, feeling small and insignificant.

Ronan cleared his throat, and I turned back to him. He was striking—even more so than the view—and I hated the way my heart sped up at the sight of him. I'd once thought he was pretty close to perfect, and I'd never quite kicked the attraction. Today, his expression was carefully blank. The indifference somehow felt worse than the active dislike from yesterday. It made me nervous. If I couldn't read him, then I didn't know what he was planning.

"Did you change your mind?" I demanded. "Are you going to press charges?" I madly tried to think of any bargaining chips I might have, but they were pitifully few. My stomach sank.

"No. That's not why I called you here. Sit down." He gestured at the seat opposite him. "I have an idea I think you'll be interested in."

I moistened my lips, nerves crowding my stomach. Despite everything, the part of me that used to fantasize about him couldn't help but wonder what he thought of me. My skirt and blouse were more flattering than the uniform I'd been in when he'd caught me snooping. Did he like what he saw, or would I always be a little girl to him?

"I have a proposition."

Unexpected arousal jolted through me.

Don't be stupid, Willow. He doesn't mean it like that.

Although what would it be like if he did?

I was inexperienced when it came to men. I'd only met up with the ones Tom tried to set me up with, but I was never interested in them. And I didn't have the time or motivation to scope out the dating scene myself now. I'd tried when I was younger, but I was never sure if guys were interested in me or my last name and the money they thought I had. I also had a bad habit of comparing them to Ronan and they never seemed to reach the standard he'd set.

It had gotten a little depressing.

"What makes you think I want to hear it?" I asked, my voice uncharacteristically husky.

His eyes flashed with awareness. Or was that my imagination?

"Because you're smart, Willow. Much more so than Tom. Probably more than anyone gives you credit for."

There was a time I would have loved to hear him say that, but while I was flattered, his choice of words concerned me. The way he'd compared me to Tom made me wonder if he was planning to play me off against my brother.

I held eye contact. "Where are you going with this?"

"Here's my suggestion." His tone was low and rumbly. It sent a shiver through me. "Work here for a month. If, at the end of the month, you don't agree that your father's company would be better off in my hands than Tom's, then I won't take it over." He stacked his hands one on top of the other on his desk. "That simple."

"Excuse me?" What on earth was he up to? "What makes you think I'd agree to work for you?"

———

I nearly had her.

"I made the reason clear enough. You want to keep the company in the family because you think that's the best thing for it. I respect that, but I believe I'm the best person to run Lennox Securities—as an extension of King's. I think you'll come to see that too, if you give me a chance. I'm willing to take the bet."

Her nostrils flared, and I could see her warring with herself. If she were completely certain Tom was managing the company well, then she wouldn't have been struggling so much internally because it would have been a no-brainer. The fact she was watching me with mistrust showed her lack of faith in her brother, whether she realized it or not. I studied her, wondering if Tom knew she was here.

"Do you actually have work for me to do?" she asked, as though that was her biggest concern. Perhaps it was the only one she could articulate. She straightened her back, and her jaw squared in determination. Fuck, that was sexy. "I think you're playing games, but if you're not, and you're telling the truth, then you should know that I value my job, and I'm good at it. I don't want to leave Lennox Securities —even temporarily—just to run errands and get coffee. If this is about humiliating me, fine, but come out and say it."

I smiled, enjoying her spark. "It's not. We don't have any social media, and I've been meaning to arrange for someone to set up accounts and build a following but I haven't gotten to it yet."

It was true, although I could've happily left it for another year or so. We got plenty of clients by word of mouth—especially once Tom had burned them.

Her lips pressed together. "Okay, yeah. I could do that. But don't you want to hear my qualifications?"

I raised a brow. "I already know them."

Her eyes widened in surprise, but then she nodded. "I should have expected that."

She nibbled on her lip, drawing my attention to the plush pink bow of her mouth. Damn, she was beautiful when she wasn't in a cleaner's uniform. Her clothes were tidy but demure. Nice, but not designer. The exact kind of thing I'd expect from someone who worked in her position, but *not* what I'd expect from the Lennox heiress. But then, I was beginning to realize that Willow wouldn't fit neatly into any of the boxes I'd tried to assign her.

"Tom would be angry," she said. "I assume that's the real reason you want me here?"

I'd be honest with her. She deserved that much.

"I can't lie, I enjoy the thought of Tom squirming because his baby sister is working for me."

She laughed without humor. "Of course you do. But what if, at the end of the month, I were to say the company is better off with Tom? My contract here would have ended, and Tom is unlikely to forgive me for taking you up on the offer, so he might not hire me back." Her tongue darted out over her upper lip. "I could end up jobless. It would be a big risk for me."

"If you did your job well, I'd bring you on longer term," I said, even though I hadn't accounted for that and found the prospect unsettling. "If you wanted to stay, that is."

My chest burned with irritation that she'd think me capable of leaving her high and dry. But then, she didn't know me, did she? To her, I was just a man with a grudge who wanted to steal her family's company.

Her shoulders rose and fell on a deep inhale. "I'd like that in writing."

I bit back a retort. "Fair enough. Although if your work is subpar, I reserve the right to let you go."

She narrowed her eyes. "It won't be."

I hid my smile, pleased by her show of self-confidence. The glow of her pretty green eyes warmed my heart and made me wonder whether I had an ulterior motive for wanting her here. I hadn't been genuinely interested in a woman for a long time, and she intrigued me. My gaze lingered on those perfect lips. I bet she tasted delicious. For a moment, I allowed myself to wonder what would happen if I seduced her. I'd make certain she enjoyed herself. But Willow didn't seem like the kind of woman who'd agree to a fling.

"Good to know." I cleared my throat. "If you were to agree, we'd pay you well." I named a figure that I knew from Zeke's research was at least double what she earned at Lennox Securities. If Tom knew she was not only employed by his competitor, but gainfully so, it would add insult to injury.

Her eyes bugged out. "That's very generous." She quickly schooled her expression. "You can't buy my loyalty though."

I shrugged. "I'm not. We always treat our employees well."

She scowled as though she wanted to say I was lying but wasn't so sure I actually was. She swallowed, and I watched the delicate ripple of her throat, unable to shut down the part of myself that wondered how she'd smell if I were to bury my nose at her pulse point. "I'll need time to think about it."

Disappointment slammed into me, shocking in its intensity. I'd told myself to expect this. She'd want to talk things over with Tom. But I'd still hoped she'd just say yes.

"Fine, but I want an answer by the end of the day."

Chapter Five

WILLOW

I was so distracted by Ronan's offer that I almost didn't notice the man behind me. It was only after he'd followed me around the third consecutive corner on my walk back to Lennox Securities that I grew worried. I glanced over my shoulder, hoping to get a better look at him, but he was wearing a hooded sweatshirt, and his face was in shadow. That in itself wasn't unusual. There was a chill in the air, and many people were dressed warmly, but it was strange that he was making all the same turns as me.

My heart rate accelerated. Perhaps I was imagining things, but I didn't think so.

I was rapidly approaching another corner—one I didn't intend to turn—but I knew this might be my best chance to get a look at him. I darted around it and into a narrow alley between two buildings. Then I ducked behind a dumpster and peered around the edge. Sure enough, a few seconds later, the hooded guy strode past. He was glancing around as though looking for someone.

Me?

He paused at the entrance to the alley. Took a few steps forward and scanned it.

I huddled against the wall, praying he wouldn't see me or hear my breathing. But a moment later, he continued on his way, muttering to himself.

I counted to one hundred before venturing out. I couldn't see the man, and I didn't want to wait around for him to come back, so I retraced my steps until I was back on the route to Lennox Securities.

My phone rang, piercingly loud to my frantic mind, and I fumbled it out of my handbag.

It was an unknown number.

"Hello?" I asked as I accepted the call. Nobody responded. "Is someone there?"

There was a muffled thud and then the call ended.

I stared at my phone, quietly freaking out.

The call couldn't have been related to the guy following me, could it? It was just too weird. But I couldn't convince myself they were unrelated. Two strange things happening at once? I didn't think so.

I speed-walked the rest of the way to the office. The fear I'd felt put any thoughts of Ronan's offer to the back of my mind, but as soon as I was inside and feeling safer, I began to dwell on it again. I couldn't understand why he would offer a solution that seemed to be to his detriment. What did he have up his sleeve?

Still, at the end of the day, it didn't really matter if he had a secret agenda. I couldn't turn him down. He was in a position of power, and he was offering a win-win—although I wasn't sure Tom would see it that way. As much as I loved Tom, he didn't always understand that compromise was sometimes necessary to get the things we wanted. He'd been raised as the heir to the Lennox empire, and in his perspective, the world revolved around him. I'd never been in the running to take over the company. Partially because I didn't have a head for business, and partially because our father had been a little old-fashioned. He'd loved me but preferred to think of me as his baby girl rather than his potential replacement.

If Tom lost his shit about Ronan's offer, this situation had the potential to go pear-shaped fast. I needed him on board with the plan so I could return to Lennox Securities after the month was done. Staying on at King's Security just wasn't a legitimate possibility.

I went directly to Tom's office and paused outside to knock. He kept the door shut whether he was in or out; I'd never understood why.

"Come in," he called.

As I entered, I was struck by the difference between this place and King's Security, where Fiona had escorted me to the boss's office. Tom didn't have an assistant because he went through them like disposable napkins. When he desperately needed help, he got it either from me or from a temp agency.

He gestured for me to sit. "What did he want?"

I gripped the arms of the chair and winced, knowing he wouldn't like what I was about to say. "He offered me a job."

Tom exploded to his feet, his blue eyes burning with fury. "What the fuck?"

"Take a breath and listen." I raised a hand and kept my tone even. My brother had always been the more emotionally fueled of the two of us. I was the quiet one. The responsible one. "He said if I worked with him for a month, and at the end of it I didn't think our company would be better off in his hands, then he'd abandon his plans to take over."

"No." He shook his head, pouting in a way that reminded me of when he'd been a petulant teenager. "He wouldn't agree to that, and no Lennox will ever work for a King."

"Something seems strange about the offer," I said. "But if there's any chance at all that he could successfully stage a takeover, then maybe we need to take him up on it." Besides, it would give me an excellent opportunity to gather intel we could use to protect our company or win back former clients.

"We can come up with something else." He picked up a paperweight and bounced it on his palm. "The answer is no."

Annoyance flared. "If it's what the company needs, then we should do it." I'm not sure when I'd decided I wanted to go forward with the offer, but now that Tom was arguing, I felt certain in my gut that it was the right thing. "It would only be for a month. Then I could come back and he'd leave us alone—assuming he's telling the truth. If he's trying to pull one over on us, then I'd have an entire month to figure out his plan and find information we could use against him."

He cocked his head, considering it, but then shook it again. "No. Absolutely not. We'll find another way."

"How?" I asked because I'd been under the impression we were pretty much out of options.

He sank into his chair. "I'll think of something."

I gritted my teeth. "If you told me exactly what was going on, I'd be able to help more." It frustrated me that he wasn't being completely open about our circumstances. "I have no idea where our money has gone or how we got into this situation in the first place. I feel like you're keeping me in the dark."

"You know everything you need to," he snapped. "This is my company, not yours." His expression softened. "You just focus on getting more customers. I'll take care of the rest."

"I'm all over the customer strategy." I decided not to argue with him anymore about Ronan's offer. It wouldn't go anywhere. I reached over the table and took his hand, which was cold and clammy against mine. "I know I'm much younger and you always felt like you had to take care of me, but I'm an adult now. I can help."

He smiled tightly. "Thank you. I'll keep that in mind." He disentangled his hand from mine. "You're very sweet."

I stood, recognizing a brush-off when I heard one. He was done talking. But I'd noticed that he hadn't given any indication of how he might get us out of our predicament. He had no ideas. No backup plan. And as I strode down the corridor, I knew I had to accept Ronan's offer. Otherwise, Tom would dig us deeper into trouble as he tried to bail water out of our sinking lifeboat.

I stepped inside my office, closed the door behind me, and withdrew my phone from my purse. Then called the number Fiona had used earlier.

"Ronan King's office. Fiona speaking."

"Fiona, it's Willow. Are you able to put me through to Ronan, please?"

"Ronan is on another call, but I'll send this one through to him as soon as the other has ended. He should be free shortly. Is that okay?"

"Perfect, thank you." I switched the phone to speaker mode and got to work while hold music played in the background.

Before long, the music cut off and Ronan's deep timbre came down the line. "Have you made a decision?"

Biting my lip, I prayed I wasn't doing the wrong thing. "Yes. I accept your offer. I'll hand in my resignation later today, serve out my two weeks' notice, and I can start with you after that."

He hummed approvingly, and the sexy rasp did all kinds of things to my insides. "You're making the right choice. But I don't want to wait two weeks. I'll give you a signing bonus if you quit, effective immediately."

My eyes widened. Wow, he was committed to seeing this through. Or did he just want to minimize delays and maximize the disruption at Lennox?

"I can't do that." I curled my fingers into my palms, hoping he wouldn't rescind the deal. "I have a contract, and I'll abide by it. I'm not going to leave them in the lurch. Two weeks, take it or leave it."

He chuckled, and I felt it to my core. "You're more stubborn than I would have thought."

I smiled to myself. I could hear the grudging respect in his voice. He may not like me sticking to my guns, but he admired it.

"Okay, two weeks."

A breath whooshed from me. "Thank you."

"No problem. And, Willow?"

"Yes?"

"There will be a confidentiality agreement. You won't be able to pass anything you learn along to anyone else, including your brother. Will that be a problem?"

"No." I'd have been a fool to expect anything else.

"Good. I'll have someone send over a contract tomorrow."

When the call ended, I packed my laptop into my bag and slung it over my shoulder. Perhaps it made me a coward, but I didn't want to be around when Tom found out what I'd done.

I slunk out the side exit, down the stairs, and out of the building. Then I caught a bus home. When I arrived at our apartment, Sage was out—probably at yoga. I frowned, noticing the book I'd been reading on the coffee table. I could have sworn I'd left it in my bedroom. I shook my head. I was going crazy.

I opened my laptop and typed a brief resignation

email, which I sent to the human resources manager rather than Tom.

Then I waited for the fireworks.

———

"He offered you a job?" Sage asked as she sipped her green smoothie.

I resisted the urge to pull a face. I drank one every now and then when she insisted, but no matter how they tasted, the texture was enough to put me off. Meanwhile, Sage lingered over them like she was enjoying a latte. Not that she'd ever put caffeine into her system. She insisted she didn't need the extra kick, and she was probably right.

"Yes, and I took it."

She assessed me in that special way she had that made me feel as though she could read my soul. "So what will you be doing for him?"

"Launching their social media presence."

She smiled. "That's a great opportunity for you. I'm glad you said yes."

"I didn't agree because of that." Although I couldn't deny being excited by the opportunity. I'd inherited Lennox Securities' stale social media from my predecessor, and trying to change anything was like swimming upstream.

"I know." She finished her smoothie and set it to the side. "You agreed because you want to protect your dad's company from becoming a wing of someone else's empire." Her brows knitted together. "Has Tom heard yet?"

"Not yet." I hesitated, wondering whether to share the other thing that had been on my mind.

"What is it?"

"It might be nothing," I said. "I feel silly, but I could

have sworn someone was following me earlier, when I was on my way back from Ronan's office."

Sage didn't laugh off my concern. She pursed her lips in thought. "Could Ronan have had someone tailing you?"

"I wondered about that," I confessed. "But I don't see what the point would be. It's the only thing I can think of though."

Unless I was going crazy.

My ring tone sounded, and I hurried to the sofa to collect my phone. It was Tom.

"My guess is that Tom just found out." I hit the Answer button.

"What the fuck were you thinking?" Tom yelled. "I told you I'd fix it. Does my word mean nothing to you?" My teeth sank into my lip while I waited him out. "Do you know how this is going to look?" he demanded, his voice steadily rising. I hoped he wasn't in the office, where everyone could hear him. "A Lennox working for Ronan fucking King. It's all kinds of fucked up."

I counted to three, making sure he'd finished, then replied, "You won't tell me what's going on, so I have to do what I can to get us out of the situation. Don't forget it's my family company too."

He snorted. "You've never been involved the way I have."

"That's not fair, Tom." Just because I wasn't interested in being the boss didn't mean I didn't care.

"I'll tell you what's not fair. You refusing to give me the benefit of the doubt. I've been working at this company since you were in middle school."

I glanced at Sage, who offered a sympathetic smile. We'd been friends for as long as I could remember, so she was familiar with Tom's temper tantrums.

He fell silent for a moment. "Of course, there is a potential upside to this," he said, finally coming around.

"I'm glad you can see that."

"You can use your access to gather information we could use against him. Perhaps get some of our clients back."

I rolled my eyes. He said it as though I hadn't suggested that exact thing earlier. Yes, I'd have to deal with the confidentiality agreement, but there would be ways around it. "I'll see what I can do."

"Good. Let's bring that asshole down from the inside."

I winced. I didn't want Ronan taking over Lennox Securities, but I didn't necessarily want to damage his business either. He'd worked hard for it, especially after Dad's death, when Tom had made it clear Ronan was no longer welcome at our firm.

"I'll do what I can to protect Lennox Securities, but I'm not going after him personally. He doesn't deserve that."

He snorted. "You're so naïve."

I didn't care what he called me. There were some lines I wouldn't cross.

"Oh," he added, "don't bother coming in tomorrow. I'll have someone pack your things and deliver them."

I flinched. "Are you…firing me?"

He scoffed. "Don't be ridiculous. I'm just speeding your plan along. The sooner your month is up, the sooner I can be sure King is off my back."

Drawing in a slow breath through my nostrils, I tried to calm my racing heart. I couldn't help but feel that he was punishing me for defying him. "What about the marketing campaign I was working on?"

"Someone else can finish it. You don't need to worry. Just get me the inside scoop on King."

Then he hung up.

"Nobody else knows what the campaign is," I muttered to myself.

Perhaps I'd be able to keep my work laptop and continue the campaign during my free time.

Sage reached across and patted my hand. "Try to view this positively. You'll be free of a work environment where you're treated poorly and taken advantage of, and you'll be near the guy you've always dreamed about. Perhaps this is the universe at work, giving you the good things you deserve, just not in the way you thought you'd get them."

"Maybe." I appreciated her looking on the bright side, but it wasn't her life that had been turned upside down.

My phone pinged, and I glanced down, wondering if Tom had maybe had second thoughts, but it was an unknown number.

Unknown: *Fiona has a contract for you. I'd like her to go over it with you in person. What time would suit? — Ronan*

"Who is it?" Sage asked.

"My new boss." Quickly, I typed a response.

Willow: *Turns out I'll be able to start tomorrow after all. Shall I come in at nine?*

The reply arrived within seconds.

Ronan: *Yes. I'm glad you changed your mind.*

I didn't feel the need to correct him. My hand trembled as I tucked the phone away, and Sage leaned in for a hug.

"It's going to be okay," she said.

But I wasn't sure I believed her.

Chapter Six

RONAN

"Sir?" Fiona's voice interrupted the conversation I was having with Kade and Zeke in my office, and I glanced at where she stood framed in the doorway. "She's here."

I nodded. "Thanks for letting me know." I'd asked her to tell me when Willow arrived, but I was surprised I hadn't felt a shift in the air to indicate that a Lennox was in my space. "Once you've gone over the contract, and emphasized the confidentiality clause, send her through to human resources."

"Will do." She smiled at me and Kade, ignored Zeke, and stepped outside.

"That woman doesn't like me," Zeke remarked. "Any tips on how to soften her up?"

I hid a grin. It hadn't taken Fiona long to pin Zeke down as the business partner most likely to cause problems. His slick way of talking did him no favors with her.

"You're fighting a losing battle," Kade told him. "Just give up. She's not interested in you." He turned to me. "While we're on the subject of bad ideas, I still think that inviting Willow to work here is underhanded and bound to screw things up."

"Noted. I promise to be on my best behavior."

Zeke formed a steeple with his hands, watching me with an expression some people would have mistaken for boredom. Not me though. His brain was constantly going a hundred miles an hour. "She's even prettier in person."

Neither Kade nor I asked when he'd seen her. If it were anywhere other than the office, we'd rather not know.

"And what?"

Zeke leaned forward. "Seducing her would be the ultimate revenge. Could you imagine Tom's reaction if you dated the precious Lennox heiress? Not that there's much of an inheritance to speak of."

I sighed. "What did I just say? I'm not messing with her."

He held up his hands. "Hey, if you genuinely liked her then you wouldn't be messing with her, would you?" He winked. "Maybe she's the one for you? Have you thought about that?"

I snorted. I was certain of many things, and one of them was that Willow and I weren't about to embark on an epic *Romeo and Juliet* love story. That wasn't my style. I was hands-off. Calculating. Efficient. I didn't get personally involved. Women like Willow didn't want men like me.

"Not happening," I said before Kade spontaneously combusted.

My friend—always a staunch defender of the fairer sex—looked like he might go up in flames at any moment. Only Zeke could rile him up like this. They weren't long-time friends, as I was with Kade. To tell the truth, it was difficult to truly be Zeke's friend because his life consisted of secrets layered on secrets. Getting to know the man behind the mask was next to impossible.

"Fine." Zeke shrugged. "I just thought I'd put it out there. She's beautiful. Seems nice. You could do worse."

"I don't want Tom for a brother-in-law. Anyway, my problems with him have nothing to do with her."

Zeke cocked his head and touched a fingertip to the metal hoop through his eyebrow. "By breaking into your office, she inserted herself into the situation. She's a player here, whether the Neanderthal beside me likes it or not."

"Fair point. But the topic is closed for discussion." I scanned my desk until I found the file I was looking for. "I need to talk to you both about the Fairbanks case."

Half an hour later, Kade and Zeke exited my office, and I stood and stretched the kinks from my back. A muscle in my shoulder twinged. While I hadn't performed any active bodyguard duty for years, I liked to keep in good physical condition. I attended more public events than either of my business partners, and if I let myself go, it might not inspire trust from potential clients. Besides, I enjoyed pushing myself in my home gym.

An errant thought drew me from my office. Before I realized where I was going, I found myself standing in the open plan area where the marketing, communications, and public relations staff were based. Willow sat at a long desk, hunched over a laptop, her chin propped on her hand, studying the screen intently. Awareness fizzled through my body. She was stunning. Zeke had been right about that. Her silky blonde hair hung down her back in a way that tempted me to wrap it around my fist.

I swallowed. Damn, I needed to get my thoughts under control.

"Can I help you?" a voice asked to my right.

I flinched, caught off guard, and turned. Imani, a Black woman in her mid-twenties and one of Willow's new colleagues, was seated at the long desk behind Willow and gave me a look that said she'd caught me staring.

Willow glanced over her shoulder, and her eyes widened.

"I just wanted to say hello to our newest recruit," I said, relieved it wasn't unusual for me to check in with new employees. In fact, I think I'd done the same thing with Imani when she started.

Willow tucked her hair behind her ears. "Everything is fine, thanks." She studied me as though she thought I was trying to catch her slacking off. "Imani has already shown me how to use the systems. Now I'm familiarizing myself with the kind of work you do so I can best determine where to focus the social media campaigns."

"She's a quick learner," Imani added, still wearing a mischievous smile. "She's going to build us a following in no time."

I nodded. "I'm certain she will." I took a step back. "I'd best return to work and let you get on with yours. Don't be afraid to ask for help if you need it."

"I won't need it." Willow raised her chin, her hair spilling over her shoulders and rippling golden in the overhead light.

Don't pay attention to her hair, I told myself. *She's an employee, like any other.*

Except for one thing: her brother was my worst enemy.

―――――

WILLOW

I flopped against my seat the moment Ronan was out of sight.

Across from me, Imani giggled. "Don't worry, he has that effect on a lot of people."

"What effect?"

Imani flashed pearly teeth. "The urge to melt into a puddle at his feet." She waved a hand dismissively. "Consider it your initiation. The three founders of King's Security are all unfairly hot, although Ronan is the most classically handsome. Have you met the others?"

I shook my head, wanting to protest that she'd misunderstood my interest in Ronan, but she wasn't entirely wrong. The man was breathtaking, and he made my pulse spike.

"That's not—"

"Sweetie." She gave me a look. "Be real. There's no shame."

"Fine," I admitted. "He's attractive."

"He's smoking." She wheeled her desk chair over, and I gave her my full attention. "Let me tell you about the founders."

"Okay." It was obvious she wanted an audience, and I was happy to listen. The more information I could gather about them, the better.

"First, we have Ronan, CEO and generally well-respected guy. He's not soft, but he's fair. Kade, who heads up the personal security division—bodyguards and the like —is his best friend from college. He's former military and doesn't talk much, but what he says is worth listening to. Serious hottie if you like them scary and built. The last member of the trio is Zeke, who joined the company from God only knows what super-secret arm of national security. Computer wunderkind, in charge of cyber. If you like your men nerdy with an edge, you might be Team Zeke."

"An edge," I echoed, not sure what she meant.

"You'll see what I mean." She cocked her head. "Where did you say you worked before coming here?"

I cringed because I hadn't mentioned the fact I'd come from Lennox Securities. It had been bad enough when the human resources staff had seemed wary of me because of my last name.

"A similar position," I said evasively. "Only it was more

of a general role, whereas here I'll be focused purely on social media."

Imani nodded, although I knew she hadn't missed my dodge. "So you basically did my general comms job at your last post?"

"That's right."

"Well, if you need someone to brainstorm ideas with, let me know." She rolled back over to her desk. "King's Security has been meaning to get someone to do socials for months now, so I've had plenty of time to think about what might work."

"Thanks." I appreciated her acceptance of me. "I'll put my thoughts together and perhaps we could compare notes?"

"Perfect."

I returned my focus to work, and so did she. For thirty minutes, I sank my teeth into information about programs and personnel. It wasn't the most thrilling reading, but any intel was good intel.

Gradually, I became aware of someone standing in front of me. I jolted to attention and clicked out of the screen, hoping he hadn't seen what I'd been looking at. My eyes widened as they settled on the man waiting for my attention. He had messy black hair, a short beard, and a piercing through his eyebrow, another in his earlobe. The darkest eyes I'd ever seen were set in a face too harsh to be considered handsome but striking all the same. My gaze tracked down his shoulders, which were clad in a leather jacket. Tattoos covered the backs of his hands and disappeared into his sleeves. Several chunky metal rings adorned his fingers. He cleared his throat, and my eyes flew up to meet his. I felt my cheeks heat with embarrassment at getting caught staring.

"How's it going, princess?" he asked, his hands remaining at his sides. "Finding everything you need?"

I broke into a cold sweat. Had he seen me snooping? I glanced at Imani, hoping she hadn't heard the comment. Fortunately, she was entranced by something on her screen.

"Yes, I'm managing." I forced myself to smile and play dumb. "I don't think we've met?"

"We haven't." A smirk played at the corners of his mouth. "I'm Zeke. Don't pay attention to what anyone says about me. I'm a big teddy bear."

Somehow, I doubted that. Everything about this man screamed danger. Even though I knew it was stupid, I wondered whether his skin would be cold to the touch. It seemed like it ought to be.

"Good to know." I wasn't sure what else to say.

His lips twitched. "Behave yourself, Willow. Not all of us are as trusting as King." He leaned closer and lowered his voice. "And remember that blood isn't always thicker than water."

With that last cryptic comment, he straightened and left. I watched him go, unsure how to react.

"Was that Zeke?" Imani asked, finally glancing up from her computer.

"Yes."

"What did he want?"

I forced myself to shrug. "I'm not sure." My guess would be that he was suspicious of me and he'd been warning me not to betray Ronan.

She raised an eyebrow, clearly not buying it. "Fine. Have your secrets." She stood, holding her purse. "Come on, I'll show you the best place to get coffee."

We took the elevator to the ground floor and exited onto the street.

"It's only a short walk."

A couple of buildings down from the King's Security office, she turned into a cafe. I followed, but just as the door swung closed, I caught a glimpse of a figure behind me. Watching us. When I turned, they were gone.

———

I was composing an email to one of our biggest corporate clients when Zeke breezed into my office without knocking. He grabbed the chair opposite my desk and dropped into it, not waiting for an invitation. I bit the inside of my lip so he wouldn't see me smile. Encouragement was the last thing he needed.

"So," he said, interrupting the flow of my fingers over the keyboard. "Your Willow isn't what I expected."

I held up a finger to quiet him while I tried to finish my sentence. Unfortunately, his statement had intrigued me, and I couldn't remember what I'd been about to type. I managed to piece something together—I could fix it later—and gave him my full attention.

"How do you mean?"

He smirked, pleased to have me hooked. "She's gutsy and interesting."

I shoved my keyboard away since I clearly wasn't going to get anything done until Zeke was gone. "Why would that be a surprise? She did break into my office, you know."

"In all the photos of her on the internet, she looks standoffish." He slid off one of his rings and turned it over between his fingers. "Her communications are carefully worded. I figured she thought she was above everyone else, but after meeting her, I'm not so sure."

"You're admitting you might have been wrong about someone?" I cocked my head. "Can I get that in a written statement, signed and dated?"

He rolled his eyes. "Not going to happen, King."

"Didn't think so." I wasn't sure why he'd felt the need to interrupt me for this character assessment though. "Where are you going with this?"

He angled his chin toward me, his smile widening. "Oh, nowhere in particular. Just that I don't trust her and I think it would be best to keep a close eye on her. If that happens to mean asking her out, then I'm prepared to take one for the team. Especially since you've already said you're not interested."

Frustration snapped like a rubber band inside me at the thought of Zeke crossing any kind of line with Willow. I would have liked to think she wouldn't fall for his particular brand of charm, but because of his mysterious past and bad-boy facade, women tended to lose their minds over him.

"Stay away from her," I ordered. "We're not playing with her feelings. That option is off the table. Got it?"

Zeke laughed. "Got it, boss man."

My eyes narrowed. He was being facetious. Technically, he was my partner, not my employee. We'd agreed at the outset that since I was the one bringing the money and the client connections, I'd be the CEO.

"Have you stopped to think about why you're so determined for her not to get caught in the crossfire?" Zeke asked.

"Because it would be wrong," I replied, ignoring the way my chest burned at the thought of Zeke touching her. Yes, *that* would be very wrong indeed.

"Sure it would." Zeke smirked. "Wrong to strike back at the criminal who snuck into your office and went through your personal files." He stroked his scruffy jaw, then said something entirely unexpected. "You're smitten with her."

My mouth dropped open. "Excuse me?"

He gave me a look. "I saw the way you visited her desk

earlier." As I began to protest, he stood and shoved his hands in his pockets. "I get the appeal. Just make sure you don't lose your edge because you have a thing for our enemy's sister."

"Fuck off." I seethed, even though I knew he'd hit the mark. "That won't be happening. In case you've forgotten, Tom Lennox is *my* enemy. Not ours. And his sister is nothing more than a tool."

Zeke stared at me, his black gaze intense. "Keep it that way. Oh, and just so you know, Lennox is *our* enemy, not just yours. We're partners. You aren't alone in this."

My rising temper ebbed. "I appreciate that."

I tamped down what remained of my anger and reminded myself that as a former spy, Zeke simply didn't know how to behave like a normal person. He was all about collecting intel and manipulating pieces into place.

"I'm not sure where I'd be without you." He shrugged, making light of what he'd said. "I like my life now, so let's not do anything to screw it up."

"Yeah, yeah." I rolled my eyes and waved a hand at the door. "Get back to work, Watts." Then I had a thought. "Wait a second. Have you found anything on Lennox yet?"

"Not anything worthwhile." He made a face. "But there's something. Trust me, I get a vibe from the guy. We'll keep looking."

"Thanks." He raised a hand as he left, and I pondered the puzzle of Tom Lennox. "What are you involved in?"

Chapter Seven

WILLOW

I felt more excited about a project than I had in years. I hated that working for the competition had gotten my creative juices flowing, but I couldn't seem to shut them off. My boss had been receptive to my ideas for the social media plan and suggested I put together a presentation for the founders so we could get the official go-ahead. I'd been beavering away since then. I hadn't even had much chance to think about how I could take advantage of my access to Ronan's computer systems like I should have. After four days, Tom was getting impatient. He wanted something to show for my presence here. And telling him that I was having too much fun making a presentation didn't seem like a valid reason for dropping the ball.

"Hey, girl."

I glanced up and smiled at Imani, who'd managed to approach without me hearing.

She scanned my work. "This is brilliant. They're going to love it." She shifted her weight. "We're all going to The Castle after work today. Want to come?"

I hesitated. "I don't know…" The Castle was a popular

bar, and I didn't really want to socialize with anyone who worked here. Things were messy enough. I needed to maintain a clear line in the sand. I was here for Lennox Securities, not to have a good time. Besides, Tom would throw a hissy fit if he found out. "I really shouldn't. My roommate will be expecting me home for dinner."

"So call her and say you'll be late," Imani urged. "Or invite her. The more the merrier. You deserve to have fun. And hey"—her voice turned sly—"maybe you'll meet the bodyguard division." She winked. "They're hunks, and they don't spend much time around the office, so you might not get to know them otherwise."

The mention of hunks conjured an image of Ronan King, all perfectly broad shoulders and sexy angles. I frowned. Perhaps I did need a distraction from him, and after a few drinks, people might say things they otherwise wouldn't. This could be a good chance to gather information and make up for lost ground.

"Okay, I'll come."

"Yes!" She high-fived me. "We leave the office at five thirty. Just stick near me and I'll introduce you to everyone."

I forced myself to smile. "That would be great."

She returned to her desk, and I put the finishing touches on the slide and checked the clock. Time for lunch. I powered off my screen and wandered to the staff kitchen area. I found my food in the fridge and chose an unoccupied table, then sat and pieced together my salad wrap.

"Mind if I join you?"

I raised my eyes. Words of welcome died on my tongue. Ronan stood over me, resplendent in a black suit and elaborately knotted tie.

"If you must."

He sank into a seat and placed a small cardboard container and a mug of coffee in front of himself. He opened the container to reveal a rice salad. "It's nice to be able to get down here. I usually eat in my office, but I had a little extra time today." He grabbed a spoon. "How are you enjoying your job?"

I glanced around. People were staring. I wished he hadn't come. They might ask questions. And I didn't want to spend more time with him, no matter how gorgeous he looked. My heart gave a flutter, making a liar of me.

"It's fine," I told him. I would not let on how absorbed I'd become in my project. "The plans are coming along well."

"Good." His eyes crinkled at the corners. He leaned forward and dropped his voice. "I know I didn't give you much choice, but I'm glad you're not hating every second of it."

I shrugged because I couldn't think of what to say. Nothing seemed adequate. I took a bite of my wrap instead.

He started on his rice. "Tell me more about yourself."

My eyes darted around again, but thankfully, most people seemed to have stopped staring. "Why? So you can use it against me?"

His eyes glinted with amusement. "Because I find you interesting, Willow."

"Oh." I didn't know how to respond to that, or to the pleasant buzz his words caused in my lower stomach. "What do you want to know?"

"You studied art in college." He took a drink of his coffee. "Were you always planning to go into communications and marketing?"

My cheeks heated, and I glanced down. How had he managed to zero in on a sore point? I didn't want to answer. Not when it would either show me for the spoiled rich girl I used to be or demonstrate what a failure I was. I didn't want him to see me in either way.

"Willow?" he prompted.

I sighed. "No. I love painting, but I'm not an artistic genius, just moderately good, so I can't support myself financially with it. When I finished school, I tried for a while, but I floundered. Then Tom needed help and I needed money for rent, so I decided to join the family company."

His dark brows furrowed. "You needed money? Excuse me for saying this, but I always assumed you were well taken care of."

"Yes, well, you'd think so, wouldn't you?" I wasn't about to explain how Tom had siphoned off the majority of my trust fund while I'd been blissfully oblivious.

His frown deepened. Apparently, he didn't like getting the brush-off. "Do you have your own place now?"

I inwardly cringed. The fact he hadn't asked about Dad's properties probably meant he knew they'd all been sold off.

"I rent an apartment with my best friend."

"What's she like?"

I hid a smile. How best to describe Sage? "She's eccentric, and I absolutely adore her for it. She has the biggest heart of anyone I know." Was that awareness in his deep brown eyes? Or was I going crazy because I'd dreamed of him looking at me that way so many times before? "Are you coming tonight?" I blurted, immediately regretting it. "To The Castle, I mean. I was told there are after-work drinks."

Disappointment flashed in his eyes. "The staff find it easier to let loose when the boss isn't there, so I don't go to any gatherings unless they're something we've organized as a company."

"Oh." Dissatisfaction weighed on me. What was that about? I should be glad he wasn't coming so I could ask more probing questions. "That makes sense."

"Be careful tonight." He looked at me in a way that would have made my teenage self swoon. "I doubt you have much experience with the type of people who go to The Castle."

"I'll be surrounded by bodyguards," I reminded him. "I'm sure I'll be safe."

His lips twitched. "Maybe it's them I'm worried about."

Chapter Eight

RONAN

I stared at the computer screen, words and numbers blurring together, then rubbed my eyes and glanced outside. Night had descended over the city, and it was a cold one. I hoped Willow had brought a jacket with her to The Castle.

Willow.

I couldn't seem to get the damn woman out of my mind. Her pert little nose. The sound of her voice. The way she moved through the hallways like she was gliding on air. I couldn't have been the only one to notice her. She was a magnet for men—not that she seemed to realize it. She was either naive or skilled at pretending. I tended to believe it was the former. She'd been sheltered all her life. First by her father, then by her brother. She probably had no idea what her pouty, pink lips made men think about.

I buried my face in my palms and growled.

Work. Get back to work.

But I couldn't concentrate. My mind was full of her.

Was she being safe? Imani might not know to look out for her. As for the bodyguards she'd mentioned earlier…

well, I hoped none of them were as taken with her as I seemed to be. Even if I couldn't fully trust her, I didn't want any of them making moves on her either. But it was impossible to believe none of them would. They didn't have to worry about the repercussions like I did.

A sudden urgency crept up on me. To see her. Make sure she was all right. A thought occurred to me. King's Security had installed The Castle's security system, which meant we had access to the camera feeds.

No. Don't do it.

Using my access to spy on a woman would be wrong. But then, I only wanted to make sure she was okay. Much as I wished I could hate her because of her connection to Tom, she was loyal to her family legacy, and I couldn't fault that.

God, I missed Frank. He'd know what to do at a time like this.

"Two minutes," I muttered to myself as I refocused on the screen and hit the keys needed to navigate into The Castle's main feed. I shifted from one camera to another, checking the screen for her, until eventually, I found her in a booth with a group of my employees, sandwiched between a pair of women. The pressure in my chest eased, and I shut the feed off.

"Creep."

I forced myself back to work but hadn't made it very far before my phone rang. I glanced at the number and sighed. Kaitlyn. This wasn't going to be fun.

"Hi, King." Her voice was brisk. All business. "I'm in town for the weekend. Want to get together?"

Kaitlyn was a partner in a small law firm in Indianapolis, but often visited Chicago for work. I'd met her through a friend, and since we were both busy people without time for a relationship, we scratched our itches whenever she was in the area. "I'm sorry, Kaitlyn, but that's not a good idea."

"Oh?" She sounded surprised. As she should have. I rarely turned her down.

I winced. "I've met someone, and nothing has happened between us, but it wouldn't be fair of me to be with you when I'm thinking about her."

"I see." Was it just me, or did she sound hurt? I supposed no woman liked to hear you preferred another woman over her. "Well, best of luck. I hope you can manage to carve some time out of your busy schedule for her."

Yeah, okay, that definitely sounded bitter.

"Kaitlyn, I'm—"

She hung up.

———

WILLOW

It was nice to be out with people. Even if I didn't know most of them and didn't really want to. They went out of their way to make me feel like part of the group. People often treated me differently because of my family, even though we'd lost our fortune. My colleagues' welcoming attitudes made me rethink my quest to pump them for information. I didn't want to be that person, did I? The one who wriggled into their good graces like a snake and exploited their trust. It didn't feel right, no matter how much I wanted to protect my family company. Whatever Ronan may or may not be up to, these were decent people and they didn't deserve that.

"Excuse me, Willow."

I looked up and found myself staring into a pair of lovely blue eyes across the table. The man smiled, and a dimple popped in his cheek. He was cute, in a boyish way, with dark-gold hair and an open expression. "I'm Oliver."

"Nice to meet you." He'd taken me by surprise, but manners had been drilled into me since birth. "How did you know my name?"

"I've seen you around the office, and I asked Imani who her beautiful friend was." His grin widened. "I've been trying to get near you all night. Would you like to dance with me?"

I blushed furiously and glanced at the dance floor. The truth was, I didn't know how to do what passed for dancing in a place like this. I'd been classically trained by a ballroom dance teacher. Club dancing was well and truly outside my comfort zone. As was flirting. Especially with this good-looking man I wasn't remotely interested in.

"I can't, but thanks for asking. It's very sweet of you."

"Ah." He nodded as though he understood. "Which of the three bosses do you have a crush on, then?"

My mouth fell open.

"I'm sorry," he rushed to add. "I didn't mean to embarrass you. It's just that most of the women at work seem to have a thing for either King, Kade, or Zeke."

"Okay," I squeaked. "But I don't. I haven't met Kade, and I've only talked to Zeke for all of thirty seconds."

"So, King?"

"No." I scrunched my nose. "That would just be asking for trouble."

"Why?"

I faltered, remembering that he didn't know my history with Ronan or who I really was. "Nothing. Forget I said anything."

He mimed zipping his lips. "You got it."

I managed to smile, even though it felt wobbly. "What department do you work in?"

"I'm in cybersecurity." He snagged a beer and took a drink. "Zeke is my boss."

"Ah, so you're crazy smart."

Clever and cute. If only I could have been interested in anyone other than the man who'd had my heart since I was seventeen. The one who was firmly in the no-touch zone.

He winked. "You said it, not me."

We conversed easily. Despite my misgivings, I asked a few questions about the way the company operated without seeming to pry, but I didn't learn anything useful. Still, by the time I called a ride to take me home, I felt good. My time at King's Security hadn't been awful. In fact, although I wouldn't admit the truth to Tom, I'd enjoyed it. I climbed into the cab and we drove in silence. I'd only had two glasses of wine, so when we arrived at the apartment building, I was steady on my feet as I made my way toward the entrance.

But then I paused. There, in the shadows at the corner of the building, stood the silhouette of a man. I stopped dead in my tracks. It *was* a man, wasn't it? Or was my mind playing tricks on me? The figure didn't move. I squinted, trying to get a better look.

Nothing.

Shivering, I hurried up the stairs and raced to our apartment. We were on the far end of the third floor. It was one of those nondescript buildings where all of the apartments looked the same from the outside. The carpet was gray, the walls dull, and tonight, it seemed too quiet. I could swear I felt eyes on me, but when I checked, nobody was there.

I slotted the key into the lock, cursing when it didn't immediately open. I jiggled it, and the lock snicked. I shoved the door inward, flipped the lock behind me, and collapsed against it. My heart thudded dangerously.

Oh God.

What was that?

My imagination must have been going haywire. I switched the light on. Sage would already be asleep. She was an early-to-bed, early-to-rise kind of person.

A shrill squeal rang out, and I jumped in fright, slapping my hand to my chest.

Shit. It was just my phone.

I answered, checking the Caller ID. "Hi, Tom."

"Has anything strange happened to you today?"

Dread crept up my spine. Perhaps I hadn't imagined the figure outside. "Strange how?"

He made a dismissive sound. "Just strange. Out of the ordinary."

"Um." I swallowed, trying to moisten my dry mouth. I went to the kitchen to get a glass of water. "Just now, I thought I saw someone watching me."

"Huh." He was quiet for a moment. "That's it?"

I thought of the man outside. "That's it. Why? What's going on?"

"Nothing you need to worry about. Just be careful."

For a moment, I'd have liked nothing more than to wring his neck. I loved my brother, but he could be patronizing, and he had a misogynistic streak. Sometimes, I wondered how the two of us could have been raised by the same man yet be so different.

"It would help if you explained what I need to be careful of."

He clucked his tongue. "Who's the head of the family business?"

"You," I said with more bite than needed. "But that doesn't mean you should keep me in the dark."

"It's my job to find solutions," he said, ignoring my remark. "Although, if you were to marry someone like

Adrian Petrov, we'd have more money than we'd know what to do with and could kiss our problems goodbye."

My stomach soured. It wasn't the first time he'd made a comment like that. I used to think he was joking, but considering the number of men he'd set me up with at society events over the past couple of years, I was pretty sure he was serious. It drove me mad that we still lived in a world where he could even contemplate the possibility of marrying me off to some creepy older man like we were in the nineteenth century.

"Or perhaps you could find a nice heiress," I said calmly. "And then all our problems would be solved, right?"

I hung up. It felt good.

Chapter Nine

RONAN

I spent the weekend reminding myself of all the reasons why I couldn't afford to be romantically interested in Willow. I managed to make it until late on Monday morning before I finally gave up and let the need to see her drive me from my office. I told myself it was because I needed to know whether she'd concede that I ran things more smoothly than Tom did, but that didn't ring true. I stopped short when she was nowhere to be seen.

"Imani, I'm looking for Willow. Is she around?"

Imani cocked her head, curious. Fortunately, she knew better than to question the boss. "She went to the print room."

"Thank you."

I headed for the print room and paused in the doorway. Willow was bent over the copy machine, trying to tug a torn sheet of paper from its teeth.

"Is everything okay?"

She jumped, clutching at her throat. "You scared me."

Suspicion crept over me. What was she doing that would warrant that reaction?

I stepped into the room. "Here, let me help."

"There's no need for that." Her cheeks flushed. "I can figure it out."

Was there something she didn't want me to see?

"I insist." I hustled forward and pressed the button that released the section of the copier she was battling with. The sheet of paper slid free, and I snatched it before she had the chance to intervene. It was a flow diagram with colored boxes and words like Insta, FB, and a few others I didn't recognize. Tension flooded out of my shoulders as I realized it was for her project. The one we'd hired her to complete. There was nothing nefarious going on here.

I handed it to her. "Here you go. In the future, if you press the button, it's much easier to dismantle."

Her flush deepened. "Thanks."

Her gaze darted to the exit, and I couldn't help but wonder why she'd been so jumpy if she wasn't sneaking around on her brother's behalf.

"Are you all right?" I asked. "You seem to be wound up about something."

"I'm fine." She smiled tightly. "Thanks for asking."

With that, she took the paper from my hand and brushed past me.

I detoured via Zeke's office and knocked on the open door. He was hunched over his computer, but a few moments later, he straightened and removed the glasses perched on the tip of his nose.

"What's up?"

"Can you look into Willow as well as Tom? Something is going on with her, but I'm not sure what." I felt a momentary pang of guilt but squelched it.

Zeke grinned. "Already have." He tapped a couple of keys on his keyboard. "I thought this might happen."

Something in my chest coiled tight. "What did you find?"

"Not much." He put his glasses back in place and scanned the screen. "She did moderately well in college and tried to make a living as a full-time artist but failed so she joined the family business instead. Oh, and here's something you might be interested in." He raised his eyes. "You're aware that her father passed away when she was nineteen and left her a sizable trust fund, but it might surprise you to know it was almost completely drained before she turned twenty-one and gained access to it."

I frowned. "Drained how?"

"As far as I can tell, her brother embezzled nearly everything. It's unclear whether she knew it was happening, but she's never taken any legal action against him."

"Of course not," I muttered.

One thing was clear about Willow Lennox: she was loyal to the Lennox family name. I didn't know what her relationship with Tom was like, except that it was friendly enough for them to attend events together, but even if they didn't get along, I doubted she'd want to cause a scandal by suing him.

My jaw tightened. No wonder she'd given up life as an artist. She probably couldn't afford to support herself the way her father had intended. Tom had screwed her out of her future.

"Anyone else in her life?" I asked. "Boyfriends or exes?"

Zeke waggled his eyebrows. "It seems that sweet little Willow is as pure as a new snowfall. She didn't date in high school and doesn't appear to have done so more than a handful of times in college. She often attends events on the arms of wealthy men who are connected to her brother but is rarely seen with the same man more than once. I assume it's all part of a smokescreen to make her look like the perfect society heiress. Except," he chuckled, "she has no inheritance."

She wasn't seeing anyone. Savage satisfaction tore

through me. I didn't like the thought of her with another man. No matter how unsuitable she might be, my subconscious said she belonged with me.

———

Someone was watching me. I could feel it.

All weekend, I'd had the strangest sensation of eyes following me, and it hadn't gone away. Now it was Monday and I was back in the King's Security office, but the feeling hadn't left. Was someone actually watching me? If so, were they working for Ronan, or had Tom gotten us into more trouble? Short of tying him up and torturing him for information, I'd done everything I could to get him to spill the truth of our situation, but he hadn't. Our company must have been in dire financial straits, that much was clear, but there was more to the story. Something I was missing. My best guess was that he owed money to someone he shouldn't.

I needed to do my own digging into Tom's affairs, in addition to the snooping I'd already been doing at King's Security. I hadn't found any mention of Lennox Securities during my time surreptitiously nosing around the intranet, but when I'd looked up the files for some of the bigger clients he'd poached from us, they were password protected. At first, I thought that was an indication of guilt, but I'd quickly realized that every client file was password protected. I'd considered mentioning this to Tom, certain he'd have ideas about how to break into them, but I'd decided not to. No matter how much trouble the company was in, I didn't believe Dad would have wanted me to stoop that low. He'd had firm ideas about honor.

I straightened and headed for the area where Zeke's cybersecurity team was housed. Anxiety squeezed in my chest. Dad probably wouldn't have wanted me to do what I was about to do either. But honestly, I didn't think I had much choice.

I scanned the people stationed at their computers, my gaze landing on Oliver, the guy I'd met on Friday. I walked over and stopped in front of his desk.

He sat back and smiled. "I'm surprised to see you in this part of the building."

I glanced at the person seated next to him and lowered my voice. "I was hoping you'd be able to help me with something."

He raised an eyebrow. "A favor?"

I nodded, knowing it was cheeky to be asking for something so soon after meeting him, but I had no one else to turn to. No one with his skillset, anyway. "Do you mind if we talk in private?"

"This sounds serious." He pushed his chair back and gestured for me to precede him into one of the meeting rooms. I sat on one side of the table, and he closed the door and sat opposite. "What's going on?"

I bit my lip. Was this a mistake?

"You can trust me," he urged.

"Okay." I set my jaw. "Can you look into somebody for me?"

He cocked his head. "Is this for work?"

"Not exactly." I cupped one of my hands with the other. They were both cold—something that tended to happen when I was stressed. "It's my brother. It would be off the books." I lowered my gaze. "I know I'm asking a lot. I wouldn't be putting you in this position if I felt like I had any other choice."

He scrubbed his palm down his face. "What are you looking for?"

I shrugged. "He might owe someone money, but he won't tell me. I've got a bad feeling and want to make sure he's safe."

"Okay." He placed his hands on the table and nodded. "As long as that's all there is to it. But you'll owe me. What's his name?"

"Tom Lennox."

He paled. "I didn't know your last name was Lennox. Willow…" He reached across the table and took my hand. "We're already looking into your brother."

"What?" I repeated, shock chilling my insides.

He glanced over his shoulder and leaned forward. "I can't share the details, but from what I've seen, you're right. Your brother owes a lot of money and he's in over his head in something rotten."

My stomach plummeted. Suspecting the truth was one thing. Having it confirmed was another. "Thank you for telling me."

I shot to my feet, my movements jerky.

Tom had dragged me into something shady, and my gut told me that Ronan was going to use it as leverage for a takeover. Why else would he order an investigation? I'd known Ronan was up to something. Damn him, and damn Tom for not being upfront with me.

"Wait," Oliver called. I stopped and looked over my shoulder. "I just wanted to let you know that it's not part of an investigation for a client."

I cocked my head, not sure what he was getting at.

He sighed and pushed a hand through his hair. "When an investigation isn't connected to a client file it's usually because one of the directors has a personal interest in the subject. If I were you, I'd talk to Ronan."

My jaw firmed. As I'd thought. "Thanks, Oliver."

Following his advice, I beelined for Ronan's office. Just as I reached for the handle, Fiona leaped in front of me, barring the entrance.

"I'm sorry, but Mr. King is busy." Her sympathetic

expression made me think she had some idea of what was going on. "I can't let you in."

I ground my teeth together to avoid snapping at her. "I need to see him."

"He's busy," she reiterated. "If you come back in half an hour—"

"Please, it'll just be a moment," I interrupted. "Look, I'm sorry, but we're overdue for a conversation."

With that, I darted around her and let myself into the boss's office, coming up short at the sight of two men seated at the table along the wall. Zeke, and a mountain of a man I assumed must be the other partner, Kade. I didn't let their appearance put me off. My hands landed on my hips, and I glared at Ronan, who sat behind his desk like a king holding court.

"When did you start investigating my brother?"

Chapter Ten

RONAN

My heart stuttered when Willow barged into my office, her eyes flashing and cheeks flushed. She looked stormy, which was a startling contrast to her usual self-containment.

She crossed her arms and stared me down, one fair brow arched. "Well?"

Zeke smothered a chuckle, and I narrowed my eyes at him.

"Gentlemen, will you give us a moment?" I asked.

"Sure thing." Zeke sauntered to the door. It could have been my imagination, but I thought I saw him wink at Willow as he passed.

My gut tightened.

Kade hesitated, glancing from Willow to me. "Are you sure that's a good idea?"

"Yes." I bit the word out, not leaving any room for doubt.

Slowly, he made his way toward the exit, but paused in front of Willow. He offered her a hand, and from the way her eyes widened, I could tell she hadn't expected it. "I'm Kade," he said gruffly. "If you need anything, my door is open."

She blinked, visibly surprised. "Thank you."

Her tone was softer than it had ever been when speaking to me, and my jaw locked in place as I managed —barely—not to snap at either of them. I shouldn't have taken Kade's offer of an olive branch to heart. I knew he hadn't wanted to involve her in our plan, so why should it bother me if he took it upon himself to keep an eye out for her?

"No problem." He nodded once and stepped past her out of the office.

Fiona appeared in the doorway. "I'm sorry, Mr. King. She wouldn't take no for an answer."

Willow's entire body tensed, and if possible, she glared harder.

"I'm sure you did your best. Don't worry about it. Willow and I have business to discuss."

Fiona's expression turned speculative. "Should I shut the door and hold your calls?"

"Please do."

She gave Willow a lingering look but did as I asked and pulled the door closed. I expected Willow to relax, but she seemed even more on edge than before.

She marched up to my desk. "You've been looking into Tom. Did you start that before or after we made our deal?"

I frowned. Clearly, we needed to check the company for leaks. "Have a seat."

She raised her chin. "If I do, are you going to be honest with me?"

I leaned back, struggling to keep a smile off my face. I loved her fiery stubbornness. It was the same stubbornness I saw in the mirror. "I'll consider it."

As she sat in the chair Kade had vacated, I reached for

my coffee and took a drink. I wouldn't let her know how unsettled her presence made me. If I gave away how badly I'd like to see her cheeks flush with passion, it could ruin everything. "I think you'll find I'm holding up my side of the bargain. I never said I wouldn't investigate your brother. I agreed not to take over the company if, at the end of the month, you're not convinced it would be better off in my hands. Those are two very different things."

She held my gaze. "But the only reason you'd be looking into him is so you could blackmail him to let you have the company."

I raised a brow. "Is it?"

"You know it is." She crossed her arms. "There would be no point otherwise."

"What about that old adage 'know thy enemy'?"

Her eyes narrowed. "I don't believe that's all this is."

She was right. Not that I'd tell her so. If I couldn't take the company, I'd settle for seeing Tom in prison. I just needed to dig up enough dirt to put him there.

"You can choose to believe me or not," I said. "It makes no difference."

She huffed. "You're not acting in good faith."

"I'm sorry you feel that way." Her accusation rankled. I'd always been a principled person, even when motivated by revenge.

She rolled her eyes. "Not sorry enough." She pursed her lips, her expression uncharacteristically vulnerable. "Can you just tell me one thing honestly?"

"Depends what it is."

"This isn't a game," she snapped.

I nodded, taken aback. "I know. Whatever your question is, if I'm able to answer it, I will."

She released a long breath. "Thank you." Then she said something that turned the blood in my veins to ice.

"As part of your investigation, have you had someone following me?"

"No." The fact she'd asked alarmed me, and I studied her features carefully. Now that I took the time to look deeper, I could see fear in her eyes, hidden behind bravado. "I swear, I haven't. Has something happened? Are you in danger?"

That wasn't part of the plan. She was supposed to have been safe.

She watched me closely, then her shoulders hunched. Many people wouldn't have noticed the change in her posture, but I was attuned to everything about her. "I believe you." She sighed. "I'm probably being paranoid."

But her voice was full of doubt.

"Why do you think someone has been following you?" I asked. She stared into space for a moment, and I grew concerned. "Willow?"

She jolted, and her eyes found mine. "I thought I saw someone a few times—outside my apartment building or behind me on the streets—but I must have been imagining it. Forget I said anything."

She stood, straightened her shoulders and hurried out of the office.

I watched her go, wanting nothing more than to call her back and demand to know every single time she'd seen something that made her nervous. I held my tongue though. I could look into things on my own if she didn't want to share.

A few seconds after she departed, Kade and Zeke reappeared. They must have been waiting nearby.

"Is she okay?" Kade asked, giving me a look that said she'd better be.

"She's scared. Seems to think someone has been following her, and given the kind of trouble Tom tends to attract, she might be right."

Kade scowled. "I'll have one of the guys check on her every now and then during the day."

His massive chest heaved, and I could tell he had something else to say. "What is it?"

"It's not too late to forget this whole thing with Willow. Send her back to Lennox Securities and return to the original plan."

Zeke sank into one of the chairs opposite me. "I saw that coming." He cocked a brow at me. "Did you?"

I ignored him. I'd had a pretty good idea what Kade wanted, but Zeke enjoyed winding people up, and it was best not to add fuel to the fire.

"Whatever this is, she's involved now," I told Kade.

"I don't like it," he replied.

I acknowledged his words with a nod, then turned to Zeke. "Remind me what you were saying before we were interrupted."

———

WILLOW

I shut myself in the office bathroom and locked the door, my mind sprinting a million miles an hour.

If Ronan didn't have people following me, then who did?

Perhaps I could have imagined the figures in the dark, but not the man who'd followed me after I got Ronan's job offer. And then there had been the strange phone call with dead air.

I leaned against the door and closed my eyes, taking a few deep breaths. None of this was going as I'd expected. I was supposed to have dug up a heap of intel to have on standby in case Ronan tried to back out of our deal. Instead, I had a feeling Ronan was looking for ways to displace my brother, and someone else was scaring the crap out of me.

I needed to talk to Tom to share my suspicions and let him know about Ronan's investigation. I headed back to my desk, grabbed my phone, and then returned to the bathroom. I couldn't risk being overheard. I dialed his number and waited for the call to connect.

"Have you found something we can use against him?" Tom didn't bother with a greeting.

I gritted my teeth. I was all for saving the family business, but he could be so single-minded it drove me crazy.

"Not yet, but there's something you should know." I considered how best to phrase it. "Ronan is trying to dig up dirt on you. I don't know if he wants to use it for blackmail or something else, but his cyber guys are on your trail."

To my surprise, Tom laughed. "Of course he's trying to unearth the skeletons in my closet. I'd do the same thing in his situation."

Something bubbled in my stomach, hot and unpleasant. I'd expected him to be grateful for the warning, or at the very least to be pleased I finally had something to report. Instead, he didn't seem to care at all.

"Is there anything for him to find?" I asked. "Shouldn't we try to head it off so we can protect the company?"

"He won't find anything," he replied, not exactly answering my question. "There's nothing for you to worry about. The best thing you can do is return the favor. You have access to his systems. Surely you can find something useful. Now, is that all?"

My stomach sank. I couldn't believe he'd dismissed me so easily. But maybe he didn't realize how dire the situation was.

"I'm pretty sure someone has been following me," I confessed. "Do you think I should be worried?"

"It's probably Ronan."

"It's not," I replied. After seeing his expression when I'd accused him of it, I knew that much.

He made an impatient sound. "Maybe you're imagining it."

I pressed my lips together so I wouldn't cry. I shouldn't be surprised. It served me right for thinking he might have my back. "I don't think so."

"Then perhaps you have an admirer."

I shook my head, stunned that he'd wave away a very real problem by implying it was either in my head or that it was a misunderstanding.

"Remember to let me know if you find anything that's actually useful." With those parting words, he ended the call.

———

FOR THE REST OF THE DAY, I DOUBLED DOWN ON SCOURING King's Security intranet for useful tidbits of information but still didn't find a damn thing. When I got home, Sage took one look at me and guided me to the sofa while she made a batch of cleansing herbal tea.

"What's going on?" she asked as she handed me a mug and sat beside me. "You look like there's a lot on your mind."

I gave her a brief rundown of everything that had happened earlier. Her expression stayed neutral as I outlined my conversation with Ronan. When I mentioned Tom, her eyes narrowed but she remained silent. That was the good thing about Sage. She never interrupted. She let you say your piece and then said hers.

"Do you have feelings for Ronan?" She intertwined her fingers around a mug of tea. "I know you used to have that crush on him. Is it possible you're angrier with him than the situation warrants because you want him to be the guy you think of him as?"

I sighed and rested my head against the back of the sofa. "Maybe. Honestly, I'm so mixed up around him that I couldn't say for sure. He's not the same man he used to be, but something about him gets under my skin anyway."

Sage hummed in thought. "Perhaps you shouldn't fight it."

I opened my eyes and stared at her. "Excuse me?"

She shrugged. "The universe is trying to bring you together. Maybe you ought to go along with it."

I rubbed the back of my neck. Sage liked to think we were all part of the universe's master plan and that there were reasons for everything, but I didn't necessarily share her view. "Not a great idea."

"What's the worst that could happen?"

I didn't even have to think about it. "He could play me, screw me over, and go forward with the takeover despite our deal." Then I might lose my most powerful connection to Dad.

"Hmm." She sipped her tea and watched me over the brim. "Don't you think your dad would want you to be happy more than he'd want you to have the company?"

"Oof." The question knocked the air out of me. "Well, yeah, but there's no guarantee I'd be happy. Like I said, it could end very badly."

"There's no guarantee of anything in life. That doesn't mean we shouldn't take risks."

I sighed. In principle, I agreed, but knowing that and acting on it were two different things. I'd dedicated years to the company, and I'd protected my heart for much longer. I'd had my first taste of men using me for my money when I was only eighteen, and even though I was no longer rich, it was difficult to unlearn that lesson. Emotion burned the back of my throat. Sage seemed to know what was going on in my head because she placed her mug on the coffee table and put an arm around me.

"You don't have to do anything now," she said. "Just take each day as it comes, okay?"

"Okay," I agreed, but even that seemed like a big ask.

Chapter Eleven

RONAN

I checked the time on my phone as I hurried out of the King's Security building and onto the steps that led down to the street. I was running late for a meeting with a client. I hated being late. I glanced up just in time to catch sight of the top of Willow's head before she bowled into me.

"Oh!" She dropped her bag and stumbled backward, her heel catching on the edge of the stair. She teetered for a moment, but I hauled her toward me before she fell. She flopped against my chest. "Thank you. I'm sorry, I wasn't looking where I was going."

"It's okay. No harm done."

I should have let her go, but instead I held on for a few moments. She smelled of vanilla again. But the way she smelled was nothing compared to how wonderful she felt in my arms. Soft and supple, her slender curves pressed against the hard planes of my body. Having her there seemed right. As if she belonged.

I shook my head. I was being fanciful. As I drew back, my gaze dropped to her lips. They parted, a puff of air passing between them, and it could have been my imagination, but it seemed as though she leaned forward. But then I raised my gaze to her eyes and froze. They were wide.

Scared.

She glanced over her shoulder and scanned the pavement.

I forced myself to release her. "What's the matter?"

"Huh?" She turned back to me, her expression distracted.

"What's wrong?" I repeated.

"Oh." She gave a nervous laugh. "Nothing. I'm just behind schedule."

"I can relate." But I got the impression there was more going on.

Her mouth set in a firm line as she bent to collect her bag, and her eyes skittered like she couldn't focus on anything. I remembered what she'd asked yesterday, about whether I'd had someone following her.

"Are you running from someone?" I asked, my gut turning over at the prospect.

She jolted, her eyes flying to mine. "No." She leaned closer and lowered her voice. "Why? Did you see someone behind me?"

"No, I didn't."

She stiffened again. "I'd better go. I don't want to hold you up." She started to push past.

"Wait," I said. She glanced back. "Are you sure you're fine?"

"Y-yes."

The stutter gave her away. She wasn't fine at all. But before I could ask what the matter was, she continued up the stairs. I frowned. If she was in trouble, we needed to know. Especially if Tom was involved.

I checked the time again. I'd be late, but at this point, I didn't really care. Some things were more important than punctuality.

I found Zeke's number and called him.

"Aren't you supposed to be in a meeting with a big wig?" Zeke asked when the call connected.

"I will be soon, but I just ran into Willow, and she's on edge. I want to be alerted if she leaves the building."

"You're spying on her now?" I could hear the amusement in my partner's voice. "I thought you were above that."

"It's for her own safety."

"Uh-huh."

"Just do it. And if she does leave, can you ask Kade to have one of his guys follow her at a distance?"

He snorted. "You're really taking this to the next level, but okay, I'll talk to Kade. He won't be happy about it."

"Tell him it's for her protection."

"If you say so, King."

"Something is scaring her," I insisted.

Zeke made a thoughtful sound. "Perhaps she's nervous because she's trying to steal our secrets for her brother. I've seen evidence she's been poking around."

"You have?" I shouldn't have been surprised. In her shoes, I'd probably do the same thing. "Do we need to be concerned?"

"I doubt it. With her level of access, there's really nothing for her to find."

"Are you sure?" I asked. "She's resourceful."

He chuckled. "I've seen the video of her entering your office. I know exactly how sneaky she is, but at this stage I don't think we need to worry."

"Okay. Thanks for letting me know anyway. I've got to go, but text me if she leaves."

"You got it." I ended the call and pocketed the phone, hoping Willow would open up to me about what was going on before it was too late.

I trembled as I stared at the envelope protruding from my bag. My name was written on the front in block letters. I'd discovered it beneath my door and opened it enough to get a glimpse of its contents, but before I'd had a chance to check properly, I'd felt the creepy sensation of being watched, and I'd had to leave. To get somewhere secure before I uncovered its contents. Where could be more secure than a security firm?

I grabbed the envelope and, with fumbling fingers, tore it the rest of the way open. Instead of emptying it onto my desk, I peered inside. Glossy photographs stared back at me. I lifted one out and felt myself go cold. It was of me, and based on the surroundings, it must have been taken during my morning walk from my apartment to work. Someone had captured that photograph without me noticing. They had been watching, exactly as I'd feared. Not that I had any idea who "they" were.

I snatched up another photo. It took me a moment to realize what I was looking at, but when I did, my stomach rolled. I was silhouetted against our apartment window, wearing my favorite tank top and yoga pants. I shoved the picture back into the envelope and leafed through the other photos. They were all of me. Walking down the street, buying coffee, at a gala with Tom and our respective dates, standing outside my apartment building with Sage.

Oh my God.

Someone had been following me. No. Worse than that. They'd been *stalking* me. Exactly as Ronan had guessed.

I searched for a letter, a note, anything to explain what this was about, but there was nothing. Desperation growing, I flicked through the photos again, scanning the backs in case anything had been written onto them directly.

Empty, empty, empty—oh, wait.

Finally, I spotted block lettering that matched the writing on the envelope. When I skimmed the text, I gagged. "My favorite" was all it said.

I flipped the photo over.

It was one of me in my flimsy summer pajamas, lying on my bed. From the angle of the image, it must have been taken through the window. But how? There were no buildings that looked directly into my room. A drone, perhaps? But why would anyone do that? Was it possible the eyes I'd felt on me had nothing to do with Tom, Ronan, or Lennox Securities? Maybe it was a garden-variety stalker, and I'd read too much into the stuff with my brother.

I turned the photo over and read those hideous words again.

My favorite.

Had some sick bastard done this for a thrill?

"Willow."

The envelope slipped from my grasp, and my hand flew to my throat. I spun around.

Imani stood behind me, grinning. "You're here."

"I-I…uh, yes." Realizing I was still holding the photograph, I tucked it inside my palm and hoped she didn't notice. "I'm sorry, you surprised me."

"I can tell." She glanced at the envelope curiously. "You were engrossed." She looked up and frowned. "Are you okay? You're really pale."

"Fine." My voice was thready, and I felt about as convincing as I'd been outside when Ronan asked what was wrong. "Didn't sleep well," I added, figuring an explanation may lessen the suspicious gleam in her eyes.

"Ah." She nodded. "Try lavender essential oil. Works like a dream."

If I'd been less scared, I'd have laughed. "My room-

mate says the same thing. I should introduce you some-
time. I think you'd like each other."

"Do it." She sat at her desk. Some of the tension eased
from my chest, and when she searched in her purse for lip
gloss, I slipped the photograph back into the envelope and
put it in a drawer, out of sight. "I love meeting new
people."

I arched a brow. "Even if they read your chakras and
say you have a muddy aura?"

Her eyes widened. "Especially then."

We made small talk for a while before getting down to
work. I kept busy until lunch and waited for Imani to leave.
When she vanished from sight, I extracted the envelope
from the drawer, stuffed it into my bag, and searched for an
empty meeting room. When I found one, I sat inside and
called the police department's non-emergency line.

"You've reached the Chicago Police Department." It
was a women's voice. "This is Fatima speaking. How can I
help?"

I glanced at the door to make sure nobody was
standing outside to overhear me. "My name is Willow
Lennox, and I'm hoping you can give me some advice."

"Of course." I heard her type something. "What's
going on, Willow?"

I lowered my voice. "For the past few days, I've thought
someone might be following me. For the most part, it's just
a feeling I get, but I did see a man once—maybe twice."

More typing.

"Has anything else happened?"

"Yes." I swallowed. "This morning I found an envelope
beneath my apartment door. It was full of photos of me." I
breathed in and out slowly, trying to ease the clench of my
jaw. "One of them was taken through the bedroom
window of my apartment."

She made a sympathetic sound. "That must have been very distressing."

"It was." Even now, I felt shaky. "Is there anything I can do about it?"

"Have you received any threats?" she asked. "Was there any kind of communication with the photos?"

"No," I replied. "One of the photos was labeled 'my favorite' but that's it."

"Hmm."

I didn't like her tone. It was hesitant, as though she was trying to figure out the best way to deliver bad news.

"Did you get a good look at the man following you?"

"No." My shoulders climbed up to my ears. This didn't sound promising.

Fatima sighed. "I'm afraid there isn't much we can do. You can bring the photographs to the station and we'll have them fingerprinted. There's a chance whoever delivered them is already in the system. We can also take a statement so there's a record in case the behavior escalates, but without an actual threat or any physical harm to yourself or your possessions, there's nothing else we can do."

"Oh." Tears of frustration welled in my eyes. I'd suspected as much, but hearing it still sucked. I cleared my throat. "I'll bring them in soon." At least that would be something useful, even if it wasn't much. "Thank you for your time."

"I'm sorry there isn't more I can do to help." I could tell she meant it.

"It's not your fault." I wasn't going to take it out on the messenger. "Can you let someone know I'll be there in the next hour or so?"

"Of course. And Willow,"—she hesitated—"take care."

"I will."

Chapter Twelve

Ronan

I was eating a sandwich and reviewing the plans for a corporate security job when a text arrived from Zeke.

Zeke: *Willow has left the building*

Immediately, I was on edge. Where was she going? To the best of my knowledge, she usually had lunch onsite and didn't leave during the day.

A moment later, another message came in, this one from Kade.

Kade: *Don't worry, I have a tail on her. He'll keep her safe if needed.*

I sighed. I'd rather watch her back myself, but Kade's guys were well-trained, and if he said she'd be safe, then I had to believe it. I replied to Zeke first, then Kade.

I sat back and tried to keep going, but I couldn't focus. I wanted to track Willow down and demand to know what she was involved in. Unfortunately, she was jumpy, and going after her like that wouldn't help. Especially since she already thought I might have someone following her. A guilty twinge reminded me that I did, in fact, now have someone following her.

I kept an eye on the ticking clock, and twenty minutes later, I received another message from Kade.

Kade: *She's at the police station.*

I leaped to my feet. What the hell?

Kade: *My guy had to wait outside. If he'd followed her, there's a chance someone would've noticed.*

She was talking to the police? Something must have been really wrong.

I strode to the window and looked out over the city. I wanted to be with her, hunting down answers, but I needed to keep myself in check. If I came on too strong, she'd freak out and back off. But I couldn't help feeling that if she was in trouble, I wanted to help. Especially if that asshole Tom was the one who'd put her in hot water.

Ronan: *Did your guy notice anyone else following her?*

Kade: *No. But I'll have him give a full report later.*

The next hour passed excruciatingly slowly.

Finally, Kade advised me that Willow had returned to her desk. I waited for another ten minutes before dropping by to check on her. I approached from behind and scanned her body. She seemed okay. Nothing out of place. I rounded her desk to avoid startling her.

"Hi, Willow."

She straightened and blinked at me owlishly. "Is there something I can help you with?"

I smiled, hoping I didn't look as tense as I felt. "I wanted to check on you after this morning and make sure you're okay. I was worried."

Her cheeks turned pink, and she gave me a pointed look, nodding toward her coworker, who was pretending not to listen. Willow's reticence, and that blush, made me ache to scoop her into my arms and keep her safe. To protect her from everything and then kiss the hell out of her. I mentally scolded myself. I wasn't this woman's white knight.

"Everything is fine," she said. "I had a rough morning, that's all."

My eyes narrowed. "Are you sure?" She'd hardly have gone to the police station without good cause.

She nodded.

There wasn't much I could do if she wasn't willing to share. I hesitated, then added, "Promise you'll come to me if you need help?"

She shrugged. "If it's something you can help with."

I pressed my lips together. That was likely the best I was going to get. I just had to accept that I couldn't shield her from the world if she wouldn't let me. But I dithered. I had no reason to stay there, but I didn't want to leave either. I liked being near her. She made me feel something I hadn't in a long time.

If she were anyone else, I'd already have asked her on a date. But because of how we'd become reacquainted, and because of who her brother was, I'd held back. But why should that stop me? If I had real feelings for her, why not let her know? She was only doing what she thought was best to protect her father's company, and I had no problem with that. Hell, I missed Frank every day.

"Willow."

She cocked her head, and the look in her eyes made me think I wasn't the only one who felt the tension between us. "Yes?"

"Would you like to accompany me to the charity gala that's happening this Friday?" I found myself holding my breath, praying she'd agree. I wanted the opportunity to get to know her outside of a work environment and to figure out what was distressing her.

Her expression became pinched, but I thought I caught a glimpse of disappointment in her eyes. "I'm already going with someone else."

My heart sank. No doubt she meant her brother and his crowd. "That's too bad."

I shouldn't have been so disappointed, but I couldn't help it. Tom Lennox ruined things even when he wasn't here. At least I'd get to see her. Maybe steal a dance or a kiss—if she was up for that.

"I'll let you get back to work."

I left before I could do something I regretted, like ask her to ditch her plans with her brother and spend time with me instead.

As Sage did my hair in preparation for the dance, I wallowed in what-ifs. What if I'd said yes to Ronan? What if I had been honest with him about everything? I'd have much rather spent the night with him than Tom and his flavor of the month. But at least Tom hadn't tried to set me up with any of his friends tonight. He loved to introduce me to "suitable" men, hoping one might stick.

"Why does Tom insist on going to these things when he has no money?" Sage asked, putting the finishing touches on a braid that curved around my forehead like a tiara.

I sighed. "Because he refuses to live within his means."

It worried me that I didn't know where the money for tonight was coming from. Events like this cost thousands of dollars per ticket, and thousands more went into looking the part. From what I could tell, Tom was basically broke. Yet he still insisted on putting on an appearance, clad in his latest designer outfit. He hadn't been pleased when I'd told him I'd be wearing a dress I already owned and would have Sage do my hair, but when I made it clear that was the only way I'd agree to go, he hadn't argued.

I checked my nails. I'd painted the pale pink polish

myself and if anyone looked too closely, they'd know I hadn't had them professionally done. And people *would* look. That's what they did at these events. They gossiped over who was wearing what, and who'd come with whom. I had no patience for it, but I'd been attending galas and charity dinners since I was eighteen, and at some point, my frustration with them had dulled.

"There." Sage patted an elegant knot on the back of my head. "All done. You look beautiful."

I smiled. "Thank you."

I gazed at my reflection, feeling oddly nostalgic. Perhaps I didn't enjoy the routine of getting dressed up for an event, but it was predictable, and I had a feeling we wouldn't be doing it up for much longer. Even if Tom maintained control of the company, things would have to change or we'd end up back in the same situation.

"Are you sure you should go?" Sage asked, gnawing on her lower lip. "You haven't seen anyone following you today? I'm worried about whoever took those pictures."

I hadn't shown Sage the photos, but I'd told her about them. Particularly the photograph of me on my bed. That had really gotten to me.

"I haven't noticed anyone." I applied lipstick and puckered up. "Maybe they saw me go to the police station and backed off."

"Maybe," she murmured, but I could tell she wasn't convinced.

My phone buzzed with an incoming text. It was from Tom, saying he was downstairs.

I stood and collected a jacket from my closet. It wasn't a cold night, but I wanted to be prepared. I tucked my purse under my arm and headed for the door.

"See you, Sage."

She waved. "Bye, Willow. Stay away from weird old men for me."

"I'll try." I took the stairs down and rolled my eyes at the sight of a limo idling by the curb. We no longer owned one, so he must have rented it. A driver, too, by the looks of it. I climbed into the back seat. "You look sharp."

His gaze flickered up and down my outfit as we pulled into traffic. "Good effort from you too, all things considered."

I resisted the urge to roll my eyes. He meant well, but he could be a shameless snob. I glanced at his date, a blonde woman with a bored expression. "I'm Willow."

She arched a perfectly manicured eyebrow. "I'm Chardonnay."

Well, okay then.

"Nice to meet you." I turned to Tom. "Is there anyone we want to impress tonight?"

Often, he had a business associate or a prospective client he wanted to wow, and it was my job to charm them so they'd sign on the dotted line with Lennox Securities.

"Petrov," he said.

I glanced out the window so he wouldn't see me pull a face. I wanted to ask if this was another of his attempts to thrust me at one of his business acquaintances in the hopes we'd click, but I held back. I'd rather not fight tonight. Things were tense enough.

We traveled in silence to our destination, The Art Institute of Chicago. When we arrived, he helped Chardonnay out while the driver rounded the car to open my door. I walked alongside them as we were escorted past the lion statues that stood guard by the stone steps. Inside, each of us was handed a glass of champagne. I looked around, taking in the grand staircases where people milled about and the quietly opulent décor—everything in tones of cream and gold. We did the rounds, circulating among his friends and acquaintances. I began to hope he'd forgotten Petrov, but then he led us to a standing table in the corner of the raised platform that ringed the room.

"Good evening, Mr. Petrov." I forced a smile but didn't offer him a hand, remembering the kissing incident from last time.

Tom gave me a meaningful look, and I ignored him.

"Willow," Petrov said, touching my shoulder. "How many times must I tell you to call me Adrian?" A shiver raced up my spine. His finger was cold and unwelcome. I didn't like it on my bare skin. But I liked the idea of calling him by his first name even less. Dad hadn't liked him and wouldn't have wanted to see us associated with him. Tom might have bought Petrov's story that they'd been friendly rivals, but I got the feeling there hadn't been anything friendly about it. "You are absolutely exquisite."

"Thank you." My tone was taut, but neither man seemed to notice or care.

"Tom." Petrov gave my brother's hand a hearty shake. "I'm pleased you came."

"Likewise. This is Chardonnay."

Petrov's slight brow raise almost made me smile. "A pleasure."

Tom pulled his phone from his pocket and glanced at the screen. "Sorry, I have to take this call. Come with me, babe?"

He stepped away, taking Chardonnay with him, and I glared at his back. The liar. He hadn't received a call. He'd ditched me with the man like a sacrificial lamb.

"Tell me more about yourself," Petrov said, resting his forearms on the table. "You are twenty-five, aren't you?"

I shivered. Why did he know my age? "Yes, I am."

I looked around for an escape route. Much as I disliked him, we had an important working relationship that was currently more valuable to Lennox Securities than it was to Petrov's firm, so I couldn't afford to offend him by being rude. However unhappy I was with Tom, I didn't want to make things worse for the company. "What would you like to know?"

He licked his lips like a hungry dog. "I've heard you like yoga. Have you been practicing it for long?"

Years of training taught me to keep a straight face, but I was shocked by the question. Who'd told him that? It wasn't as though I kept it secret, but I spoke to few people outside of work.

"My friend Sage teaches it. She started making videos a few years ago, and I was her first student. I'm nowhere near as skilled as she is, but I'm passably good."

"I'm sure you're better than passable." He caressed my bare upper arm, and my skin crawled in response. "In fact, I suspect you're something of a prize."

Chapter Thirteen

RONAN

The moment I entered the gala, I knew she was here. I stood near the entrance and observed the people gathered. Finally, my gaze snagged on her, tucked into an upstairs corner with another man.

My eyes narrowed. Where was Tom? The man touched her, and I scowled.

She was beautiful tonight in a demure gown of the palest pink. Combined with the braid along her crown, it made her appear regal. Like a princess who'd deigned to grace us with her presence. Funny, because that's how I'd always thought of her. As a princess. Untouchable. But I longed to touch her anyway.

I studied her date, and my eyebrows shot up. The man was much older than her, with silver hair and a bulldog face. He was eying her as though she were dinner. Meanwhile, she edged away. Subtly, of course, because Willow Lennox was the epitome of good manners—to everyone other than him. Her eyes flicked around as though she was trying to figure out how to make a clean break from him.

Not okay.

Couldn't he tell she didn't want his hands on her? Or did he not care?

Probably the latter. Men who attended galas like this tended to be entitled asses. But I didn't have to stand by and watch some jerk make her uncomfortable. I surveyed the floor once more, searching for Tom, and found him standing by the bar with a statuesque blonde. He wore a smug, self-satisfied smirk. I wanted to wipe it from his face. My intuition told me he'd set Willow up and forced her into a one-on-one conversation with a man she couldn't be less interested in.

Bastard.

I needed to know who the guy was and what he meant to Tom. In the meantime, my gaze returned to Willow just in time to see the silver-haired man—there was something familiar about him—trail a finger down the side of her face.

Enough was enough.

I strode over to them and put a proprietary arm around her waist. Willow whipped her head up to look at me. For a moment, I thought she'd say something snarky, but when recognition hit, she relaxed. Her apparent trust in me felt good.

"Sweetheart," I said, silently encouraging her to play along. "There you are. I thought I'd lost you." I kissed her cheek, surprised by the gut punch of lust brought on by the simple act of brushing my lips over her silky skin. "I promised Anton Rogers I'd introduce you." I name-dropped the richest asshole here, knowing it would bother her admirer. I turned to him but kept my gaze steely as recognition set in. He was Adrian Petrov—a big name in the corporate security industry and a former competitor of Frank's. We'd met once or twice, but it had been in my former role, and so long ago I doubted he'd remember. "I'm Ronan King."

charge of the company, and the company is Dad's legacy. Making sure his memory is honored means more to me than nearly anything."

His expression softened. "I get it. He was a good man."

"The best." I felt my eyes start to well up, and I offered him a hand, in need of distraction. "You're right. We should dance."

He led me down one of the grand staircases and onto the dance floor, where he placed one hand on my hip and the other on my shoulder. We swayed together. The steps of a waltz came easily to me from years of childhood lessons. I'd been raised for this life. My mother had put a lot of effort into making sure I could hold my own in social settings before she passed away. It had been the one thing she'd done with me. Seeing me swirl around the floor in the arms of a handsome billionaire would have been her dream come true.

Ronan kept pace easily, and I smiled to myself. He must have taken classes because I knew he hadn't come from the same privileged background I had. He'd been a scholarship kid who'd clawed his way into the big leagues.

I inched closer until I could feel the hard planes of his body shift with each step and shut my eyes. I enjoyed dancing with him, whatever his reasons might be. He smelled clean and masculine—not of aftershave, as Petrov had, but of good, old-fashioned soap and hard work.

My chest brushed his midsection, and my nipples tightened in response. Heat pooled between my thighs. I might have been a virgin, but I knew what it felt like to want a man. I didn't let on though. I simply existed in the moment and let myself fantasize that this could be more than it was. That he honestly cared for me. That we were on a date, and soon, he'd take me home and kiss my cheek as he bid me farewell.

"You're beautiful."

My eyes flickered open, and I blinked up at him. His gaze was serious. Almost tender.

"Beautiful, and strong," he murmured, low enough that no one else could hear. It felt like we were in a bubble, separate from the rest of the world. "Why do you hide behind a persona?"

I frowned. "I'm not hiding anything."

His lips pursed. "People think you're cold. A proper, polite princess."

I laughed. "Then people are deluded. I'm no princess."

"You are," he said. "You just don't see it."

Tingles began low in my belly and traveled upward. "You think you know me?"

He gave a tiny shake of his head. "I think very few people truly know you."

Someone bumped into him, knocking us both to the present.

I glanced around, suddenly aware of Tom standing near the bar with murder in his eyes.

Ronan followed my gaze. "Let me give you a ride home. My conscience won't let me leave you with him when he's looking at you like that."

"It's okay. Wouldn't be the first time I've had to deal with one of his tempers."

"But you don't have to. Why not let him cool off and see him tomorrow?"

Wouldn't that only be delaying the inevitable?

At this point, did I even care?

"You know what? I'd like that. You can drop me off outside my apartment." I didn't want him to think he'd be getting an invitation to join me inside.

"Perfect. Come on." He took my hand and led me from the floor.

I kept an eye on Tom. He was fuming but didn't try to stop us. Ronan extricated his phone from a pocket and fired off a message—to his driver, I assumed. The moment we got outside, a shiny black car pulled up to the curb.

"What's your address?" Ronan asked as we slid inside.

I gave it to him, and he passed it along to the driver. I drew my phone from a hidden pocket in the dress and sent Tom a message.

Willow: *Heading home. See you tomorrow.*

A moment later, a call came in. Tom's name flashed across the screen, but I ignored it. I wasn't going to give him the chance to yell at me in front of Ronan. After a while, he gave up. I relaxed. But then a text arrived.

Tom: *What the hell were you thinking? I can't believe you left with that man in full view of everyone. Do you know how hard I've worked to assure Adrian you aren't dating him?*

My jaw dropped. What the hell did it matter if Adrian Petrov thought I was dating Ronan? Whatever Tom's business plans with the tycoon might have been, if he intended to use me to tempt more money or assistance out of Petrov, I wasn't interested. Perhaps I hadn't been clear enough on that front.

Willow: *I don't care if Mr. Petrov thinks I'm with Ronan or anyone else.*

I powered off the phone, some of the tension easing from my shoulders as I cut off Tom's only means of contacting me. It was childish, and I knew I'd have to deal with him later, but not tonight.

"Is everything okay?" Ronan asked.

"Better now."

"Good."

We sat in silence, but it wasn't uncomfortable. For my part, I didn't know what to say, and he seemed happy to exist in the quiet. That shouldn't have surprised me. The man I remembered from my youth hadn't been the chatty type. He'd been thoughtful. A trait that was far more attractive than it sounded.

Had he felt our connection tonight?

At one point, I'd wanted to kiss him. I still did. Being in his arms was everything I'd imagined as a girl and more. My insides twisted. He was supposed to be the enemy, but if that were true then he wouldn't have come to my rescue tonight or taken the time to remember Dad fondly with me. The truth was far from straightforward. But what was clear was that I had a chance with the man of my teenage dreams, and if I let it pass, I'd regret it.

"We're here."

I glanced up, surprised. I hadn't realized we'd been traveling for so long. "Thanks."

"No problem."

I opened the door and got out. He did too. We paused by the car, and I realized this was my opportunity. I may not get another. Tentatively, I rose onto my toes and brushed my lips over his. The kiss was soft and fleeting. I heard a quick intake of breath and pulled back, my mind already reeling. Perhaps I'd overstepped.

But then his palm curved around my cheek, and he drew me to him, capturing my lips. I ran my hands over the hardness of his body and the breadth of his shoulders. He tasted faintly of mint. The tip of his tongue tickled the seam of my mouth, and I opened, sighing as he deepened the kiss. Our tongues stroked, and our breaths came in gasps. He pivoted and flattened me against the side of the car, bracketing my face with his forearms.

"You are so lovely," he murmured, nuzzling the juncture of my neck and shoulder. If not for the press of his body, my knees would have given out. "Inside and out." I tilted my head to give him better access, and his lips feathered along the side of my neck. "You need to go into your apartment before I get carried away."

"Do I have to?" I whispered. "Carried away doesn't sound so bad."

He straightened. "Yes, Willow, you do." He kissed my forehead. "I'll walk you to your door."

"No." I'd be too tempted to drag him inside. "But thanks for everything. I'll see you next week."

"Take care of yourself." He stepped aside to let me pass, then waited on the sidewalk while I entered the building.

I reached my apartment feeling more exhilarated than I had since I was a teenage girl crushing on my father's protégé. Only this time, it wasn't a hopeless case. This time, I had a chance. Or more accurately, I might have a chance if we could figure out how to get out of the tangled situation we'd gotten ourselves into.

Chapter Fourteen

WILLOW

"So?" Sage demanded the second I walked through the door. "How did it go?"

I slipped off my shoes and collapsed onto the sofa. "Better than expected."

Her eyes lit up, and she settled beside me, drawing her knees to her chest. The hood of her unicorn onesie flopped over her eyes. "What happened?"

"I kissed him."

She flinched. "Who, Tom?"

"Ew, no!" I waved a hand. "Ronan. Tom supposedly got called away right after we started talking to Mr. Petrov, but Ronan saved me. We danced, he gave me a ride home, and I kissed him outside."

"Go, you!" Sage held up her hand for a high five. "Except for the whole Petrov thing, it sounds lovely. You basically got your date after all."

I rested my head on her shoulder and smiled. "I know. I actually think I might want to see where things go with him, even though he wants to steal my family company. I can't seem to help but want him."

Sage gave me a look. "That's great. I don't understand why you thought you and Ronan couldn't be together and just keep it separate from what's going on with your companies."

"Because things are messy and the world doesn't work that way."

She pursed her lips. "It should."

A knock sounded at the door.

I raised a brow. "Are you expecting anyone?"

"No. You?"

I shook my head, my pulse picking up as I wondered if Ronan had come back. "Who is it?"

The knocking stopped. A moment later, the entire door smashed inward and crumpled to the floor. Sage screamed. I scrambled off the sofa as a massive man appeared in the doorway. Debris crunched beneath his boots as two other men followed him in.

I exchanged a wide-eyed look with Sage. "Run!"

I took off for my bedroom, which was directly behind the living room, and she raced right, toward the bathroom. I slammed the door and stumbled to the window, but I'd forgotten it didn't have an emergency exit and there was nowhere I could go, short of falling to the concrete. I lunged for the closet, but before I could reach it, an arm encircled my waist and yanked me into a bruising embrace.

"Let me go!" I yelled, lashing out ineffectually with the back of an elbow.

The man grunted. I flailed, trying to kick him in the knee, but I couldn't reach it from my angle. I heard a shriek and a curse and hoped Sage was having more luck than me.

The brute hauled me into the living room and tossed me on the sofa. I straightened, mouth open to speak, and he backhanded me across the face. Pain blossomed on my cheek.

I touched the hot skin with the tip of a finger, hardly able to believe he'd hit me. Fear churned in my gut.

These men had burst into our apartment and attacked us. They were masked. They acted like they had no problem hurting people. But I had no idea why they were here, who they were, or what they wanted.

I didn't wait to find out.

I sucked in a lungful of air and screamed, hoping to alert the neighbors. The brute who'd backhanded me clapped a hand to my mouth and pressed. Hard. I whimpered into his palm. He leaned close, his eyes alive with excitement. He *enjoyed* this.

"Don't make another sound or I'll cut your pretty tongue out." His breath was warm and fetid. Near the bookshelves, the third man, who'd stayed out of the fray, snorted in amusement. If I had to guess, I'd assume he was the leader.

There was another curse from the other room, and I looked over in time to see a second man, short and stocky, enter with Sage tossed over his shoulder. He dropped her to the floor, then bent and secured her wrists with flexicuffs. That done, he headed toward me, shouldering Brute out of the way.

"Wrists together," he ordered.

I didn't comply.

Shorty extracted a knife from his pocket and flipped the blade out. "Now," he snarled.

With a gulp, I did as he said, even though it seemed like the worst possible move. I had no self-defense training, so what other options did I have? I couldn't take on three grown men, and Sage didn't look like she'd be much help. She was rocking back and forth, her expression blank.

"What do you want?" I demanded as he pulled the plastic uncomfortably tight.

The leader stepped away from the bookshelf, where he'd been examining our reading choices, and cocked his head. His impassive face was somehow more terrifying than his companion's excitement.

"Your brother owes our boss money." His rough voice grated on my nerves. He sauntered forward, cast a look at Sage, and returned his attention to me. "He needs motivation to pay."

Slap!

His palm cracked across my face. Warmth spilled down the side of my eye. His bulky ring had cut my skin. Blood trickled in a slow but steady stream, and my head spun. I didn't do well with blood.

Oh God. We were in trouble.

"Leave her alone," Sage cried.

She crawled over to me and started to raise her hands as if to touch my face, but then remembered they were cuffed. Something flashed, and we both looked up. Brute held a phone aimed at us. He snapped a second photograph.

"Do you think that's enough?" he asked the leader.

Leader considered us for a moment. "Trash the place," he said. "Make sure to get another photo on your way out." He stalked to the exit, only glancing over his shoulder for long enough to wink. "Play nice, girls. And, Willow?" A shiver crawled over me at his use of my name. "No cops, or Tom takes a long dive from a high building. We can make it happen. *Capiche?*"

"Yes," I whispered, wondering who on earth my foolish brother had gotten involved with.

To Brute, he added, "Hands off the blonde, but anything goes with the brunette."

Sage paled.

"I won't let him hurt you," I promised.

Her frightened look told me she knew it was a promise

I couldn't keep. Shorty shoved the bookshelf over and upended the coffee table.

I squeezed my eyes shut and tried to make myself small. Questions ran endlessly through my mind. I felt sick. Who did Tom owe? And how much? People didn't destroy apartments and assault women for small sums of cash. A sinking sensation told me he was in well over his head.

Brute advanced on Sage, licking his lips. She pressed herself into the base of the sofa as though wishing she could vanish. I forced myself to move despite the pain that licked along my nerves, sheltering her with my body. For some reason, this guy had been ordered not to hurt me, and I wouldn't let him get to Sage without defying that order.

"Out of the way." He nudged me with his foot.

"No." I curled protectively around my best friend.

He leaned down and sneered nastily. "I said move, bitch."

I stayed where I was. Shorty strode into my bedroom, and I heard something crash. Brute glanced at the door, then grabbed me by the shoulders and tried to lift me from Sage. I clung to her with every bit of strength I had.

"Hey, fuckwit," Shorty said a moment later. "Hands off the blonde, remember?"

He scowled. "It's not her I want."

"Come on." Shorty nodded at the exit. "We need to leave. Someone might have called the cops."

"But—"

"Forget about her."

Brute grunted in disappointment but straightened and lumbered away.

Beneath me, Sage's limbs loosened with relief. I waited until I was certain they'd both left before scrambling off her.

"I'm so sorry. Are you okay?"

"Don't worry. They didn't hurt me." She studied my face. "You're not bleeding much, but you should get the cut taped shut."

I shook my head. "If we go to the hospital, they'll ask what happened."

"And?" She widened her eyes. "If we don't, you could be scarred."

"Not a big deal." A scar might make men like Petrov less interested in me.

"What about the police?" she asked.

The only reason they hadn't arrived already was because our neighbor across the hall worked night shifts and the one to our left was on vacation.

"You heard him," I said. "If we call the police, they might do something to Tom."

"Willow." She sounded exasperated. "Tom can take care of himself. He's the one who dragged us into this mess. We need to look out for ourselves. Do you think, if the situations were reversed, he'd hesitate?"

I paused, considering her words. My brother was all the family I had left. He wasn't perfect, but no one was. Surely I should at least give him a warning first.

"I'll call him." I realized that my hands were still bound. I headed for the kitchen drawer and managed to open it and grip the handle of a pair of scissors. There was no way I could cut my own binds, so I made my way back to Sage. "Hold your hands out."

She cringed. "Please don't stab me."

I bit the tip of my tongue as I concentrated on lining the blade up with the indentation between her wrists. Then I held my breath and snipped. Her hands came free.

"Phew!"

She took the scissors from me and cut the band off my wrists. "There you go."

I winced as circulation returned to my fingers. I hadn't even realized it had been blocked.

I rubbed them, then turned on my phone. It buzzed with messages from Tom—all of them angry. I tapped one and hit Call Back then held it to my ear. It rang and rang, but he didn't answer.

I tried again. Damn, he must have been ignoring my calls because I'd ignored his, but now wasn't the time for stupid games.

I sent him a text message.

Willow: *Call me ASAP. It's urgent.*

We waited. Minutes passed with no reply, and my chest began to ache. Tears of frustration pricked my eyes.

"We have to tell someone," Sage said gently. "Even if it's just for the insurance. The door will need replacing, and the landlord is going to be upset. Not to mention, that guy was going to…" She trailed off, but my mind filled in the blank. She had every right to be angry and scared. She'd been threatened with far worse than I had.

"Can we give Tom until tomorrow to get back to us?" I asked. "He might have turned off his phone, and he'll probably hit the bars after the dance is finished. We can try him again in the morning and if he doesn't answer, I'll pay him a visit. He's probably ignoring me because he's angry, but what if he's not? What if they have him?"

I was asking for a lot, and we both knew it. Strange men had kicked down our door and terrorized us. Waiting to report the incident until tomorrow might not look great when the police asked why we hadn't called immediately. But Sage was my best friend, and she was strong. She'd endured a lot in the past, and I was hoping she could hold out for a while longer now. I'd do nearly anything for her, and I was counting on the fact she felt the same.

"Fine." She sighed. "But if we haven't heard from him by lunch, I'm calling the cops. What happened isn't okay."

I hugged her. "Thank you. I'm sorry about this."

She touched my forehead and tutted, not acknowledging my words. "If you won't see a doctor, then at least let me patch you up."

She moved around things strewn across the floor as she went to the bathroom, returning with a first-aid kit and a cloth. She set them down, took her phone from her pocket, and snapped a few photos of my face.

"For the police," she explained.

I nodded, mentally kicking myself because I should have thought of that. She knelt in front of me and, with soft strokes, cleaned the blood from my face. My cheek throbbed when she touched it, and from how hot the skin was, it must have started to swell.

"You're going to look terrible tomorrow."

"At least it's the weekend." Not that I'd be staying here. The apartment no longer felt safe. A sense of menace lingered. I was getting out at first light. Sage finished with the cloth and spread salve on my skin. Probably one of her home remedies. Last, she used a bandage to close the small cut above my brow.

"We can't stay here," I said as she tucked things back into the first-aid kit.

"We shouldn't leave when we can't lock the door to keep our things safe," she countered.

"No one is going to come down this end of the hall unless they're visiting us," I reminded her. "And nobody would visit this late at night."

She nodded reluctantly. "Okay. I'll say an incantation to ward off intruders and dispel the negative energy, then we can go."

"Sure."

If that was what she needed to feel comfortable, I wouldn't argue. Instead, I packed a few things in an overnight bag while she wandered around the apartment with incense. She left crystals at each of the windows and the door. When she completed her ritual, we took a cab to the nearest hotel and huddled together on the bed.

Neither of us slept.

Chapter Fifteen

The morning after my spectacular kiss with Willow, I found myself back in the office, reading my emails, when I noticed movement on one of the security cameras. I liked to keep them running so I could see who was around on the weekend. I watched as the top of a blonde head made its way into Zeke's office and hovered above his desk. I leaned closer, studying the image intently. Blonde hair, graceful movements…I was almost certain it was Willow. But what was she doing?

I got to my feet and was halfway across the room before I realized I'd moved. I took a calming breath and slowed my pace. If I rushed in, I might not get to see what she was up to. I carried on in a more measured way, wondering what had brought her in to work on a Saturday —and more specifically, into Zeke's office.

I approached from behind, my gaze tracking down her slender back as she reached for one of the drawers and pulled. It didn't budge. I paused, watching as she tried another. My stomach clenched as I realized why she must be here. She was trying to find something to use against me. Ammunition to make me back off from Lennox Securities. I'd hoped we were past that after the kiss, but apparently not.

I cleared my throat. "Good morning."

She jerked in shock and spun around. "Shit!" Her eyes were wide and panicked. "It isn't what it looks like."

I was pretty sure it was exactly what it looked like, but when I caught sight of her face, her motivation for being here no longer mattered.

"What happened to you?" I hurried to her side.

One of her eyes was swollen shut, the skin around it blue. Her other cheek was bruised, and there was a bandage on her forehead that couldn't quite conceal the split skin.

Someone had hit her.

Fury roiled in my gut. "Who did this?"

She touched her cheek. "Nobody you need to worry about."

I narrowed my eyes. "Tell me."

"I can't. It's complicated."

"Please," I beseeched. "I'm asking as someone who cares about you."

The fact she was holding back made me suspicious. Was this the result of a run-in with Tom? Had he hit her because she'd left the dance with me? I felt sick at the thought. I hadn't thought he'd go that far.

"I can't tell you," she whispered. "Not now. But maybe later. There's someone I need to track down first."

"Tom?"

She didn't answer, and frustration flared, twisting and heating in my gut. I burned with the need to keep her safe. To protect her.

"Is that why you're in here?" I asked. "You can't find Tom and you thought we'd have something you could use to hunt him down?"

She winced. "It sounds stupid when you put it like that. But I already knew you were looking into him, so I thought maybe you'd be keeping a record of his location."

The knots in my chest loosened at the knowledge she hadn't been trying to spy on me. At least, not today.

I held her gaze but gentled my tone. "He's in trouble?"

Her lips parted, and the lower one wobbled, but then she seemed to get a hold of herself.

"So am I," she replied. "But it's not your problem. I'm sorry for snooping. I didn't know what else to do, and if I can't find Tom then I have to call…"

I wished she'd finish the sentence. Who would she have to call?

"What's going on, Willow?"

For a long moment, she didn't say anything, and I began to worry she was going to ignore me, but she moistened her lips and spoke again. "I have to go."

Her words set off a series of uncomfortable sensations in my chest. I reached for her hand, but she pulled it away. "You need my help. Let me in."

She slung her bag over her shoulder. "What I need is to find Tom."

She was shutting me out.

"Don't leave."

But she pushed past me, heading for the exit.

I didn't know where I was going—certainly not back to the apartment—but I couldn't handle Ronan's questions or his gentle touch for a second longer. If he spent another minute looking all concerned and righteous on my behalf, I'd break down in tears. I wasn't equipped to deal with his version of caring. Especially when I didn't deserve it. I'd seen his face when he'd first arrived. He'd thought he'd caught me committing corporate espionage. And while that wasn't what I'd been doing—*this time*—I couldn't claim innocence on the whole. I'd betrayed the trust he'd shown by bringing me into King's Security. I may not have found anything to use against him, but it wasn't for lack of trying.

Whatever happened next, I knew I wouldn't be continuing the subterfuge. The panic I'd felt when I'd seen who'd discovered me had made what I'd already known in my heart all along undeniably obvious. Lying and scheming wasn't the way to protect my company. It wasn't ethical, and Dad wouldn't have approved. I was more than a little ashamed it had taken me this long to realize it.

I reached the elevator and jabbed the buttons, listening to his footsteps as he followed. The elevator doors opened; I stepped inside and prayed for them to shut quickly.

"Willow," he called.

"I'm fine," I yelled back.

I saw his face as the doors drew together and knew he'd have been able to put his arm inside and stop me if he wanted, but he didn't. Thank God.

I arrived in the foyer, swiped my access card, and rushed down the front steps. I wasn't sure whether Ronan was following close behind me, but I didn't care to find out. I glanced in each direction, and during my moment of hesitation, a white van pulled up alongside me. The door opened, and two men in black hoods leaped out.

I stumbled backward.

Not again.

One of them lowered his shoulder and rammed into my midsection. I found myself hanging over his back, the pavement swimming beneath my face. I bit my lip and focused. I wouldn't let these men manhandle me two days in a row.

I shoved my knee into his chest. "Let me go!"

It was daylight, and people were around. One of them had probably already called the police. I lashed out and listened to my abductor grunt when the blow struck true. A thump sounded nearby, and I lifted my head to see the other, black-masked man slump to the ground.

"Put her down." I recognized Ronan's voice above the rushing in my ears. My would-be kidnapper froze.

"You won't risk hitting her." I could tell from his voice that it was the man from last night. The one who'd wanted to hurt Sage.

"I won't hit her." Ronan sounded confident. "My aim is excellent. Now put her down, or I'll shoot."

Shoot?

Goddamn. He had a gun, and he'd aimed it at my captor. I just prayed he didn't hit my butt instead since it was level with the guy's face. I forced myself to relax, just in case. Tensing muscles usually only made an injury worse. I was used to guns. Dad had insisted I learn to shoot when I was a teenager because he'd believed women should be able to defend themselves. But I'd still rather not have one aimed in my direction.

Suddenly, my captor dropped me. I landed in a heap on the concrete. Pain burst through my body. The man in the mask hauled his friend into the van and they screeched away from the curb before the door had even swung shut.

"Willow?" Ronan knelt beside me. "Are you all right?" He touched my shoulder, and I realized I was trembling. Shivers racked my entire frame. Slowly, I checked each of my limbs. They seemed to be working. I staggered to my feet. "You took quite a fall."

"I'm okay," I rasped, my throat drier than I'd expected. "Sore and shaken, but okay."

"Okay?" he demanded in disbelief. "Do you realize someone just tried to abduct you from the street? Who were those men?"

"I don't know."

"Come on." He put an arm around me. "Let's get you inside."

I didn't argue. I felt very exposed out here. I let him guide me, surprised when he led me to a room on the ground floor instead of into the offices. He stuck a key in the lock and opened the heavy metal door.

"What's this?" I asked.

"One of our safe rooms. We have three in the building. Until we know who those people were, I'm not taking any risks with your safety." He switched on the light, ushered me inside, and locked the door behind us.

I scanned my surroundings, not taking in much other than the fact there were no windows.

"Sit down." He gestured at an armchair in the corner. "I need to make some calls."

I did as he asked and listened while he talked to his business partners, then to the police to report the attempted kidnapping.

I sighed, knowing I was going to have to come clean about the break-in last night.

I tucked my feet beneath me and tried to get warm, but my fingers and toes were icy. I shivered, pressing my lips together. A sweat broke out on my forehead. Something was wrong. I shouldn't have been so cold.

"Uh, Ronan? Do you have a heater or anything?"

He took one look at me and said a brief goodbye to whomever was on the phone. "Shit. You're going into shock."

He went to one of the cupboards, grabbed a fleece blanket from it, then carried it across the room and draped it over my lap. Next, he shucked his jacket and settled it over my shoulders. I liked the fact it smelled of him.

"Hold on a moment." He returned to the cupboard and came back a moment later with a lollipop.

I raised a brow, not sure if he was messing with me. "Are you serious?"

"One hundred percent." He handed it over. "Your body is having a shock reaction. Sugar will help." I peeled the wrapper off and popped it into my mouth. "Are you okay to stand?"

I got up. He took the seat, then patted his lap.

"I'm not sitting on your knee," I told him.

He rolled his eyes. "There's nothing sexy about it. You're cold, and my body heat will warm you."

I hesitated, then told myself I was being silly. In the grand scheme of things, it didn't matter that we'd kissed last night or that my body always reacted to his presence. This wasn't personal. He'd seen a problem and was trying to fix it. I lowered myself onto his lap. His warmth immediately saturated the fabric between us.

"You're hot." His lips twitched, and I cursed my runaway mouth. "You know what I mean."

"I do." He ran his hands up and down my arms to get my blood moving. "I need to know who's after you."

I closed my eyes.

He'd been well and truly dragged into the Lennox family mess now, and he deserved answers, even if I didn't want to give them.

Opening my eyes, I took a leap of faith.

"I don't know who they are, but Tom owes their boss money." I felt him stiffen at the mention of Tom, but when he didn't say anything, I continued. "Three men came to our apartment last night. They kicked down the door and tied us up." I didn't look at him. I still hated that we hadn't been able to fight back yesterday. "I don't know who their boss is or how much Tom owes him. I've suspected the company was in financial trouble for a while, so I'd been trying to bring in more clients, but I could never get him to talk about it. He's like a vault when he wants to be."

Ronan grunted in disapproval. One of his hands curved around my face and caressed the side of my cheek. "The men who came to your apartment did this?"

"Yes." I longed to lean into his touch, but he seemed to be doing it unconsciously, and I feared he'd stop if I drew his attention. "They hit me and trashed the apartment."

He exhaled slowly. "Did they do anything else?"

"They didn't sexually assault me." My voice was stronger than I thought possible. "If that's what you're asking. One of them wanted to hurt my roommate."

"Damn," he muttered. "Is she all right?"

"As much as she can be. They manhandled her and cuffed her but nothing worse, thank God."

His arms circled my waist, and he held me close. "What did the police say?"

"We haven't called them yet." He stiffened, but I soldiered on. "They threatened to throw Tom off a building if we did. Sage wanted to contact them immediately, but I got her to agree to wait until I'd had a chance to speak to him. Now he's not answering my calls and when I went past his place, he wasn't there."

I didn't look at Ronan because I didn't want to see his censure. I knew I'd messed up. We should have called the police immediately and trusted them to protect Tom.

"The men who tried to grab you now, were they the same ones from last night?"

"I think so. I recognized one of the voices, but they all wore masks, so it's impossible to say for sure."

He nodded. "How certain are you that it was the same voice?"

I thought about this. "Ninety percent."

Was it my imagination, or did his arms tighten around me? Perhaps I just wanted that to be the case because, despite the awful situation, I couldn't help reacting like a teenage girl with a crush around him.

"I can't believe Tom would put you in this position." He sounded frustrated. "If he owes money to someone dangerous, he's a fool not to sell the company and pay them off."

I didn't say anything, but secretly, I agreed. The family company—Dad's legacy—meant a lot to me, but it wasn't worth endangering our lives. We could always start over. The Lennox name carried weight. Not as much as it used to, but enough to bring a few clients and potentially a seed investor.

"He's running out of choices," Ronan muttered. "Why wouldn't he sell?"

"Tom will fight like a wild dog when he's cornered. He doesn't back down. Especially when he thinks you're the one trying to take the company from him." Finally, I voiced a question I'd always wanted to ask. "Why do you hate each other so much?"

Chapter Sixteen

RONAN

"I'll tell you about Tom and me later." I didn't want to think of her brother when she was on my lap. Without exception, Tom Lennox made me angry, and I'd hate to take it out on her. I was already worked up from the adrenaline spike of seeing those men try to shove her into their van. Time had slowed, and I'd wanted to rip them limb from limb. If the guy who'd had her hadn't given up, I'd gladly have shot him as well as the other. Willow didn't deserve to be hurt just because her brother was an asshole who didn't pay his debts.

An insidious voice whispered in my mind that if they hadn't tried to take her right in front of me, I might never have known how bad the situation was. They might have come for her again, and I wouldn't have been there. I couldn't stand the thought.

"Has anything else happened?" I asked.

She hesitated, scanning my face as though trying to get a read on me. "Some photos were pushed under my door recently. They were all of me."

My chest burned. "Do you think someone is stalking you?"

"Yes." I could hear the strain in her voice and hated it. "There was no note. I took them to the police and they checked for prints but there was nothing else they could do. Maybe it's not about me though. It might be a scare tactic for Tom to pay up."

Fury raged in my veins. It pissed me off that the cops couldn't do anything about a woman being stalked. A good portion of our clientele were stalking victims whom the police couldn't legally protect. It made me sick. But stalking was a far cry from the transactional nature of the crimes from last night and this morning. Those were about money. This was not. While it would be too coincidental for them to be happening at the same time, I wasn't sure how they might have been related.

"Thanks for telling me." It took every bit of willpower to sound calm. "Do you have any idea who Tom might owe money to?"

"No." She curled up smaller. "I wasn't even certain he did until yesterday, although I had a pretty strong suspicion."

Someone banged on the door, and she flinched. Then, as if noticing our position, she scrambled off my lap and wrapped the blanket around herself like a shield.

"King? It's Kade. You in there?"

I went to the door and undid both locks to let him in. "Thanks for coming."

"No problem." He glanced over my shoulder at Willow, who was pale but had stopped trembling. "How are you doing, Willow?" His voice was gentle, as though she were a frightened animal.

"Okay," she replied. "All things considered."

"Good." He stepped into the room, and Zeke appeared behind him, clad in a leather jacket and black jeans. Zeke's eyes flicked from me to Willow, then narrowed. He'd read the undercurrent of tension between us. "Is there anything I can get for you?" Kade asked. "A hot drink maybe?"

Her lips curved. If I weren't finely attuned to her, I might have missed it. Damn, why hadn't I thought of that?

"A coffee would be wonderful, thanks."

"I'm on it." Kade bustled back through the doorway, presumably going to the in-house café.

"We should head up to the office," Zeke said. "I assume that's where the police will go."

"Most likely." I hadn't told my Chicago PD contact about our safe rooms. There were some things I liked to keep quiet. "You're right. We should go." The threat had passed, and now that all three of us were here, an enemy would have had to be insane to try their luck at abducting her. I turned to Willow. "Bring the blanket. I'll restock later."

She flashed that almost-smile again.

We walked in a convoy to the elevator and rode it up. I led the group onto our floor and looked around before sending a message to Kade to let him know where we were.

"We can use my office," I said.

Zeke nodded. "You take her there. I'm going to grab my laptop and pull up the roadside security footage."

Our company oversaw security for the entire building, which meant we had cameras everywhere.

He broke away from us, and I dropped into step beside Willow. "Do you need anything to eat? The police will want to take a statement, and you might be busy for a while after they arrive."

She shook her head. "I don't think I could make myself eat anything. The coffee will be fine."

A buzz sounded overhead, alerting me that someone else had entered the foyer via the elevator. I rested a hand over the holster of my gun and shoved Willow behind me. It was probably the police, but better safe than sorry. The door from reception inched open, and a badge appeared around the corner, held up by someone who knew better than to surprise me.

"It's Detective Lee."

I relaxed. "Come in, Jo."

Joanna Lee lowered her badge and entered the office. Her olive-toned face didn't crease into a smile. She wasn't the type for anything as informal as that. Detective Lee was by-the-book.

"Heard you had some trouble, King."

"We did. I was just taking Willow to my office. Why don't you come through?"

Joanna nodded, her long, black ponytail bobbing over her shoulder. "I left two officers outside to shut off access to the area. The crime scene techs will be here soon to check for evidence, but considering it's a busy street, I doubt they'll find much." She gestured to a uniformed young woman behind her. "This is Officer Matthews. She's trained in evidence collection and will process Ms. Lennox. After that, I'll take her statement."

Officer Matthews smiled and raised a hand. I lifted my chin, acknowledging her. The kid looked no older than twenty, but Joanna didn't suffer fools, so if she was here with her, then she must have been good at her job.

I led them to my office and gestured for them to sit at the table along the wall. I dragged my chair around the desk to join them. Before they could begin, Kade returned with coffee and set it in front of Willow.

She smiled gratefully. "Thank you."

"No problem." His cheeks reddened, and he dropped into a seat at the table.

Joanna raised an eyebrow. "Are we expecting anyone else?"

"Zeke is getting the security footage," I told her.

"We'll need a copy."

"Of course."

She turned to Matthews. "Would you like to take Ms. Lennox somewhere more private for processing?"

"Here is fine," Willow interjected, glancing my way. "I feel safer with everyone around."

"Okay, then." Joanna indicated for Matthews to begin.

We sat in silence while Matthews photographed Willow and checked her body for evidence. Willow sat stoically throughout as though having a stranger touch her was nothing new.

"Are you okay?" I asked at one point.

She raised her eyes to mine and shrugged. "It has to be done. No point making a fuss."

It was a pragmatic reply, but I couldn't help feeling that she was bottling everything up, and I didn't like it.

Shortly after, Zeke came in with his laptop and passed Joanna a flash drive. "Here is the recording."

"Thank you, Ezekiel."

He winced, and I noticed Kade hide a smile.

Finally, the poking and prodding ended, and Matthews handed Willow a tracksuit and a plastic bag to put her clothes in because they'd become evidence. She took the items and left the office, returning minutes later in the shapeless gray outfit. She handed Matthews the bag and sat.

Joanna turned to Willow. "Are you ready to give a statement?"

Willow sipped her coffee and nodded. Her hands trembled.

Joanna pulled a recorder from her pocket and placed it between her and Willow.

"This is Detective Joanna Lee interviewing Willow Lennox at 12:45 p.m. on Saturday, March 27." She looked at Willow. "Can you state your name for the record?"

Willow moistened her lips. "Willow Lennox."

"Good. Now please tell me everything that's happened, in your own words."

We all listened while Willow recounted what she'd told me earlier, including the envelope of photographs she'd taken to the police station. Kade caught my eyes, and I could see how pissed he was about the entire situation. My friend hated women being endangered more than anything else. It had gotten him into trouble in the past.

"Do you have any idea who your brother might owe money to?" Joanna asked.

"No." Willow seemed to shrink in her chair. "I'm sorry, I wish I did. I know Ronan has been looking into him. He'd have more idea than me."

Joanna nodded and glanced at me. "We'll want copies of any information you're able to share."

"Zeke will provide our file on him," I replied.

She turned back to Willow. "Is there anyone you've noticed Tom spending a lot of time with? Meetings at the office or late-night phone calls?"

Willow scowled. "I'm not around him much outside of work, and I haven't noticed anything out of the ordinary except he's on edge and very sensitive about money."

"Tom doesn't talk to you about his problems?" Joanna asked. "You're his sister. His only family."

One of Willow's eyes twitched. She'd hit a nerve. "I assure you, I'm aware of that, but I'm telling the truth. I don't know who Tom might be involved with. I don't even know where he is."

"Come on, Willow." Joanna leaned forward, her expression intent. "*Think.* You know Tom better than anyone. If he was in trouble, where would he go? Who would he turn to?"

Willow's eyes flashed with temper. "I have no idea."

"I don't buy that," Joanna pressed. "Dig deep. Does he own any real estate?"

"There's his condo. The Lennox Securities office. I think that's all, but it's not as though we share confidences."

"Why not?"

"Maybe it's the age gap. Maybe it's the fact I was Dad's favorite. Or it could be just that he hates showing weakness to anyone."

Joanna shook her head. "And if there were more to it than that?"

"If there is, then I don't know about it." Willow's voice cracked, and I shifted uncomfortably, exchanging a look with Kade. She'd been through enough today without an inquisition. "I've told you everything I can."

Joanna met her gaze levelly. "You're sure there's nothing else?"

"My brother clearly doesn't trust me, and he doesn't want me involved in running the business. So yes, I'm sure there's nothing else." Air hissed between her clenched teeth. "As I've said, I have no clue where he might be, or who he might be with. That's God's honest truth, and wishing I knew more won't make it happen."

I cleared my throat. "Willow has told you as much as she can. Why don't we call an end to the interview?"

Chapter Seventeen

WILLOW

"I think that's a good idea." My voice shook with emotion. I needed to end this conversation and try to get in touch with Tom. Perhaps he'd drawn me into his bullshit, but he deserved a heads-up that someone was coming after him—if he didn't already know.

I stood and paced to the window, refusing to make eye contact with anyone. I found his number and called it. No answer, same as this morning.

"Call me back as soon as you get this," I said. "You're in danger." Then I hung up, silently cursing the position my self-centered brother had put me in. "Please find him," I said, turning to Detective Lee, who'd remained seated. "He's not an angel, but he doesn't deserve to die."

She nodded briskly. "We'll try, but we don't have a lot to go on."

I pressed my lips together. "I'm sorry I wasn't more help."

"We'll work with what we've got. If you think of anything else, let me know." She slid a business card onto the table. "Until we get new information, you're our priority. We'll send crime scene techs to your apartment to collect evidence—provided there's still something to find." She paused. "You should have called us last night."

"I know." Then something occurred to me, and I gasped. "Oh my God. Sage!"

Her forehead wrinkled. "Excuse me?"

"My roommate," I explained. "She was there last night. Is it possible they'd have gone after her?"

The detective considered this. "Given your theory that Tom owes them money, it's unlikely, but not impossible."

"I'll get her," a gruff male voice barked. Kade. He stood. "Where will she be?"

I rattled off the address, then impulsively hurried over and hugged him. He stiffened against me, and I backed away, feeling awkward. "Thank you. Sage is very important to me."

Kade nodded. "We'll keep her safe. I'll be back as soon as I can." He started toward the exit.

"Kade," Ronan called after him.

He turned. "Yeah?"

"Let us know when you have her."

"I will." He lifted a hand as he left.

I sent Sage a quick message, letting her know that someone would be coming to get her and that I'd explain everything when she arrived.

Detective Lee's phone rang, and she stepped outside the office to answer it.

"Are you okay?" Ronan asked as he came to my side and touched my shoulder. A jolt ran through me at the contact, and I resisted the urge to lean into his body and let him support me. I was the furthest thing from okay, but I'd been raised by Frank Lennox, and I wouldn't wilt under pressure.

I lifted my chin. "I'm managing, but I'll be better once I know Sage is protected."

"Good." He moved away and went to his desk, where he and Zeke spoke in hushed voices.

Officer Matthews sidled over while I watched them. "Is he your boyfriend?"

I couldn't mask my surprise. "Who, Ronan? No, he's my boss."

Although we may have muddied the water on that score with the kiss last night.

She pulled a face. "Awkward. Sorry. I thought I sensed a vibe between you. My mistake."

"No problem." I tried to dismiss the comment, but it unnerved me. The truth was, Ronan had been the yardstick I'd used to measure every man I met, and I wanted for there to be something more between us.

"I'm sorry this is happening to you," Matthews added.

I caught her eye, surprised once again. "Oh?"

She shrugged. "Seems unfair that you're a target because your brother doesn't take responsibility for his actions."

I narrowed my eyes. The young cop barely looked like she'd left high school, yet she sounded more mature than Tom ever had. "How old are you?"

She laughed. "Twenty-two, but Joanna says I'm an old soul."

I could see that.

The office door swung open, and Detective Lee re-entered. "We have the results from fingerprinting the photographs." She crossed the floor and held up her phone to show me the screen. "They came back to this guy. Do you recognize him?"

I studied the image. The man—Mark Orlov, according to the name beneath the mug shot—had close-cropped brown hair, a brutish face, and a mean glint in his eye. "I don't, sorry."

"Are you sure?"

I looked closer. "I have a good memory for faces. Dad drilled it into me. I don't know him. But the men who attacked me wore masks."

She pursed her lips. "Could he have been one of them?"

"Maybe." I didn't want to commit to anything when I hadn't seen any faces. "He's the right build." I felt useless and hated it. I racked my brain. "Perhaps if I could hear him. All three men spoke last night, and I definitely remember their voices." I shivered. "I can't get them out of my mind."

"Good idea." She smiled, and I felt vindicated after how supremely unhelpful I'd been so far. "The fingerprint is enough to bring him in for questioning, and I should be able to get a recording of his voice to see if you can identify him."

I nodded. "Let me know as soon as you do."

"I'll be in touch." She jerked her chin at Matthews. "Do you have everything you need?"

"Yes, ma'am."

Was it just me, or had Detective Lee's nostrils flared at the word ma'am? I hid a smile.

"We'll be on our way then." She tipped her head to Ronan and Zeke. "Keep me informed if you learn anything."

"You got it, Jo." Zeke winked at her, and she gave him a schoolmarm look. "See you soon."

Then she and Matthews left.

"Do you have to toy with every person you meet?" Ronan asked Zeke.

Zeke shrugged. "Only the ones who need to loosen up." He turned to Ronan. "I need to talk to you." He glanced at me. "In private."

Ronan rounded his desk and placed his palm on my

lower back. The heat from his hand was oddly reassuring. "Will you be okay here until we return?"

"Yeah." Although the jackhammering of my heart made me realize I didn't want to be alone. I wasn't about to show my weakness though. I'd done enough of that already.

"Keep warm," Ronan said. "If you need something to eat, I'll get it. Don't leave the office."

My nostrils flared. I wanted to protest that he didn't need to be so bossy, but he was right. Being here was the safest thing. "I won't."

The two men walked out, and I sank to the floor and drew my knees to my chest. Somehow, I'd managed to hold everything together, but now I could freak out in peace. I rested my head on my knee and blew air out through my teeth. What was Tom thinking, getting a loan from a person dangerous enough to kidnap me when he didn't pay? My brother must have known who he was getting into bed with.

I reached for my phone and sent him a message.

Willow: *Someone tried to abduct me. This is serious. The police are involved.*

Next, I sent one to Sage.

Willow: *Are you okay? Has your ride arrived yet?*

I counted the seconds until my phone buzzed again.

Sage: *What's going on? The silent giant won't tell me anything.*

Willow: *It's complicated. Like I said, I'll explain when you get here.*

Finally, half an hour later—at which point Ronan and Zeke were still gone from the room—I caught sight of Sage through the small window set into the office door. I raced out and launched myself into her arms.

"I'm so glad you're okay."

———

"The friend is here," Zeke said, glancing at his computer, where the security footage was displayed.

I followed his gaze and watched the two women embrace. Willow was slim and ethereal, while Sage was shorter, curvier, and brunette.

"Let's run them through the plan," I said.

Zeke and I had already decided we'd be putting a protective team on Willow. Even if she hadn't asked for it, we took care of our own, and whether she liked it or not, she was one of us now. Personally, I didn't think watching over her was enough. Anytime she was out of sight, my nerves went crazy.

As we approached my office, the women and Kade came into view in the corridor just outside. I immediately noticed that Kade had an unusual expression. Something was off with him, but I couldn't put my finger on it.

Willow was speaking rapidly to Sage. Updating her on the situation, I supposed. She looked up, and her lips curved as she saw us coming. That slight change felt like a punch to my gut. It left me winded and confused, but strangely, I liked it. Her happiness, however minor or fleeting, lit me up.

"Sage." Willow spoke louder, presumably for our benefit. "This is Ronan, and his other business partner, Zeke."

The brunette turned, and without warning, launched herself at us, her arms open wide. She wrestled both Zeke and me into an embrace, then broke away. "Thank you for saving my Willow. I don't know what I'd have done if you hadn't been there." Her lower lip wobbled, and I worried she'd break down in tears, but she took a deep breath and stilled the tremble. "I told her we should go to the police, but she was worried about Tom."

"You're welcome," I said. "I'm sure she mentioned it already, but we've spoken to the police now."

"Good." Sage's eyes narrowed, and the directness of her gaze caught me by surprise. Apparently, the yogi had a hidden layer of steel. "I hope they catch those men and make them rethink their major life choices."

Before she could say anything more, my phone rang. I extracted it from my pocket. "King."

"Ronan, this is Detective Lee. The crime scene techs have finished at Ms. Lennox's apartment. They said the door will need to be replaced. It splintered when the offender kicked it down and the damage is irreparable."

"Damn." I was definitely not okay with sending Willow and Sage back to a place where they'd be sitting ducks if anyone came looking for them. "Anything else worth noting?"

"There's blood on the floor that corroborates Willow's story. Nothing major. Just what could be expected from a shallow head wound."

My gut churned. I hated the idea of Willow bleeding. "Thanks for the update. I'll let you know if we find anything. If you need to speak to the roommate, she's here with us."

"We'll have to get her version of events," Joanna said, as I'd expected.

"Of course. I'll pass her contact details along."

We ended the call. The group around me had fallen silent, no doubt waiting to hear the latest. I filled them in on what Joanna had said, then hesitated, hoping they wouldn't object too hard to what I was about to suggest. "I'd like both of you to stay at my place until we know you're safe. My penthouse has top-of-the-line security. There are too many variables if you return home."

Willow blanched. "We can't put you out like that. You've already done too much. Sage and I will rent a hotel room for the night. No one will know where we are."

I sighed. "Can I speak to you alone?"

I led her into my office and gently closed the door so we were out of sight of the others. Any question died on her lips as I brushed my mouth over hers and breathed in the scent of her.

"Willow," I urged. "Please let me do this for you. I won't be able to concentrate on finding whoever is behind it if I'm worried about you. If I know you're there, I'll be able to focus."

"Oh." She tilted her head, her brow furrowing in bemusement. "You're that concerned about me?"

"I am." I didn't want to come on too strong, but she needed to know where I stood. "There's something between us. It doesn't make sense, but we both know it's there." I waited for her to nod before continuing. "I need you safe."

"That's surprisingly sweet." She touched her lips chastely to mine, and the scent of vanilla invaded my senses. I ached to haul her into my arms and kiss her until she went boneless, but now wasn't the time. "Okay, I'll come. But I can't just sit around. I need to keep busy. Do something useful."

I reached down and intertwined my fingers with hers. "That's fair. You should talk to Sage about coming too, just to be safe."

"I'll do that now."

We went back out to the others. I noticed my partners glance at our interconnected hands, but no one said anything. I stared at Zeke, daring him to comment as Willow extricated her fingers from mine and pulled Sage aside.

"What's going on between the two of you?" Kade asked, edging closer. "I hope this isn't about Zeke's cock-eyed idea of revenge sex."

"It's not," I assured him, although I suspected he already knew that. "I like her."

Zeke rolled his eyes. "Anyone would. She's stunning, brave, and loyal. I just hope you know what you're doing."

Willow and Sage rejoined us. Sage raised her chin. "I'm overdue to visit my grandparents in Wisconsin. I think it's time I do that."

I was already nodding, but Kade disagreed. "You could be a target too."

"Unlikely," I said. "Since Willow was the target of the attempted kidnapping, I'd say it was more a case of Sage being in the wrong place at the wrong time last night."

Kade shook his head. "I don't like it. They could use her to get to Willow."

I paused. He had a point.

Seeing that he'd caught my attention, Kade carried on. "I'll escort Sage to her grandparents' place and lose anyone who might be tailing us. She can drop me off at the nearest airport once we're there and I'll fly back."

I studied him with interest. Escorting a client to a safe location was a reasonably common part of the job, and one that any of his staff could manage. Why had he volunteered to go himself?

I looked at Sage. "What do you think of that plan?"

She shrugged. "If it keeps the silent giant happy, then it's fine." One side of her mouth hitched up. "Of course, he should know that I like to listen to the sounds of nature while I'm traveling."

Kade groaned, swiping a hand down his face. "You mean I'll be stuck with hours of birdsong?"

"Or something like that. More than you can handle?"

"No." He thrust his shoulders back. "I've survived worse."

We all fell silent, aware that no one else in the room could claim to have more experience with adversity than our former military companion.

Well, except perhaps Zeke. But he'd never confirm or deny anything.

I cleared my throat. "It's settled then. Kade will go with Sage to her grandparents' place. Once she's there, she'll check in with Kade at 10 a.m., 2 p.m., and 6 p.m. every day to confirm she's okay. Does that work for you?"

Sage nodded. "Perfect."

Chapter Eighteen

WILLOW

"Let's go to your apartment so you can pack," Ronan said, glancing from me to Sage. "Both of you. I don't want you to have any reason to go back later."

"Okay," I agreed. Honestly, having a couple of people with weapons nearby would be comforting.

"I'll follow you," Kade said. "Then the wild child and I can continue to Wisconsin."

Wild child?

I looked at Sage and raised a brow, but she just rolled her eyes.

"I'll stay behind and work on pulling what I can from the security footage," Zeke said. "Call if you need anything."

We took the elevator to the ground floor, and Ronan guided me and Sage to a black Honda Civic.

"What, no Lexus?" I joked to cut the tension.

"This is better for getting around unnoticed." He unlocked it electronically and climbed into the driver's seat. I got in opposite, and Sage sat in the back.

"Are you sure you'll be all right without me?" she asked quietly.

"I'm sure." Even though I would have preferred to have her company, I wasn't willing to expose her to more risk. She reached forward to take my hand, and we gripped each other until we arrived outside our building.

"Let's do this," Sage said, stepping out.

Kade pulled up behind us and we made our way up the stairs and along the corridor, pausing outside the apartment, where police tape crossed the open doorway.

I glanced over my shoulder.

Kade's face had turned thunderous. "The assholes are lucky they're not still here, or they wouldn't be walking out alive."

"Come on." I took a deep breath and ducked under the tape.

Sadness welled inside me at the sight that greeted us. Furniture was overturned, powder dusted most surfaces, and a few drops of what looked like blood had soaked into the carpet—presumably mine.

I swallowed and picked my way through the mess without stopping to think about it. If I did that, I'd break down, and now was the time to be strong. I went to my bedroom, grabbed a suitcase from the closet, then started shoving things in it. Clothing, jewelry, my favorite shoes. I didn't know when I'd be back, and to be honest, I didn't think we'd ever be able to live here again. I'd never feel completely comfortable.

"Willow." Sage appeared in the doorway with a backpack over her shoulder. She'd changed into a loose-knit boho-style blouse and denim cutoffs. "You okay?"

"We're going to have to move."

She nodded. "I know. We should make sure our insurance company fixes everything as soon as possible, then hand in our notice. There's an unrestful energy about the place."

She came into my room and closed the door behind her.

"What's up?" I asked, zipping my suitcase.

"Don't waste this opportunity to get to know Ronan." She spoke quietly. "The universe has a funny way of working, and maybe this is how it's chosen to bring you together. He seems like a good guy."

"Yeah, he is." I sighed. "Just as much as he always was." And while I wasn't sold on Sage's theory about a matchmaking universe, I'd take advantage of our time together to find out if there really could be something between us.

We sorted out the last of our things and exited the apartment, not having to duck beneath the tape this time because either Ronan or Kade had torn it off. We all made our way downstairs. Sage and I embraced on the sidewalk.

"I'm sorry about all of this," I muttered.

"It's not your fault." She squeezed tighter. "Stay safe. I know I have orders to check in, but I'd like it if you could do the same since you're more likely to be in danger than me."

"Of course." I kissed her cheek. "Say hi to your grandparents for me."

"I will."

We broke apart and each went to our separate cars. She gave me a little wave as I climbed into Ronan's vehicle. We pulled away from the curb, and moments later, she was out of sight. I relaxed into my seat, suddenly exhausted.

"Kade will keep her safe," Ronan promised.

I curled cold fingertips into my palms. "He'd better."

His eyebrows shot up. "Or he'll answer to you?"

"Damn right."

He chuckled. "You don't curse much, do you? At least, not out loud."

I huffed. "According to the law of Frank Lennox, ladies shouldn't curse."

He rolled his eyes. "One of the few things we disagreed on. I think ladies should be able to say whatever the hell they like, the same as men."

I grinned and snuck a sidelong peek at him. "Agreed." We drove in silence for a few minutes, but curiosity got the better of me. "Do you miss him?" I asked. "My dad, I mean."

For a long moment, I thought he wouldn't answer. Then all of his breath left on a whoosh. "Every day."

I could hear the pain in his voice. The grief. Somehow, it made me feel less alone. "Me too."

"Frank was a special guy." He clutched the steering wheel tighter, his knuckles whitening. "A true gentleman."

I blinked, trying not to tear up. "He just had this way of talking to people as if what they had to say really mattered."

"Yeah." He cleared his throat. "That was one of the things I liked best about him. He didn't care who my parents were or how I'd been raised as long as I was good at my job."

My heart skipped, and I held my breath, hoping he'd expand on his childhood. There was so much I didn't know about him. But he stayed silent, and before long, we arrived at his penthouse, which was located in a forty-story apartment building with a glass façade within the Chicago Loop. The elevator ride to the top floor was fraught with tension. I glanced at Ronan, wanting to close the distance between us but not certain how. When we reached the top, we passed through a small foyer that separated the elevator from the penthouse. Ronan unlocked the door and let us into a spacious living area. I looked around, mentally comparing it to my own apartment, but there wasn't even a comparison. Everything here was just so, from the expensive white leather chairs to the exquisite rugs and the art adorning the walls. Once upon a time I'd have fit in, but now, I was completely out of place.

Ronan steered me down a hall and to a closed door. He tapped on the wood. "This will be your bedroom for as long as you're here. There's a bathroom attached. Feel free to use anything you find and let me know what else you need." He paused, then brushed a kiss over my temple. "I'll give you some time to settle in. I'll be in the living room."

"Okay." His tender kiss had shaken me, but I tried not to let it show. "I appreciate everything you're doing, especially when I wouldn't blame you for not wanting anything to do with my mess."

He drew the backs of his knuckles along my cheekbone, and I tried to ignore the goosebumps that erupted all over my body. "We'll find whoever is behind this, then we'll track down Tom and make sure his problems don't touch you again."

I shivered. "From your mouth to God's ears."

He pulled away and I gripped the door handle to steady myself. Then I took a breath and entered. The bedroom was beautiful, with off-white walls, a massive bed in the center, and an impressive view of Chicago from the window.

I wandered over and stared out.

Thinking back to a week ago, I'd never have believed I'd end up here. So much had changed, and I wasn't sure what to make of it. Somewhere out there, Tom was laying low, and I hoped he was all right.

———

When Willow vanished into the bedroom, the first thing I did was text Kade to arrange a guard for the door into the penthouse. Then I ordered pizza, advising them to notify me when they were in the lobby below. Once that was done, I went to my bedroom. I stripped off my suit and changed into a pair of jeans and a plain black T-shirt.

The sound of running water came through the wall. I tried to tune it out. I didn't want to think about Willow naked or wonder whether her legs were as long as they seemed to be.

Groaning, I dragged a hand down my face. I also didn't want to imagine the slight curve of her hips and the creamy smoothness of her breasts. For God's sake, the woman had been traumatized. The last thing she needed was me fantasizing about her. I was ashamed for letting my mind even go there.

I hung my suit and returned to the living area, where I grabbed my personal laptop from the coffee table and flopped onto a sofa. I booted it up and went down a virtual wormhole, investigating the man whose fingerprints were found and delving deep into Tom Lennox's life, trying to discover whom he owed money to.

I hadn't found much by the time I heard feet padding down the carpeted hall. I glanced up to see Willow enter the room. She paused just inside the doorway and brushed a damp lock of hair behind her ears. With her face scrubbed clean, she looked very young. She crossed her arms, and I noticed she wasn't wearing a skirt or dress as she usually did. Instead, she was wrapped in a soft gray sweater and yoga pants. Comfort clothes. My protective instincts went into overdrive. I wanted to seal her in a bubble and make sure no one ever popped it.

"Hey," I said belatedly.

"Hi." She smiled shyly and gestured at the sofa. "Mind if I join you?"

"Not at all."

Her feet were bare, her toenails painted pale pink. She tucked them beneath herself as she sat. "What are you doing?"

I glanced at the computer, and my stomach soured. I didn't want to open the topic of her brother right now. Fortunately, my phone buzzed before I could reply. I checked it. "I ordered pizza. It's downstairs now. Don't leave the apartment while I'm gone."

She gave me a wry look. "Where would I go?"

"Good point."

I headed out, pleased to see Sean, a muscular Black man, standing guard at the door. "Thanks for coming in on your weekend."

"No problem, King."

I nodded respectfully, and he returned the gesture. "The primary goal is to protect Willow," I told him. "Someone is after her, and we're not sure who."

"Got it." He adjusted his stance. "I've only met her once, but she seemed like a sweet woman. Don't worry, nobody will get past me."

"Thank you, Sean." I took the elevator to the ground floor to collect the pizza. When I returned to the living room, Willow hadn't moved from her position on the sofa. I placed the pizzas on the coffee table and went to get us each a plate. "I wasn't sure what you liked," I said. "So I got pepperoni, cheese, and vegetarian."

Her eyes widened. "Any of those is fine. I'm not fussy."

We each grabbed a slice. Willow didn't say anything while we ate. The adrenaline rush from earlier must have left her hungry. Finally, two slices in, she wiped her fingers on a napkin and looked at me.

"So," she said. "Is now a good time to tell me why you and Tom have this weird little war going on?"

I swallowed a mouthful of cheese pizza and felt it travel in a hard ball down my throat. I'd rather not talk about Tom, but I supposed she deserved the truth. I put the slice of pizza down. "How much do you know about our history?"

"Not much," she replied. "You used to both work for my dad, but after he died, you left the firm and struck out on your own. I get the feeling Tom may have driven you out."

"He did, but our issues go way further back than that. Did you know Tom and I went to high school together?"

"I thought you might have—I knew you'd gotten a scholarship to a good school, but I wasn't certain which one."

"Horton Academy," I confirmed. "I worked my ass off in elementary school for that scholarship. But when I got there, Tom bullied me relentlessly."

"Why would he do that?"

I gave her a look. "Why does any bully do anything? It makes them feel good. I was an easy target because Mom and I were dirt-poor. I never knew my father, and Mom had a job, but it didn't pay well. Some weeks she had to turn tricks to keep food in our stomachs."

She gasped and clapped a hand to her mouth. "That poor woman."

I gritted my teeth. I hated pity, and so did Mom. "Not anymore. She's pretty well-off these days. But yes, the boys at school used to pick on me because of that."

I felt something brush against my fingers and glanced down to see Willow place her hand on mine. "I'm sorry," she said. "That must have been awful."

"It was." I wouldn't sugarcoat it. "But she's the one laughing now. She no longer has to work. She started her own charitable foundation and spends her days either working on that or volunteering at a homeless shelter because that's the kind of person she is."

"You love her very much." It was an observation rather than a question, so I didn't bother responding. "Did my father know about the bullying when he hired you?"

"He never came out and said it, but he asked after my mother often enough that I wondered."

"If things were so tight, how did you manage to go to college?" she asked.

I smiled wryly. "The same way I got into Horton. I earned a full ride to Harvard."

Her eyes widened. "Tom got rejected by Harvard. I can't imagine he took that well."

I snorted. "He didn't, but as long as I didn't have to deal with him anymore, I didn't care how he took it. I never expected to see him again. When I graduated, I received several job offers. I considered turning down Frank's because of my history with Tom, but his was objectively the best offer and there was something about him that I liked."

At that, she smiled. "He had that effect on people."

I couldn't deny it. I'd admired my mentor more than anyone else. "In the end, I figured that Tom had surely grown during our years apart so things would be different."

"But it didn't happen that way?"

I gritted my teeth. "He hated being treated as my equal. We were judged on our merits, and I respected the hell out of Frank for that, but Tom didn't like it."

She squeezed my hand. "Dad respected you too. He thought of you as his protégé."

Unexpectedly, the words hurt, and I couldn't hold back a bitter response. "If Frank respected me so damn much, why'd he leave me in such a crappy position? Tom tossed me aside the moment he could."

Her fingers jerked where they rested against my skin. "He *fired* you?"

I rolled my eyes. "Well, I didn't leave Lennox willingly. Frank meant a lot to me. I wouldn't have abandoned his legacy like that."

Her eyes darkened with sorrow…and was that a hint of anger? "Tom had no right to do that, and I'd have smacked him over the head if I'd known." She pursed her lips, her eyes glistening with emotion. "I knew he'd made things difficult, but I had no idea he'd gone that far. You'd just lost your mentor. How could he do that to you? It's thoughtless and selfish."

Which, in my experience, summed up Tom.

"He was an asshole," she continued. "Actually, scratch that. He *is* an asshole. I know Dad wouldn't have wanted things to happen the way they did. It's just that his death was so sudden. No one thought he'd drop dead of a heart attack." Her voice trembled, and I turned my hand over and cupped hers.

"I know. Unfortunately, the fact is it did happen, and we have to live with that." Something occurred to me. "How do you know he thought of me as a protégé? Did he say so?"

Her cheeks flared fire-engine red.

Intrigued, I leaned closer. "Tell me."

She bit her lower lip. "He did. I remember because I paid attention any time Dad mentioned you. I had a massive crush on you. He used to tease me about it, but not in a mean way."

I stared in shock. "He never said a word."

Although it stood to reason my boss wouldn't have told me his teenage daughter had the hots for me. It would have made me uncomfortable. But still, I couldn't fathom why a pampered princess would have held me in such high regard in the first place. And did the feelings she'd had for me still linger?

I hoped so.

I wanted Willow Lennox, and I intended to have her. I could be patient though. Tonight wasn't the time to make a move.

"Thank God." Her blush deepened. "If he had, I'd have died of embarrassment. It was bad enough that Tom knew."

"Ah." Yet another thing for her brother to hold against me. "Well, you might have been embarrassed then, but you don't have to worry now. You're a beautiful woman and anyone would be lucky to have you."

Her answering laughter was a little too loud. "Okay, so you know my big secret, and I know yours. Time for the really important stuff." From her tone, I could tell she was trying to lighten the mood. "Who was your first epic crush?"

I went along with her change of topic. Considering the day she'd had, I could understand why she needed to veer away from the deeper stuff. "Jessica Alba."

She gave me a look. "When did you realize it wasn't going to happen?"

I grinned, enjoying the way she teased me. "About the time she got married. I was heartbroken. Cried for days."

She laughed harder and rested her head on my shoulder. "Stop! I don't believe you, but it's still too much."

I tilted my head until my cheek sat on the top of her damp hair. "Has anyone ever told you that you're sadistic? You're getting far too much joy from my broken heart."

"I am," she admitted, wiping her eyes on the backs of her hands. "Thank you. I needed to laugh."

I breathed in her sweet scent and silently admitted to myself that I was beginning to need *her*.

Chapter Nineteen

WILLOW

Sleep eluded me for hours. I should have crashed the second my head hit the pillow, but I couldn't turn off my hyperactive mind. Instead, I lay in the luxurious bed and wondered how I'd come full circle to being infatuated with Ronan again. Somehow, he'd become my safety blanket. I curled up, cuddling my knees close. I'd felt so protected when he'd held me earlier. Now that I was alone again, all of my worries came crawling back.

Where was Tom and why hadn't he reached out?

What did the men who'd attacked me this morning want with me?

Was I intended to be a hostage or a message?

A muffled thud made me flinch, and my pulse soared before I realized it was Ronan next door. He must have been awake, too. Either that or he was a restless sleeper. I ached to comfort him. My heart hurt from what he'd told me earlier, and I hated that Tom and I had brought this trouble to him.

I slipped out of bed and tentatively headed to the hall, where I knocked softly on his bedroom door. He murmured in response, and I edged the door open and padded inside.

"Ronan?"

A shadowy figure sat up. "Is something wrong?"

"No, nothing like that." I bit my lip, wondering if it had been a mistake to leave my bed. But no, I needed company, and so did he. "I've been lying awake, staring at the ceiling. I can't shut my brain off. I know this is presumptuous, but can I join you?" It was just as well he couldn't see my flaming cheeks in the dark. "I feel safer when you're near." Realizing he might mistake my meaning, I hurried to add, "This isn't me making a move on you."

"Too bad." The soft words curled in the space between us like smoke. They tempted me. Made me wonder if he felt the same intense level of attraction between us that I did.

He shuffled over and drew the covers back. "Come here."

I climbed in beside him.

He immediately pulled my body against the curve of his and rested his arm over my waist. "Is this okay?"

I went limp with relief. It felt good to have him close. "Yes. Thank you."

His breath tickled my ear. "I'm glad you came. I like having you here." He kissed the back of my neck. A zing of pleasure raced through me. "I won't let anyone hurt you."

That was the last thing I heard before I fell asleep.

———

RONAN

I woke with my arms full of woman and wished the

moment could last forever. Unfortunately, I hadn't woken by coincidence.

Someone was in the house.

I edged from the bed, yanked a T-shirt over my head to accompany my boxers, and crept out of the room. I tiptoed down the hall, but once I reached the kitchen, I rolled my eyes and stepped out of hiding.

"How'd you get in?"

Zeke looked up from the stove, where he was scrambling eggs. "Good morning to you too."

"I never gave you a key."

I trusted Zeke on a professional front, but when it came to personal matters, the guy was a shameless snoop.

He winked, and a dimple popped up in his cheek. "I have my ways. Just so you know, the guards have changed shift."

"Good." I hoped Sean was getting a decent sleep after standing watch all night.

"So." Zeke returned his attention to the eggs, turning them over and then removing them from the pan. "How did the night go?"

His tone told me he was asking about more than how I'd slept.

"Uneventful." There was no reason for him to know we'd shared a bed. No reason for *anyone* to know. It was between us.

He laughed. "Whatever you say."

"Ronan?" The soft voice carried down the hall, and Zeke smirked.

"In here," I called.

A moment later, Willow appeared in the doorway, wearing a tiny pair of pajama shorts and a thin cotton tank top with no bra underneath.

My mouth went dry. Damn, she was the hottest thing I'd ever seen.

I might have been pressed up against her all night, but seeing her state of attire was different from feeling it. Especially since I'd tried to keep my hands on strictly PG regions of her body.

Her eyes widened, and she crossed her arms over her chest. "Zeke. I didn't realize you were here."

He laughed, and luckily for him, didn't take advantage of the opportunity to check her out. If he had, I might have needed to cut his eyes from his face. "Nor did Ronan."

"Why don't you go get changed," I suggested, my voice tight. "I will too. Zeke can finish cooking breakfast." I met his gaze. "I assume you're making enough for all of us?"

"Of course."

I placed my palm on the small of her back and guided her out of my business partner's sight. "Sorry about that. He tends to show up uninvited." That was, in fact, how he'd begun working with me in the first place. I stopped at her door. "I'll make sure Kade is on his way here. Then we can debrief while we eat."

She nodded, still blushing furiously. "Thanks. See you soon."

With that, she vanished into her room.

––––––––

WILLOW

Just my luck that I'd wander out in lightweight pajamas when Zeke was around. He probably thought I'd slept with Ronan in a less-than-innocent way. He might have even believed I was taking advantage of his friend's generosity. I didn't think Zeke trusted me. I sighed as I went into the bathroom. I'd just have to take him as he came and show by my actions that I wasn't a bad person.

I showered, dressed in a skirt that fell to my ankles, and

applied a coat of lip gloss. I took a deep breath and returned to the kitchen, where I found Ronan, Zeke, and Kade seated around a table with plates of scrambled eggs. A spare plate sat at the empty side of the table. Assuming it was for me, I slid onto the chair and inhaled the scent of coffee.

"That smells amazing."

"Of course it does," Zeke said. "I made it."

I pressed my lips together to mask a smile. I hadn't quite figured out the dynamic between these men yet, but it had taken all of twenty seconds to realize Zeke had an ego the size of Jupiter.

"How did the trip go?" I asked Kade. "Is Sage with her grandparents?"

He stopped wolfing down his eggs and nodded. "Safe and sound. She actually followed through on her threat and made me listen to nature sounds too." His expression said exactly how distasteful he found her choice of music. "For *hours*."

This time, I couldn't hide my smile. "Did you feel calm by the time you arrived?"

He rolled his massive shoulders. "No, I felt like ripping the stereo out. There's only so many waterfall tracks a man can be expected to listen to. But does she see that? Oh, no. She advised me in no uncertain terms that the soundtrack would be good for my blood pressure."

I privately agreed. But for all of his complaints, there was a certain fondness in his tone. Perhaps Sage had grown on him.

Zeke laughed. "She's a cheeky one."

"She's an eccentric," Kade said.

"There's nothing wrong with that." I silently dared him to disagree.

He dipped his chin. "The most interesting people are

eccentric. I didn't mean it as an insult. She's an unusual little thing, that's all."

"Well, okay then." I dropped the topic. Sage wouldn't disagree with his assessment, and unless he was badmouthing her, I had no problem either. I picked up my cutlery and tasted the egg. "Mm, this is good."

Zeke shrugged with false modesty, as if to say I should have expected that.

"Do we have any updates?" Ronan asked. He'd finished his breakfast and pushed his plate aside. He leaned onto his forearms.

"Tom is in the wind," Zeke said. "We'll find him, but he's making it difficult. We've managed to track down Mark Orlov, the guy who left his fingerprints on those photos."

"Good," Ronan grunted.

"One of my men is shadowing him," Kade added. "We won't lose him."

Ronan nodded. "Zeke, what say you and I have a conversation with Orlov?"

"Me?" Zeke's eyes widened. "Wouldn't you rather have The Incredible Hulk by your side in case the conversation isn't friendly?"

Ronan's gaze settled on me and warmed a fraction. Something tickled at my insides. "I'd rather Kade stay with Willow. If someone was to find her, I'd prefer they have to go through him than you."

Zeke's eyes flashed with humor. "Right. Got it."

"I'll keep her safe, King." Kade's lips curved in what might have been a smile. "We can practice some self-defense moves." He turned to me. "I'd rather you didn't need them, but it's better to know them and not need them than to need them and not know them."

"I'd like that." I was sick of being on the back foot. That stopped now.

His teeth flashed. "We'll start as soon as they go."

To my surprise, Ronan got to his feet immediately. "No point in delaying."

Zeke frowned and gestured at the remainder of his meal.

"The sooner the better," Ronan added.

Kade nodded. "Agreed."

With a last longing look at his eggs, Zeke got to his feet. Ronan rounded the table and stopped in front of me. I stood, unsure what he wanted, but then he kissed my forehead. Heat licked up my cheeks. I darted a look at Kade and Zeke, but Ronan didn't seem to care if they'd witnessed our private moment.

"I'll be back soon," Ronan murmured. "You're safe here."

"But will you be safe out there?" I countered. "I don't want anything to happen to you."

Zeke snorted. "King can take care of himself."

"And Zeke used to work for a government organization that he's not legally allowed to tell you about," Ronan added, caressing my cheek with the pad of his thumb. "We'll ask some questions and be back to you in no time, okay?"

I narrowed my eyes. "You'd better."

"I promise I'll get your lover home in one piece," Zeke said.

My eyes shot to him. *Lover?*

Neither of us had said anything about that.

Ronan rolled his eyes. "Don't mind him. He's digging for dirt. It's what he's best at." He bent and brushed his lips over mine, then he straightened, all business. "Zeke, we'll go to the office first to gear up, then you can tell me where to next."

His friend saluted irreverently. Despite myself, I

laughed. He might have been a bit of an ass, but he was a funny one.

"Bye," I whispered as they gathered their things and headed for the exit. "Be safe."

When the door closed behind them, Kade slid the lock into place. "Finish your breakfast and change into activewear if you have some. Let's see what you've got."

I gulped, wondering what I'd gotten myself into. "Okay."

Chapter Twenty

RONAN

Zeke and I geared up and checked our perp's location. Apparently, Mark Orlov was at church.

"Maybe he's praying for forgiveness?" I suggested, unlocking the car and loading a supply bag into the back. Zeke programmed our destination into its GPS, and I slid into the driver's seat while he claimed the passenger side.

"I don't think he's getting it," he said. We sat in silence for all of two minutes before he cleared his throat. "So what was that wonderfully domestic scene with Willow about?"

I sighed. "You're a terrible gossip."

"Do I look like I care? Let me hear it."

I wondered how much to say. "I like her. She's beautiful, smart, and loyal. It's just a shame that her loyalty extends to her brother."

"You going to let that stop you?"

I shook my head. "I'm planning to date her. But before you ask, nothing happened last night. Not that it would be your business if it had."

He wound down the window and rested his arm along

the frame. "I burned all my bridges to join you, King, so it is my business. I just hope she isn't part of some long con Tom is running. This could all be a setup."

"It's not." Of that, I was certain. Willow's fear was genuine.

He hummed in the back of his throat. "Just because you believe it doesn't make it so. I don't want to believe it either, but she's been sticking her nose into places it doesn't belong. We can't be certain she's trustworthy."

"Recently?" I asked, recalling he'd mentioned previously that she'd been digging around.

He hesitated. "There hasn't been any evidence in the past few days, but she's been busy with her own problems so that doesn't necessarily mean anything."

Perhaps not, but I hoped it did anyway.

"It doesn't surprise me that she was looking," I said. "But I don't think she's trying to manipulate me, and honestly, all I care about at the moment is making whoever is behind this regret it."

Zeke dropped his arm from the frame and wound the window up as we neared our destination, an elegant stone church. "I guess I'm going to have to trust your judgment."

"Good." In our line of business, we needed to trust our partners implicitly. "Looks like service is still in progress. We can park outside and wait."

I had no doubt we'd recognize the man on sight. Zeke had a near-photographic memory, and I'd made a point of studying Orlov so I'd know who I was coming for. Nobody tried to steal Willow out from under me.

I parked on a side street, and we locked up, checked our weapons, and made our way to the front entrance. We were hoping to do this peacefully, but if Orlov put up a fight, we'd be ready.

We stood on the sidewalk—Zeke to the left of the entrance and me to the right—so we could cover as much ground as possible. There was a chance Orlov would slip out a side entrance, but as far as we knew, he had no reason to be aware we were pursuing him.

The longer we waited, the more impatient I grew. I wanted answers, damn it. Eventually, people began to filter out onto the street. I scanned the faces, searching for Orlov. I skimmed over a bruiser of a man with short hair, and my gaze bounced back.

That was him.

"My side," I murmured into the headset, so Zeke would know I'd sighted him. "Tall, short hair, walking in my direction." As I spoke, Orlov looked up, and we locked gazes. He froze. Then, like a rabbit that had sighted a hawk, he ran, shoving through his fellow parishioners. "Coming to you now."

"I see him," Zeke replied. "Giving chase."

I bounded through the crowd and spotted Orlov and Zeke breaking away from the group. Orlov was aiming for an alley. I sprinted after him, determined not to lose sight of him for a second. He rounded the corner, with Zeke and me on his tail. We veered around another corner, then another, the alleys growing progressively narrower and darker. Finally, we reached a dead end. Up ahead, Orlov cursed loudly. His path out had been blocked by a chain-link fence.

He turned, expression thunderous. "Are you armed? Because if not, you're fucking stupid. Do you know who I am?"

I slowed to a walk and lifted my jacket so he could see the gun strapped to my body. "You're Mark Orlov. Long rap sheet. If I had to guess, you're hired muscle. We'd like to know who did the hiring."

He opened his mouth to spit a retort, but then something flickered in the corner of my vision, and he fell back a step, clutching his chest. His mouth gaped as he stared in shock. Blood began to soak through his shirt. He dropped to his knees. I spun, searching for the shooter, while Zeke maintained cover. I couldn't see anyone. Whoever had fired the shot was either gone, or it had been long distance, in which case we had no hope of catching them. We were better off trying to question Orlov.

"Call emergency services," I said to Zeke—needlessly, since he was already dialing.

I knelt at Orlov's side. He'd slumped to the ground and stared sightlessly, struggling to drag in a breath as blood gurgled up his throat.

Fuck.

If I didn't do something, he might not make it, and then we'd be back to square one. I ripped off my jacket, folded it, and pressed it to his wound. "Don't you dare die."

He garbled something unintelligible.

"Tell me who hired you," I demanded as his blood soaked through my jacket and drenched my hands. "Tell me!"

His chest rose and fell with shuddering heaves. "N-not…"

"Not what?" I pressed harder, hoping like hell he'd survive until an ambulance could arrive.

His lips moved, but no sound came out. I leaned closer, hoping to catch a hint of his words.

"Not about the mmm…" His jaw went slack.

He was dead.

————

WILLOW

"It's been hours," I said to Kade, who glanced up from the book he was reading. After our self-defense session earlier, I'd showered, changed, and retreated to my room to work and try to contact Tom again. "Something must be wrong."

He closed the book, and his expression spoke volumes.

"What is it?" I asked. "What happened?"

"They had a problem, but they're talking to the police, and they'll be here as soon as they can."

"The police?" A boulder lodged in my throat. "Something went badly enough that the police had to get involved?"

"Unfortunately, yes."

"And you didn't tell me?"

He winced. "There's nothing you can do, and I saw no reason to stress you out. You've had enough of that over the last few days."

"No reason to stress me out?" I huffed, scarcely able to believe what I was hearing. "I don't like to be kept in the dark. I'm not made of glass, and I have a right to know what's going on."

He nodded. "Yes, you do. King will tell you everything as soon as he's back."

I straightened my spine. "Did he ask you not to say anything to me? Is this because neither of you trust me?"

I couldn't blame them if that were the case. I had been trying to find information to use against Ronan prior to all of this going down.

He watched me warily, as though worried I might lash out. "Just wait until he gets here and he'll explain."

"Why don't *you* explain?"

He held my gaze, not wavering for a second. "You're personally involved with one of my friends. I respect that connection enough to let him share the news."

I deflated. "This is because of me and Ronan." Not that there technically was a me and Ronan yet. But I wanted there to be, and I think he did too.

"Yes."

I sighed heavily. "I still don't like it, and you wouldn't either if you were in my shoes."

He inclined his head. "Maybe not."

A shrill ring interrupted us. I jolted in surprise and patted my pocket for my phone. My heart leaped into gear as I pulled it out. It was an unknown number.

"I don't know who it is," I said to Kade. "Should I answer?"

"Yes." He stood, businesslike. "Put it on speaker."

I accepted the call and hit the Speaker button. Meanwhile, he retrieved his own phone and tapped the screen several times.

"Who is this?" I asked.

"Willow?" It was Tom.

I nearly dropped the phone. My eyes jerked to Kade's.

"Tom," I said aloud, in case Kade wasn't familiar with my brother's voice. Kade nodded to indicate he understood. "Are you okay?" Questions bubbled inside me, spilling over each other, but only a few managed to break free. "What's going on? Where are you? Who's coming after me?"

"Not now." His tone was terse. "I'll tell you when I can see you in person. First, I want to know why the hell Ronan King is sticking his nose into my business."

"*Excuse me?*" After everything that'd happened, he had the nerve to ask?

"Don't play the fool. I know you better than that."

"I wasn't," I snapped. "I just can't believe you'd actually have to ask." I turned my back to Kade, embarrassed he could hear the way Tom was speaking to me. "Someone tried to kidnap me yesterday. Ronan is the only reason they didn't succeed, and now he and his business partners are working to keep me safe."

I waited for the relief. For the gratitude. No matter what his personal feelings toward Ronan were, surely he could see we owed him. It was time to put the past aside and figure out the best way we could all come out of this in one piece.

Tom uttered a string of foul words. "Assuming it was who I think, you should have gone with them. They wouldn't have hurt you, but who knows what they'll do now?"

I pressed my fingers to my temples, which throbbed at his unspoken admission that he'd been keeping things from me. "You know who it is?"

"Yes, and you wouldn't have been in any danger."

I gaped. He was deluded if he believed that. "They broke down my apartment door and then tried to snatch me off the street."

"He would have told them not to harm you much. They need you alive or you're no good to them."

My jaw dropped at his use of "much". As if a few minor injuries would have been acceptable. "Who is 'he'?" I closed my eyes. "Even if you're right that they wouldn't have hurt me more than they already did, did you think about the fact that Sage was there? They had no problem with the idea of hurting her."

Behind me, I heard Kade grumble.

"I'm sorry." Tom's tone had gentled. "I fucked up. I never meant for you or Sage to get caught in the crossfire. Please believe that. I owe money and now they're coming to collect but I'm broke."

"Why didn't you tell me? I could have helped."

"I'm hoping you still will."

I tried to swallow but couldn't. His tone scared me. "How?"

He was quiet for a moment. "I've found a way out. You're not going to like it, but it will allow us to keep a twenty percent share of the company and have all of our debt wiped clean. It's the best I've come up with."

"Keep twenty percent of the company? So we'd be selling thirty-one percent of the company shares that are in your name to someone else?"

"No, we'd be selling twenty-five percent to Adrian Petrov. He's already purchased the six percent of the shares from me and bought out several smaller shareholders."

"You've already… What?" My mind spun. I couldn't believe what I was hearing. He'd sold off part of the company and not told me? No wonder Ronan had thought a takeover was possible. By selling anything to Petrov, Tom had made us vulnerable. We no longer held more than fifty percent of the company within the Lennox family.

He sighed. "How do you think I've been able to keep us afloat for so long?"

I felt sick. How could he do this to me? Especially when he knew how strongly I felt about Dad's legacy and how hard I'd been working to stop Ronan from taking it over. Betrayal burned hot in my veins, and tears prickled my eyes.

"Willow, say something," Tom prompted.

I clutched at my chest. A comforting hand landed on my shoulder, and I shrugged it off. Kade was trying to help, but he needed to leave me alone so I could digest this. "You absolute asshole."

"He'll let us buy them back in the future."

As if that made it any better.

I shook my head. "Men like him want to be in control. They don't do things out of the kindness of their hearts."

He huffed. "Adrian has been good to us, Willow. He's richer than a king and he's willing to bail us out for a majority share of the company and your hand in marriage."

What. The. Fuck.

"My hand in marriage?" I demanded. "Are we living in the Dark Ages?

Marry Adrian Petrov? Not only no, but *hell* no.

"It wouldn't have to be forever. Just for a while. You'd have plenty of good years left after he either divorces you or passes away."

My mouth opened and shut. Tears spilled silently down my cheeks. What the fuck sort of screwed-up reality had I landed in?

"It's for Dad," he said. "To protect his legacy."

No, it wasn't.

I realized in that moment it had never been about Dad. Not any of it.

The predicament we found ourselves in was entirely Tom's fault. He'd lost the company money—whether through bad management or something else, I didn't know —and he was trying to save himself. Perhaps he felt bad for making it my problem too, but not bad enough to find a solution that would work for me. He was selfish. I'd always known that, but I'd let him use my loyalty to Dad against me.

Dad wouldn't want this. He'd rather lose the company than sign me up for a lifetime of misery.

"The answer is no." I sounded much colder than I felt. "I've been used as a pawn for long enough. I'm not marrying that pervert just because you got yourself into trouble. I'm done trying to fix your problems."

I jabbed the End button and flung the phone across the room. It hit the wall with a crash and dropped to the floor. It rang again, but neither Kade nor I moved. I couldn't bring myself to look at him.

"I'll be in my room," I said bitterly. "Waiting until someone deigns to tell me what's going on."

Chapter Twenty-One

RONAN

"So you chased him into the alley, and then someone else shot him?" Joanna clarified.

"Yes." It was the third time I'd answered some variation on the same question.

"But you didn't see the shooter?"

"No. If you think I'm lying, you're welcome to test my hands for gunpowder residue. I didn't shoot Orlov."

She nodded. "We will. It's standard procedure; you know that." She glanced at the voice recorder, silently reminding me that she couldn't give the appearance of favoritism.

I sighed, frustrated that she was in here with me rather than trying to hunt down whomever had shot our only lead. I understood the necessity though. It was the same reason she'd had to collect my blood-stained outfit—to make sure my story aligned with the evidence.

"Do you have any idea where the shooter was hiding?" she asked.

I shrugged. "My best bet is that they were on a roof, or in one of the surrounding buildings, but I couldn't say for sure." I hesitated, then added, "It's possible his boss heard he was wanted for questioning and decided to take him out before he could talk."

She nodded. "That's certainly an option." But she wouldn't say more. Not to me. Or at least, not yet. "How did you know where to find him?"

"Zeke tracked him down yesterday, and Kade had a man keeping an eye on him."

She wisely didn't ask how Zeke had tracked him down. "Did he say anything to you before he died?"

"Nothing helpful. All he said was 'not about the m—' but he didn't finish the sentence."

"Hmm." She looked thoughtful, and I wondered if her mind was traveling down the same track as mine. If there was a hidden motivation behind the attacks on Willow— assuming that's what the guy had been talking about— then what was it? Did Orlov's employer want Tom's company? Or perhaps they wanted access to Tom himself to make a statement. Whatever the case, if it was worth killing someone over, then Willow was in more danger than we'd imagined.

My phone rang. I glanced at the screen and saw Kade's name. "Do you mind if I take this?"

She shook her head. "Interview ended at 3:38 p.m." She switched off the recorder and gestured for me to accept the call.

"You free?" Kade asked.

"Almost."

"Good, because we need you back here. Tom called Willow."

Fury flooded my body. "He'd better have a fucking good explanation for all this."

"Not so much." Kade's tone told me more than his words. Whatever Tom had said, my friend didn't like it, which meant I wouldn't either. "He also didn't give away any information we can act on. I'll tell you more when you get here."

"Thanks for the update. I'll be there as soon as I can."

When I caught Tom Lennox, he was going to regret dragging his sister into this mess.

The line went dead, and I turned back to Joanna. "Am I free to go?"

"Yes." She cocked her head. "What was that about?"

I debated whether to answer, but Joanna was a good cop and we needed her on our side. "Tom Lennox called his sister. According to Kade, he didn't say anything we could use to find him."

She nodded. "I'll need to speak with Willow to follow up."

I stood. "I'll get her to call you."

She followed my lead, and we left the interrogation room. Zeke was waiting outside, having apparently already been released.

"We need to get back to the penthouse," I told him without preamble.

He frowned. "What's wrong? You seem ruffled." He glanced at Joanna. "What did you do to him?"

She pursed her lips. "It wasn't me. He got a phone call."

"Ah." Understanding lit his features. "The lovely Willow." He gave her a wink. "Our great and mighty King has caught feelings."

She ignored his comment, and so did I.

The drive home seemed to take forever. Zeke gave me a hard time, but I didn't care. I was anxious to see Willow and make sure she was all right.

Zeke dropped me off at the front of the building, and I jogged to the elevator. I arrived in the penthouse foyer to find the same guard from this morning standing watch. He nodded as I passed, but I didn't stop for conversation.

A blur of color caught my eye as soon as I opened the door, and then Willow was in my arms. I closed my eyes as I embraced her. It felt so right to hold her this way. The tension eased from my body because she was, at the very least, physically safe. I kissed her forehead, never wanting to let her go again.

———

WILLOW

"I'm so glad you're okay," I said. "Kade reported something had gone wrong but wouldn't tell me what."

He raised his head and met my gaze. His eyes burned with a strange kind of fervor. "Let's sit down and we can talk about it. I want to hear what happened with you."

I bit my lip. The last thing I wanted to do was replay my conversation with Tom, but he needed to know, so I supposed there was no avoiding it.

"Where's Zeke?" Kade asked from behind me.

"Parking the car." Ronan continued to hold my gaze. "I wanted to make sure you were all right, so I left him to sort that out."

My stomach fluttered. Once upon a time, I'd dreamed of having him look at me like this. As though I were something precious. In the face of my conversation with Tom, I didn't feel conflicted about my attraction to him. Tom had betrayed me. He'd sold part of our company to a man I knew had been a rival of Dad's. Then he'd tried to sell me off too. Everything else was moot at this point.

"I'm okay," I told him.

He searched my face. "I want to hear everything." He slipped his hand into mine. "Come on."

He led me to the living room, sat, and hauled me onto his lap. I squirmed, unsure what to make of the display of affection in front of Kade.

"Please." Ronan's lips caressed my ear. "I need you close."

I softened. "Okay." His words started a warm glow inside me. Nobody had ever said that to me before.

I rested my head on his shoulder, and we sat in quiet until Zeke barreled into the room. He came to an abrupt stop at the sight of us and raised a brow.

"What happened with Orlov?" Kade asked, breaking the silence.

"We waited for him outside the church," Ronan said, his chest vibrating beneath my cheek. "Chased him down a series of alleys, but as soon as we cornered him, someone shot him. He died at the scene. We didn't see the shooter."

I stiffened. "He was shot right in front of you? Are you okay?" I inspected him. "Did you get hurt?"

"I'm fine," he said softly.

"He's been through worse than that," Zeke added. "Seeing someone get shot is practically your usual Sunday. Right, King?"

The blood drained from my face. "It had better not be."

"He's joking." Ronan's eyes snapped to Zeke's. "Cut it out."

I glared at Zeke and then turned to Ronan. "What happened next?"

"I tried to save him." His expression went taut. "I failed. Just before he lost consciousness, he said, 'it's not about the m—' but never finished the sentence." He looked around at the others. "My best guess is that he meant it's not about the most obvious thing: money. Thoughts?"

"Sounds like a reasonable assumption to me," Kade replied. "Money is what everyone's been saying all along. If that's not the motivation though, then what is?"

"The company," I suggested.

"It's a possibility," Ronan agreed.

"I think Tom pissed off the wrong person and they want to punish him." Zeke didn't look up from studying his fingernails. "I'm sorry, Willow, but your brother has made a lot of enemies, and now a man is dead."

I heard the accusation in his voice. He thought the death today was on Tom's hands. I couldn't fully disagree. Tom hadn't been the one to hold the gun, but he'd certainly contributed to the situation.

"It could be someone who hates Tom," I admitted. "There are plenty of people who fall into that category."

Including Ronan. But I wasn't about to say that when I was curled on his lap. My judgment might not have been flawless, but I knew beyond a shadow of a doubt that Ronan had nothing to do with this, except for casting himself in the role of my protector.

"Tell them about the phone call," Kade prompted.

I tried to shift from Ronan's knee while I recounted the awful call. Sometimes, distance served me better during difficult conversations than sympathy or physical comfort. But he refused to let go.

"Stay," he urged.

"I need to be able to think," I replied, sliding off and settling beside him on the couch. "Like Kade said, Tom called earlier."

"I hope he fucking apologized," Ronan grated out.

I glanced away. "At first, he was upset you'd interfered with the kidnapping. He's worried they'll retaliate."

"Fuck that."

I didn't meet his eyes. I was too embarrassed by how little regard my brother seemed to have for my well-being. "He confirmed that he owes people money. He said he'd organized for Adrian Petrov to deal with all of his outstanding debt in exchange for a majority share in the company and marrying me."

"No way in hell," Ronan growled.

"That's what I said."

"Believe it or not, she's making it sound better than it was," Kade offered, and I shot him a look. He held up his phone. "I have the whole thing recorded."

I didn't want him to play it, but I understood the necessity, so I bit my tongue.

"Do you want to leave the room while we listen?" Kade asked, his expression gentle.

"No." I straightened my shoulders. "I can handle it."

Ronan stroked the back of my hand. "You're not alone."

He had no idea how good that sounded. Despite technically being on the same team as Tom for years, I'd never really felt like it was us against the world. He'd always had his own agenda. But Ronan made me feel like I had support if I needed it. His eyes burned with an icy anger I'd never seen, and I knew it wasn't directed at me. Somehow, his rage was soothing.

"Thanks." I steeled myself and nodded to Kade. "Do it."

Kade pressed the button, and I heard my voice ask, "Who is this?" I gritted my teeth as we relived the conversation I'd had earlier. The betrayal felt like a festering wound that Kade had just exposed for everyone to see. When the recording ended, the room was silent.

Finally, Zeke cleared his throat. "Well, I think it's safe to say your brother is a monumental dick." He pursed his lips. "I'm sorry for suspecting you might be involved. It turns out, he's just a bastard who doesn't mind throwing his sister under the bus to save himself." To my surprise, he winked. "If you need someone to toss him beneath an actual bus, I'm your guy. Just say the words."

Despite myself, I smiled. His levity was what I needed at that moment. "You thought I was plotting against you?"

"I considered it a possibility."

I wondered whether to admit the truth. I didn't want to lose these men as my new allies or jeopardize my connection with Ronan, but they deserved to know what I'd been up to. It wasn't fair of me to keep secrets when they were going out on a limb to help me. Besides, if I didn't say anything and they found out another way, they might not be so forgiving. With an empty feeling in the pit of my gut, I decided it was time to put everything on the table.

"Actually, I was." I wet my lips. "I'd hoped to find something I could use to make you guys back off Lennox Securities. When I first arrived, I scoured through the files I had access to, but I couldn't find anything useful. Eventually I made the decision to stop looking because it didn't feel right." I glanced at Ronan, afraid of what I might see on his face. "I knew Dad wouldn't have approved, and I was beginning to care for you, even if I didn't want to admit it."

"You were trying to spy on us from the inside?" he asked.

His expression hadn't changed. He didn't let go of my hand, which was a good sign.

"Yes."

A muscle in his jaw ticked. "I wish you hadn't, but at least you've come clean."

"I'm sorry." I hated his disappointment. With a sense of horror, I realized he didn't seem surprised. "You knew," I accused.

His lips pressed together. "Zeke told me. Apparently, he's been keeping an eye on you."

"Oh." I felt foolish. Of course he had. Hadn't he warned me not to betray Ronan soon after I started? I'd suspected he might have an inkling of what I was up to even then. I bounced my knee, wondering how this revelation would change things. "Are you..." I cleared my throat and tried again. "Now that you know, are you going to throw me out of your apartment?"

I hated the thought. I didn't want to be on my own, but more than that, I didn't want to be without Ronan.

"Do I need to?" he asked. "Are you still spying on us?"

"No!" The word burst from me with more force than necessary. "I mean, no," I repeated more quietly. "Tom is out of control and isn't respecting Dad's memory, I can see that now." I squeezed his hand, wishing my own was less clammy. "I'm with you, Ronan."

I just hoped it wasn't too little, too late.

His mouth lifted into a halfhearted smile. "Then we're okay. Your loyalty is one of the things I respect most about you, and while I don't like what you did, I understand needing to do what you thought was protecting Frank's company."

My muscles softened with relief. Thank God.

Ronan slipped an arm around my waist. "Anything else to get off your shoulders?"

"No, not that I can think of."

"Good. Here's what I really need to know. If this comes down to a situation where it's either you or Tom getting hurt, are you okay with us doing what it takes to make sure you're the one left standing?"

I considered the question. What had started as a potential corporate takeover had become a dangerous minefield with far higher stakes. Enemy forces were circling, and things could get ugly.

"Yes." I felt the word deep in my heart. I didn't want anything to happen to Tom, but it was time to put myself first. "As long as you remember that he's my brother and regardless of what he's done, I care about him."

He nodded. "We'll make sure he survives, but there's a good chance his life is going to burn down around him."

I managed to nod. Tom had exposed me to danger

without much forethought. He was out for himself, and that meant I needed to be too.

"Now that we've got that out of the way," Zeke said, drawing my attention away from Ronan, "why do you think Adrian Petrov wants you as well as the company?"

"He's an old creep," I answered. "He's been showing interest in me since I was barely legal. I don't know if it's an ego thing or what, but maybe he figured he may as well see me thrown into the deal. Tom has dropped a few hints about him lately, but I've always ignored them."

Chapter Twenty-Two

____

RONAN

If my jaw got any tighter, it might snap.

Adrian Petrov was at least thirty years older than Willow, and he'd been leering at her since she was a teenager? That was not fucking okay. Nor was the fact that Tom hadn't done anything about it.

"Of course you ignored them," I growled. "Nobody can force you to marry someone you don't want to."

If I had my way, Tom would never be able to upset her again. She deserved better.

"I know. Apparently, he hasn't gotten the message." She looked around the room. "Thank you. All three of you. I appreciate what you're doing for me more than words can say, and I'm sorry about what I tried to do when I started with the company."

Kade's cheeks flushed, and Zeke smirked. Neither of them seemed to know how to respond.

"I mean it," she added. "Other than Sage, nobody has had my back like this since Dad died."

Kade and I exchanged a look that said we'd both like

to introduce her brother to our fists. General human decency shouldn't have been something to celebrate.

Zeke ran a hand through his shaggy hair. "You said this guy Petrov has been sniffing around you for years. Is it possible he set the whole thing up so Tom would hand you over without a fuss?"

She burst out laughing. I scowled. I didn't find anything about the situation funny.

"God, no," she exclaimed. "He's a creep, and I'm sure he's taking advantage of his chance, but it's not like he's obsessed with me or anything. I'm just a pretty accessory he'd like to wear on his arm. Perhaps a way to one-up Dad from beyond the grave. They were business rivals."

I wasn't as sure of that as she was. I doubted she realized the lengths to which a man would go to have her. But it didn't matter what Petrov was willing to do because she was mine and I wouldn't let him lay a finger on her.

"I still think we should look into him," Zeke said.

I nodded. "I agree. Just to be on the safe side."

"I'll get on that now." He stood and shoved his hands into his pockets.

Kade stood too. "If everything is okay here, I'll head home. I'm only a phone call away. The guard changed ten minutes ago, so you're all set for the night."

"Thanks, man." I released Willow and walked them to the door. "If anything happens, I want to know immediately."

Kade nodded. "You got it."

"Don't worry," Zeke added, clapping me on the shoulder. "We'll keep your girl safe."

"I appreciate that." I didn't deny she was my girl. We were past that. "Don't forget to get some sleep. You're no good to anyone if you're a zombie."

Zeke rolled his eyes. "Even as a zombie, I'd be smarter than most people."

"Arrogant ass," Kade muttered as they left the apartment.

I took a moment to thank Sean for returning to duty and headed back to the living room.

Willow had vanished from the sofa, and my heart crashed around in my chest, zooming from zero to a hundred as worst-case scenarios ran through my mind.

I stormed into the kitchen, finally breathing again when I saw her standing at the counter with a mug of tea clasped between her hands. I took the mug from her and set it on the counter, then drew her close and pressed my lips to hers. She tasted faintly of spice—perhaps from the tea.

I crowded closer, needing more of her.

More, more, more.

As if I could ever get enough. I'd be craving this woman until the day I died.

I moaned deep in my throat. I couldn't stand the thought of her in danger, but I couldn't verbalize my fears, so I'd have to show her instead. I grabbed her by the hips and lifted her onto the counter, then stepped between her legs. She laughed breathlessly. I twined my hand into her hair and dragged her lips to mine, plundering her mouth. But then I felt her shiver, and I froze. It could have been from lust, but it also could have been the result of shock or any number of things. She'd had a terrible day and here I was getting into her space.

I backed off and scrubbed a hand over my stubble. "Should we cook dinner?"

———

WILLOW

Wait, what?

My brain lagged, still caught up in the wonder of that

kiss. Ronan King was the sexiest man I'd ever had the pleasure of making out with. Not that the list was very long.

"Dinner?" I panted, trying to gather my wits from the floor.

"Yes." He stepped farther away, and I slid down from the counter, my knees nearly collapsing beneath me. He lunged forward, but I steadied myself in time and held up a hand to keep him at a distance. He was right; we'd gone too far, too fast.

"Do you have any ciabatta?" I asked, trying to think of what I could pull together based on the things I'd seen in his refrigerator and pantry.

He blinked blankly. "What's that?"

"Men." I heaved a teasing sigh. "You're all hopeless."

I went to his pantry and found a loaf in the breadbox, then dug around until I found the other things I needed.

"What are you doing?" he asked, hovering behind me.

"Making bruschetta. It won't take long, and after the day we've had, I think we deserve something nice."

"Do you need help?"

"No." I waved him out of the kitchen. "It won't take long."

"You know, when I suggested we make dinner, I didn't mean you had to do it."

I smiled. "I know. But it's nice to have something to do."

True to my word, fifteen minutes later I served up bruschetta with a salad on the side. We sat at his table and ate, neither of us speaking much. I kept an eye on him, noticing how his shoulders stayed up near his ears. They were tight. In fact, his entire body was rigid.

I finished eating and wiped my fingers on a napkin.

"You look tense. Would you like a shoulder rub?" It was the least I could do, considering I was the cause of his stress.

He shook his head. "No. It's just,"—he sighed—"it's not every day that a man dies in front of me."

My stomach dropped. "I'm sorry. I can't even imagine how that must have felt."

And it was all my fault. He wouldn't be involved in this mess if not for me.

"It's something I could happily never experience again." He buried his face in his hands. "I just keep picturing the way the light faded from behind his eyes, as though someone had flicked off the switch." His shoulders shuddered. "I've seen men die before, but not up close. It got to me."

"That would get to anyone. I know it won't help with the memories, but at least let me give you that massage. You guys have done everything today and I hate feeling useless. I'm not used to doing nothing."

He looked up and met my eyes. "Is that really a good idea after what happened earlier?"

I raised my chin. "We can behave like adults." Maybe.

"Okay." He pushed his chair back. "Let's do the dishes first."

Together, we tidied up and packed the dishes into the dishwasher, then I ordered him to his bedroom while I dashed to the spare room to dig through my toiletries. I returned to find him sitting on the edge of his bed.

"You'll need to take your shirt off and lie facedown."

He yanked his shirt over his head, and my jaw fell open. I snapped it shut again before he caught me staring, but honestly, his torso was absolute perfection. Smooth muscles, nicked in places, and dusted with dark hair. Tattoos encircled one shoulder and wound down his arm. I wanted to lick every inch of him. But that wasn't what we were here for.

I pointed to the bed and he lay down, his arms thrown carelessly above his head. For a moment, it struck me how much trust it took to let his guard down like this. I hoped he knew that after the past two days, I'd cut my arm off before I'd hurt him.

I cleared my throat and climbed onto the bed. Then hesitated. I'd imagined straddling him, but I hadn't considered the reality of what that would involve. He had a glorious bubble butt, and if I sat on him the way I'd planned, I'd be pinning my crotch against it.

"Everything okay?" he asked, his muscles tensing and reminding me of why I had to suck up my discomfort and do this. Lately, I'd been taking while he'd been giving. That needed to change.

"Yes, of course." I slung a leg over him and sank into position, trying to ignore the heat of his flesh between my legs. I reached into my pocket and withdrew the small vile of massage oil Sage had given me, dripping it onto his back. He flinched in surprise. "Sorry."

I recapped the bottle and pocketed it, then rubbed the oil into his skin. It smelled of eucalyptus and something else I couldn't put my finger on. I breathed it in and set to work, stroking along each of his muscles to loosen them up.

His skin was smoother than I'd expected, and he seemed to sink deeper into relaxation with every glide of my hands, except for when I focused on a knot. Given the way he groaned, I didn't think he minded the brief discomfort because of the relief it brought him. I found myself seeking out those knots and pressing closer to him with each ragged sigh. What the hell was wrong with me? Ronan had seen a man die today, and here I was, riding his butt like a hussy.

Desperate for a distraction, I traced one of his scars with a finger. It bisected his trapezius muscle over his shoulder. "How did you get this?"

He stiffened. "Nasty story. Are you sure you want to know?"

I hesitated. I'd only asked the question idly, but yes, I wanted to know all there was to know about him. "Yes."

He turned sideways and glanced up at me. "I accidentally interrupted Mom with one of her johns. He was angry. Used a switchblade on me."

My heart squeezed. "How old were you?" I didn't really want to know, but felt I needed to.

"Eight."

A lump lodged in my throat. At eight years old, children should be playing with their toys, not being hurt by grown men. "That's awful."

He closed his eyes. "Mom defended me. She stood up to him even though he was bigger and had a weapon. She kicked him out and refused to see him again, no matter how much he threatened her. She took me to the hospital and made sure I had the best medical care she could afford, despite the fact it meant she could barely eat for weeks. That's the kind of person she is."

I swallowed, horrified by the thought of what he and his mother had endured. Nobody should be put in that situation. Meanwhile, I'd lived a charmed life with holidays in Europe and every material thing I asked for. Shame bubbled up inside me. At the time, I'd never considered there might have been people out there who went hungry. It was completely outside of my sphere of experience.

"She sounds like a wonderful woman." My voice was thick, my tongue clumsy. "What's her name?"

"Natalie." His lips curved up, and the tension flowed out of his body again. "The first thing I did when I started earning good money was to buy her the kind of home she deserved. She gave up so much for me."

Would it be weird for me to say I'd like to meet her? Probably.

I kept my mouth shut, but I couldn't help thinking I understood some of why Ronan hated Tom so much. Tom came from a place of privilege but never seemed to appreciate it.

"I'm glad you were able to do that for her."

He sighed. "I'd take care of her forever if she let me, but she doesn't want that, so instead I helped her start a charity that gives financial advice to women in need."

I remembered him mentioning her charity previously. Something tickled my cheek, and I swiped at a tear. The last thing Ronan needed was me falling apart on him.

"That's amazing." I decided I didn't care if I sounded weird. "I'd love to meet her one day."

He hummed, but I didn't know if it was in agreement or something else. "I think she'd like you."

I laughed. "I doubt that."

"Really." His eyes snapped open. "Why would you believe otherwise?"

"Because I'm the antithesis of what she stands for. A spoiled former rich girl whose biggest problem is that I'm probably going to lose the family company."

He was quiet for a moment, then asked, "Is that how you see yourself?"

I rolled my eyes. "It's the truth. I've been very lucky in life."

"Interesting."

I shimmied backward and dug my thumbs into his butt cheek. Sage said people carried a lot of tension there. Ronan groaned, and I figured I must be on to something, so I doubled down, hoping he'd be too distracted to finish his thought.

I didn't get that lucky.

"When I look at you, I see a woman who is loyal to the people she cares about. You lost your mom and dad when you were young, and your brother doesn't truly appreciate you, but you haven't let that define who you are. You're a hard worker, a skilled artist, and you don't expect anything you haven't earned."

Oof. His words hit me right in the heart. "I like your version of me better than mine."

Suddenly, he flipped over, and I was straddling his crotch rather than his ass.

He sat up and curved a hand around the side of my face. "Willow, that's not a different version of you. It's how you actually are."

His face angled toward mine, and my breath caught in my lungs. He paused as though giving me time to move away. Instead, I leaned closer. Our lips met softly. I placed my hands on his chest and felt the beating of his heart. Strong and steady, just like him. We explored each other tentatively, and even though there was none of the heat from our previous kisses, it slayed me because of how real it was. There was no question of whether we'd been caught up in the excitement of the moment. What was happening between us meant something, and neither of us was shying away from it.

"Ronan," I breathed as our lips parted.

"I'm here," he murmured. "I see you, and I'm not going to let you go."

Chapter Twenty-Three

RONAN

I battled for my sanity as Willow's hot center rested atop my raging erection.

"That might be the sweetest thing anyone has ever said to me." She studied my face, apparently unsure how to react. My heart ached for her because this woman should have been swimming in a sea of compliments.

She grabbed my shoulders and kissed me, riding the ridge in my pants as though she intended to get me off when she probably didn't even realize she was doing it. She pulled back, her breath warm on the side of my neck.

"Wow." She laughed. "That feels amazing."

"I have to be honest," I rasped. "If we don't stop soon, I might get carried away."

She tensed, and her forehead furrowed, just now noticing our position. "Oh, God. I'm practically giving you a lap dance. Sorry."

"Don't be." I smiled wryly. "I like it. A little too much."

She reached between us and ran her hand over the outline of my cock. "I want to be with you."

I grabbed her chin and raised it so I could see her eyes. "Do you mean that?"

"Yes." Soft, but certain. "I've never been more sure of anything." She bit her lip. "I spent my teenage years daydreaming about you, but the reality is better than the fantasy."

"I'm no white knight, princess. I hope you know that."

Her lips firmed. "You've been rescuing me since day one. You just don't realize how rare you are."

"Nor do you." I released her chin and brushed my mouth over hers. "Our first time should be romantic. Not on the heels of a day like today."

She shook her head, her expression nearly giddy. "Don't you get it? Our first time will be perfect because it's us. That's the only thing that matters."

I groaned and dragged her back onto my lap. God help me, but I was going to take what she offered whether it was the right thing to do or not.

WILLOW

Ronan grabbed the hem of my shirt and tugged it over my head. I reached behind myself and unsnapped the clasp of my bra. It fell away, baring me from the waist up. His awed expression made me feel like a goddess.

"You're beautiful." He kissed my shoulder and pressed another kiss to my collarbone, his facial hair rasping against my skin. The delicious sensation sent a cascade of shivers rippling through me. Slowly, he worked his way down to my nipple and laved it with his tongue. I clutched the back of his head and moaned. If these were the preliminaries, how good would the main course be?

His hand slipped beneath my waistband, delving into my panties. He slicked a finger between my folds. "You're wet. So good." He withdrew his finger and sucked it. My eyes widened. That, I hadn't expected. "I want to see your pretty pussy."

I stripped off as fast as humanly possible, although my movements were less graceful than I'd have liked. I lay back and let him look at me. I'd always thought I'd be shy the first time I was with a man, but the way his eyes darkened gave me confidence.

He wanted this. He wanted *me*.

"Now you," I said more boldly than I felt.

He nodded and divested himself of his bottoms. My eyes locked on his cock, and I swallowed.

Uh-oh. That thing was significantly bigger than I'd imagined. I mean, I'd known it was large when I rubbed against it, but seeing it in the flesh really drove the fact home.

"I'm not sure this is going to work. Did I mention this is my first time?"

He held my gaze, his own softening. "I thought it might be. You're sure you want this?"

"Yes, completely." The last thing I wanted was for him to stop.

"Good." He smiled. "Trust me, sweetheart. I'll give you what you need. We just have to make sure you're ready." He grabbed my hips, hauled me to the edge of the bed, and shouldered his way between my thighs.

I stared at him, breathing heavily. He parted my folds with his fingers, then licked down the center. My hips bucked, but he pinned them with his arms and growled in the back of his throat.

"You're the most heavenly thing I've ever had on my tongue."

I fisted the sheets, my entire body contracting around him. A rumble vibrated against my needy flesh, and I levered myself onto my elbows so I could watch him. His dark head blocked my sex from view, and when he caught my eyes, his pupils expanded and he looked at me like a starving animal. But his movements didn't falter. He maintained strict control, even while his eyes burned into mine, turning me into a hot mess.

"The way you look at me…" I couldn't verbalize everything I saw in his dark gaze.

"I want you." He pressed a finger against my entrance and slowly worked it inside, filling me. I could barely breathe. This was, without a doubt, the most intimate experience of my life. "But first, you have to come, baby." He crooked his finger and rolled his tongue over my clit. "*Come.*"

As if my body had been awaiting his command, I arched my back and buried my fingers in his silky hair as pleasure overtook me.

"Don't stop," I pleaded as he maintained his rhythmic licking and thrusting. "Don't stop, don't stop—oh my God!"

"That's my girl." He worked me through my orgasm, then placed a gentle kiss on my pussy. I didn't even stiffen as he rolled a condom on. My nerves were well and truly gone.

He smiled tenderly, and every part of me throbbed in response. "Let me know if I do anything you don't like."

"I will." My lips curved in a smug smile. "But I doubt I'll need to."

I was convinced he was a sexual unicorn. Even if I had no one to compare him to, I doubted most men as handsome and sought-after as him were generous lovers. Yet here he was, making sure I was taken care of first.

His jaw flexed. "Let's hope I can live up to your expectations."

I shuffled up the bed, and he climbed over me, holding

himself up as he aligned us. He rocked forward, inching into me, and I gasped and tightened reflexively.

He dropped to his elbows. "Relax, sweetheart. I'm going to make you feel good. I promise."

I exhaled, and my muscles went limp. He shifted deeper until there was no denying the connection of our bodies. But he still wasn't all the way in.

"Do it quickly," I said.

He looked pained by the request, but thrust all the way into me nonetheless. He groaned. "You feel amazing. Are you okay?"

I breathed slowly, the air having been forced from my lungs, but as I considered his question, I realized it didn't hurt. I'd felt only a moment's discomfort. I smiled. "I'm good."

"Thank God."

He pushed into me again, making love the same way he did everything: carefully and thoroughly.

I captured his mouth and wrapped my legs around his back. He might not have known it, but Ronan had claimed me that night, and I wanted him as deep as I could get him for as long as I could keep him there.

My head fell onto the pillow, and I moaned. His lips journeyed up my neck, then he slid a hand beneath my head and angled my face up. I opened my eyes and found him looking at me as though I were the most wonderful thing he'd ever seen. His mouth hung open, and he picked up the pace, panting as he raced toward the finale.

He nudged my sensitive clit again. Our eyes locked together as we reached our peaks at the same time. I fought to keep my eyes open so I could watch him take pleasure from my body. I felt him jerk inside me, and my channel clasped around him as I came. We stayed in suspended animation for a few moments, slowly floating down to earth. Then he brushed a kiss over my skin.

"You good?"

I smiled dreamily. "Absolutely perfect."

He rolled off me, disposed of the condom, and came back to gather me in his arms. "You're not going anywhere tonight. My bed is your bed."

I snuggled closer. That was exactly how I wanted it.

Chapter Twenty-Four

WILLOW

Warmth. Comfort. Support. That's what I felt as I woke in Ronan's embrace.

I wriggled until his hold loosened, then rolled over and took in the sight of his early morning face. His features were softer in sleep, but no less handsome. Tenderness welled within me, and I kissed his cheek. His eyelids fluttered open, and his eyes took a moment to focus on mine. They were completely unguarded.

I kissed him again, this time on the lips. "Good morning."

His mouth curved into a heartbreaking smile. "Morning."

His rough voice slid over me like velvet.

"It's Monday," I said sadly. "Much as I'd love to stay here, we have to go to work."

His gaze turned flinty. "I don't want you to leave the penthouse."

My eyes narrowed. "Will *you* be staying?"

He hesitated.

"That's what I thought." He wanted to leave me here

while he went into the office to, among other things, fix my problems. Well, that wasn't going to happen. "I want to come with you. Won't I be safer surrounded by trained security staff than here by myself?"

He considered the question, and I could see that he wanted to argue, but he couldn't deny the logic of what I'd said. "If you come in, I'll expect you to check in with me every hour so I know you're safe, and to not leave the premises without an armed guard. Preferably Kade."

I rolled my eyes. "Kade owns a third of the company. I doubt he has time to run around after me."

"Ask him." His expression dared me to do just that. "He'll make time. Kade has a thing about women in danger."

It seemed he wasn't the only one.

"Okay," I conceded. "If I want to leave the office, I'll ask Kade to accompany me." The point was moot anyway because I didn't plan to leave. I wasn't a fool. If I set foot outside, it could be poaching season with me as an endangered species. "Do we have a deal?"

His lips twitched. "You drive a hard bargain." He thrust his hips against me until I could feel his erection. I whimpered, and his pupils dilated in response. "But yes, I agree. Just please keep my sanity in mind before you do anything risky." He smoothed my hair back from my face. "If you were hurt, I'd lose it."

"I won't do anything stupid," I promised, pressing a kiss to the center of his palm. I broke away and rolled out of bed. "Let's go."

An hour later, we arrived at the office. I noticed several people glance at us as we walked past, and one openly stared. Before we went our separate ways, Ronan kissed my forehead.

"Be safe," he murmured. "Don't forget to check in with me in an hour. If you don't, I'm coming to find you."

"I will," I promised. "I'll be fine. Try not to worry."

When I got to my desk, Imani leaped up and raced over.

"Are you okay?" she asked, running her hands up my arms as though to check for broken bones.

"Yes." I frowned. "Why?"

She stepped back and scanned me from head to toe, lingering on my cheek, which was still bruised, and my forehead, where the cut was slowly healing. Her hand flew to her mouth. "What happened? Everyone is saying you're in trouble, but no one seems to know why." To my surprise, she hauled me into a hug. "I'm so glad you're in one piece. I was worried."

Tentatively, I hugged her back, surprised by how nice it felt to know she cared. "I'm okay." I eased away from her, although she kept a loose grip on me. "Some men trashed my place on Friday night, and then the same guys tried to snatch me off the street on Saturday morning. Fortunately, Ronan was there. If not for him, I don't know what would have happened."

Her eyes widened impossibly further. "Why are you even in the office today? You should be locked away in a safe house, or at least given paid sick leave. I mean, you were nearly freaking kidnapped. Surely no one expects you to work."

I explained to her the same thing I did to Ronan. She didn't look convinced, but nor did she argue.

"I'm here if you need anything," she said.

"Thanks." I smiled and squeezed her hand. "How was your weekend?"

"Nowhere near as exciting as yours, thank God. I had a blind date, which didn't go well. The guy was a looker, but he was a little too sure of himself, if you know what I mean." She sat and gestured for me to do the same. "Tell me more about what happened."

I opened my mouth to speak, but a throat cleared to the left, and I flinched in surprise. I hated that someone had been able to approach without me noticing. I glanced up. It was the woman from reception, and she held a massive array of flowers bound in blood-red paper.

"Delivery for you."

"For me?" I squeaked, ogling the bouquet. They must be from Ronan. Who else would do something like this? But he didn't seem the type to be flamboyant in a professional setting.

The receptionist winked. "Aren't you a lucky girl?"

She set the flowers on my desk but hovered while I read the card. The more I read, the colder my insides became.

My dearest Willow

Please do me the honor of joining me for dinner at The Sauvignon Steakhouse tonight at 8 pm to discuss our upcoming nuptials. I look forward to making you my bride.

If you need to call me, you can do so using the number below.
Adrian

At the bottom, he'd scrawled a number. Just looking at it made me feel sick. Even after I'd told Tom 'no' in no uncertain terms, he'd clearly called Petrov and given him the go-ahead. Tears prickled in my eyes, and one slipped down my cheek. My brother had gone completely crazy if he thought I'd let him do this to me. I didn't even know who he was anymore.

I ripped the card off the flowers and spun away, halting when I realized that both Imani and the receptionist were still watching me.

"Excuse me," I muttered and brushed past them.

I found an empty meeting room, shut myself inside, and dialed the number on the card.

Petrov answered on the first ring as though he'd been waiting for me. "Do you like the flowers?"

I didn't respond. I was burning with anger because Tom must have also given him my phone number. There was no other way he could have known it was me. We hadn't spoken over the phone before.

"I'm not marrying you," I stated bluntly. "Tom lied. I've already told him it won't be happening."

Petrov laughed. "Yes, it will."

"No." My heart hammered forcefully against my rib cage. "My brother may have gotten himself into trouble, but I refuse to give up my freedom to get him out of it. We're living in the twenty-first century. Women can't be bought and paid for."

"They can, and frequently are," he replied as though bartering women were an everyday occurrence. What the hell was this man's deal? "Let's get something straight. I allowed you to speak to me disrespectfully because you're clearly angry, but I won't tolerate more of it. I *will* see you at the steakhouse tonight."

I shook my head. "No, you damn well won't. You won't see me tonight at all. You won't be marrying me. And if I have anything to say about it, you'll never so much as set eyes on me again."

He spat something in Russian. It sounded angry. "Tell your beloved brother that our deal is off." His voice was dangerously low. "If there's no wedding, I'll take what I'm owed another way."

The call ended before I could respond. I stared at my phone, breathing hard.

Oh my God. That was a threat.

What if Petrov was behind everything?

"Our offices will house a number of high-end jewels." The man opposite me steepled his hands and watched me over them. "They are worth millions of dollars, making them a tempting target for thieves. We need to be sure that nobody will be able to get to them."

I nodded. "While I can't make any guarantees, our systems are the best on the market. They're sensitive, customizable, and we have professionals monitoring the alarms twenty-four-seven."

He nodded, and his heavy brow furrowed in thought. "I've asked around about you, Mr. King, and everything I've heard is good. You were trained by Frank Lennox, is that correct?"

"Yes." The door opened before I could say anything more, and Fiona stepped inside. I raised a brow. She knew better than to interrupt me unless there was an emergency.

"Mr. King, may I have a word with you?" She widened her eyes to communicate that it was important.

"Excuse me for a moment." I stood and walked over to her. "What is it?" I asked quietly.

"Willow is waiting outside. She's very pale. I thought you'd like to know."

Fuck. Something must have gone wrong.

"Thank you, Fiona. I'll be out in a moment." I returned to my chair, and Fiona closed the door as she left. "Yes," I repeated, picking up where I'd left off, "I was trained by Frank Lennox, but I left the company after he passed away to go into business on my own."

He cocked his head. "Is it true that Tom Lennox fired you?"

I ground my teeth together. "Tom and I don't see eye

to eye. If that's a deal breaker for you, then I'm sorry, but that's just the way it is."

Sometimes connections meant more to people than quality of work. Disappointing, but an indisputable fact.

"Not at all." My prospective client smiled. "I'm afraid Tom isn't half the man his father was. The Lennox name doesn't carry the same weight it used to." He stood and extended a hand. I reached over to clasp it. "I'm looking forward to doing business with you. I'll have my people get in touch."

"Thank you." I escorted him to the door, impatient for him to leave. "Have a good day."

But before the man could go, his gaze alighted on something to the right of my door, and he beamed. "Willow, is that you?"

I turned to follow his gaze, and my gut clenched.

Willow stood with a bouquet of flowers clasped to her chest, practically vibrating. She was as pale as Fiona had said, but it wasn't fear that burned in her eyes. It was fury.

"Roger." She summoned a smile, but I could tell it was difficult for her. "It's nice to see you." Her eyes flickered from Roger to me, and I could see her realizing why the man was here. She blinked, silently taking the hit.

"What on earth are you doing here?" Roger asked jovially. "Scoping out the competition?"

She cleared her throat. "Actually, I work here."

She didn't mention the job was temporary, and that gave me hope. I liked having her around. Maybe she'd want to stay.

"Well, that's perfect," he exclaimed. "I can continue to support the Lennox child I actually respect while working with a better firm."

"You're signing on with King's Security?"

"That's right." He had the decency to look chagrined. "I'm afraid Lennox just isn't what it used to be. Times have changed. But you must know that or you wouldn't be here."

She nodded and flashed her teeth. "I'd hate to hold you up, Roger." She glanced at me. "I know how busy you are. But it was nice to see you."

"You too, Willow." He took her cue and continued walking.

"Fiona," I called. "Can you please see Roger out?"

"Of course." She hurried after him.

I gave Willow my full attention. "Come inside." She entered and set the flowers on the table. I shut the door behind her. "Who are they from?"

She thrust her hand out, and I noticed a card clasped tightly between her thumb and forefinger. I took it from her and scanned the text, growing angrier with each word.

I raised my eyes to hers and noticed that her cheeks were damp. She'd been crying.

"Fuck," I cursed. "I'm going to blacken your brother's eye when I get my hands on him." He was trying to use his sister as a bartering piece, and I wouldn't stand for it. "I'm sorry. He's a user."

I thought she might crumple, but instead her expression turned steely. "Every time I think he's hit rock bottom, he finds a way to sink lower. When will it stop?"

"When we make it stop," I tell her. "Did these arrive just now?"

"Maybe five or ten minutes ago." She hesitated. "I called him."

"Who, Tom?"

"No." Her tone was bitter. "Petrov."

Something knotted in my gut. "You should have come to me first. Talking to him could have put you at risk."

She shrugged. "I'm used to taking care of myself. But as it happens, you might be right. He said something that got me thinking."

My mind caught on the first part of her statement. It saddened me how much she'd grown accustomed to tackling things alone. It was difficult to believe I'd thought of her as a spoiled princess. But then the second part of what she'd said sank in. "What did he say?"

She pressed her lips into a thin line. "That the deal was off and he'd be taking what he was owed another way."

Something clicked into place. "Is it possible that Petrov is behind everything?"

She cocked her head. "I wondered the same thing."

My fingers curled into fists. If Petrov had been the one terrorizing her because Tom owed him money, and her brother was still trying to force her into marrying him, then Tom was going to wish he'd never been born.

"Perhaps Petrov thought that if he kept up for long enough, Tom would somehow conjure the money or beg for it from someone else," I suggested.

"Honestly, I have no idea what's going on in Tom's head. It was bad enough that he raised the possibility of paying his debt with a bigger portion of the company... and me. But this?" She swiped at her eyes. "It feels like he's a stranger. I don't know him anymore."

I gathered her in my arms. "I doubt he knows himself either."

She made a disdainful sound. "He's been growing more distant for years, but I figured it was normal to drift apart as we got older. I should have known something was seriously wrong. Perhaps I could have fixed things before it got this far."

"There's no point playing what-ifs."

She wriggled free of my embrace. "You're right. Have you found anything on Petrov?"

"Not that I've heard. I'll check with Zeke." I grabbed my phone from my desk and summoned my partner with a brief call.

He strode into the office a few moments later, the tails of a cape-like coat fluttering behind him. I eyed the strange outfit but didn't comment. Questioning Zeke's choices generally didn't lead anywhere useful.

"So?" I asked. "Have you found anything on Petrov?"

He waved a hand in a so-so gesture. "Nothing conclusive, but a few things about his businesses don't add up." He perched on the edge of my desk and glanced at the massive array of flowers on the table. "Your buddy Petrov isn't as legitimate as he first appears."

Chapter Twenty-Five

It felt like my whole world had been upended. Tom, who was meant to be protecting Dad's legacy with me, had decided to back me into a corner in the hopes of saving himself. Meanwhile, our supposed rival was protecting me.

I sank to the floor and crossed my legs. "What evidence do you have that Petrov is shady?"

Zeke assessed me with a single look. He had the most unnerving way of doing that. "Like I said, nothing concrete. Just a few paper trails that don't add up."

Ronan nodded. "Dedicate as many resources as you can to finding out what he's up to."

"Is there anything I can do?" I asked, hating to feel so useless.

"Not unless you want to go behind enemy lines as a spy," Zeke said.

My heart stuttered. If it meant ending this nightmare, I could do that. "Okay. What do you need?"

"No," Ronan snapped. "He was joking. Weren't you?"

Zeke held his palms up. "Of course. I'd never suggest a

civilian put themselves at risk." He winked at me. "I'm just enjoying the opportunity to make the boss man sweat."

Ronan grunted. "Get back to work."

To my surprise, Zeke complied without any smart-ass comments.

Ronan turned back to me. "Bring your laptop in here. You can work from my office for the rest of the day. I don't want you out of my sight until I know you're not in danger."

"If I do that, it will look like something is going on between us," I argued.

He gave me a look. "Something *is* going on between us."

I huffed with frustration. "Do you really want people knowing we're together? Won't that be a bad look for you, since you're technically my boss?"

"Frankly, I don't care how it looks." He took my hands, his expression serious. "If the rumor mill decides we're having a workplace romance, that's fine by me. I want more of you, and I don't care who knows it."

I debated how to respond. I liked that he wanted a relationship and wasn't afraid to say it, but then, he was the boss. I still had time left on my contract, and I was the one who'd have to deal with muttered comments in passing and the loss of respect from my coworkers. That's assuming my contract was actually upheld after all of this was done. Who knew what would happen, or if there'd even be a need for the deal Ronan and I had originally struck. That possibility seemed to become less likely each day.

"What's going on in that head of yours?" he murmured.

"Far too much for me to be able to think clearly." I bit my lip. "I'll bring my laptop in here because that's the smartest thing to do and I'm not one of those people who cuts off their nose to spite their face. But you and I need to talk about where this thing between us is going and what we're going to tell people."

"Okay." He leaned forward as though to kiss the tip of my nose but stopped himself. "We can talk later. I want you to be comfortable."

"Thank you." I smiled and then turned toward the exit. "I'll be back in a few minutes."

He raised his chin. "If you're not, I'll come looking for you."

Warmth filled my belly. As someone who'd never relied on anyone since Dad died, knowing there was another person who cared about me was a heady feeling. I was smiling to myself as I arrived back at my desk.

Imani shot to her feet when she saw me coming. "Is everything okay? You seemed really upset when you left."

I felt a prick of guilt for letting her worry with no explanation. "I'm not exactly okay, but I will be."

"All right." She didn't seem to know how to take that. "I'm here if you need support."

"Thank you." I gave her a quick hug. "I'll be working elsewhere for the rest of the day. Why don't I give you my number in case you need to get in touch?"

"Yes, please." She handed me her phone, and I entered my details into it, then passed it back. "Where are you going?" she asked as I started gathering my things.

My cheeks flamed. "Ronan's office. I think the man who sent those flowers might be the same one who tried to abduct me. Ronan wants to keep an eye on me to make sure I'm safe."

Imani's eyes narrowed. "That creeper! I hope Ronan lets him know where things stand." She waggled her eyebrows. "So is something going on between you two?"

"Maybe." I held up a hand as she squealed. "But please, don't mention it to anyone."

"I won't." She grinned. "I'm just pleased that something good might come from all the crap you're going through."

"Me too." I collected the things I'd stacked on top of my closed laptop. "I'd better get back before he sends out a search party."

She nodded. "I'll text later."

I made my way back to Ronan's office, ignoring the eyes on my back. I knocked once on his door, then eased it open and peeked inside. He was on the phone, but he waved me in.

"Nothing illegal, as far as I know," he said to whoever he was talking to. "But I thought you'd like to be kept in the loop." He ran a hand through his hair. "Okay, yeah. Sounds good. Talk soon." He hung up and pocketed his phone.

"Who was that?"

"Detective Lee," he replied. "Just updating her on the latest turn of events." He jerked his thumb at the flowers.

"Oh. Thank you." The prick of guilt from earlier was growing into a ball in my stomach. "I'm sorry my problems are taking up so much of the company's resources. It doesn't seem fair to everyone else. You really don't have to do so much for me." I could take care of myself. I needed to be able to stand on my own two feet.

He strode over as I placed my stuff on the desk that had been dragged in for me to use and took my hands. The warmth in his expression instantly made me feel better.

"You have nothing to apologize for. Everything that's happened is on Tom." He kissed my forehead, and my eyelids fluttered closed. It was the sort of sweet, affectionate kiss I'd always longed for. It said I meant something to him. "We'll get to the bottom of this and then you'll be free of Tom's problems. I promise you'll be safe. I wouldn't be able to live with myself if anything were to happen to you."

———

As I held Willow close, I battled internally over the next step. If I was serious about keeping her safe, then the simplest way to do that would be to pay off Tom's debts. But that would mean protecting an asshole who'd done nothing to deserve it. A man who'd bullied me as a child, fired me when I was grieving the loss of my mentor, and tried to force his sister to marry someone in order to pay his debts. Every part of me rebelled against the idea.

I brushed some hair from her cheek. "I need to talk to Zeke. I'll be back soon. Don't go anywhere."

"But I was planning a downtown shopping spree," she said, tongue in cheek. I was glad she could find humor in the situation. Her smile softened. "Don't worry, I'm not moving."

I kissed her once more, then headed straight for Zeke's office. I couldn't help but think what a remarkable change there had been in my relationship with Willow over the past few days. I hoped we were building a solid foundation for things to come, but I had a niggling fear that she might not need me so much once everything had been resolved. I wouldn't push her though. I'd fix things and then hope she wouldn't be done with me afterward.

"Hey, King." Zeke stopped hammering on the keyboard as I entered. "What's up?"

I jammed my hands in my pockets. "Have you found proof Tom Lennox is involved in anything illegal?"

Getting Tom locked up wouldn't solve Willow's problems, but having dirt on him would be useful as leverage to make him go along with our plans.

Zeke leaned back and interlaced his fingers behind his head. "A few minor things but nothing that would get him serious time." He hesitated, which was strange because I'd never known him to hold back on offering his opinion. "I'm always a fan of a good revenge plot, but if you're serious about Willow, then maybe you shouldn't start your relationship by trying to have her brother arrested."

I sighed. The man spoke sense, but we were running out of options. "Keep digging. I want whatever you can get, just in case."

"On it, boss."

"Thanks. I appreciate you taking the time. I know you're busy."

He straightened, all traces of humor vanishing from his face. "I'm never too busy to help the guy who gave me a second chance."

"You don't owe me anything," I reminded him, but he narrowed his eyes and shook his head, dismissing my words. "Let me know if you find anything big."

I nodded and returned to my office. If my instincts were right, shit was about to hit the fan. I shut the door behind me and locked it so nobody could interrupt then dragged my chair over to sit near Willow.

"I have to ask you something, and I need you to be honest with me," I said.

She turned her chair to face me and curled her hands together on her lap. "Okay. I'm listening."

"Good." I studied her closely so I could see any micro-expressions that might flicker over her features. "I know it hasn't been a month, but can you see the difference between how I run this company and how Tom runs Lennox Securities?"

Her mouth tightened, but she nodded. We were off to a solid start.

My palms sweated, and I wiped them on my trousers,

surprised by how anxious I was to hear the answers to my next two questions.

"Which approach do you think is more like Frank's—his or mine?"

"Yours," she whispered.

Her answer soothed something inside me. "Look at me."

Her eyes locked on mine, allowing me to read every doubt and fear she had. She didn't try to keep them from me. "Does this mean you want to go ahead with the takeover?"

"Do you trust me?"

She inhaled sharply, and my heart battered my rib cage while I awaited her reply. Her lips parted, and her eyes searched mine. "I do."

I released the lungful of air I'd been holding. Thank God. I didn't know what I'd have done if she'd answered in the negative. "Then I'll offer to pay whatever debts your brother owes in return for full ownership of the company —or at least anything he hasn't already given up. Not because I think Tom deserves to lose everything, but because I want to preserve your father's memory and protect you. That's all I've ever wanted. Tom is ruining his reputation bit by bit and you know it."

She sighed, unsurprised by my comment. She knew her brother wasn't a good businessman. I think she'd always known, but loyalty to the Lennox name had prevented her from doing anything about it. "Honestly, Tom doesn't deserve the company. He is willing to give it away to one of Dad's oldest rivals. I'd rather you have control than Petrov."

"So, you're okay with the plan?" I asked, wanting to make sure we were completely clear.

She drew in a shaky breath and nodded. "Tom has lost all rights to Lennox Securities. You have my blessing."

"Thank you." Her words gave me hope that we could get through this and have a future together on the other side.

Chapter Twenty-Six

Willow

"Are you ready?" Ronan asked, a couple of hours later. His eyes were filled with concern. He knew this was going to be hard on me, but I was going to do it anyway because this was the easiest way to get our message to Tom.

"Yes. I've got this." I straightened my shoulders. I'd opted to stand rather than sit because standing made it seem more like I was in control.

"You do." He cupped my face between his hands and kissed me, then stepped back and nodded to Zeke and Oliver, who'd set up a station to record and trace the call in case things didn't go the way we wanted.

Zeke pressed a button and nodded. "Go for it."

I used my phone to call the number Tom had contacted me from yesterday. I felt a pang of guilt for what I was about to do, but when I met Ronan's eyes, the awful sensation subsided.

This was the right thing. It was time for me to put myself first.

I half expected Tom not to answer, but after a few rings, he did.

"Willow, how are you?"

As if he cared.

A potent combination of rage and hurt sizzled along my nerves. He wasn't even brave enough to admit what he'd done.

Across the room, Oliver caught my eyes. Both he and Zeke had headsets so they could listen to our conversation.

"Not great, actually. It turns out my brother is trying to coerce me into a marriage I've already refused." I placed my free hand on my hip. "How could you do that?"

"I didn't have a choice." His voice was strained. "I told you how dangerous our situation is."

"*Your* situation," I reminded him. "And I told you I wouldn't marry Petrov, yet he seemed to be under the impression we're engaged. Lucky for you, I fixed that."

"What did you do?" He sounded panicky.

"Did you expect me to go along with your lie?" Angry tears welled in my eyes, but I blinked them back. He didn't deserve them. "I told Petrov there wasn't going to be a wedding."

Deathly silence followed.

"Tom?"

"You've killed us both," he said baldly. "All you had to do was go along with it for a little while and everything would have been fine." Each word grew louder than the last. "Petrov would have let me off the hook and treated you like the goddamn princess you think you are. You'd have had all the dresses and jewelry you could ever want. Holidays in Europe. A fucking house in the Maldives. A husband who would leave you alone most of the time to enjoy it. Yeah, that sounds like a real fucking hardship."

I gaped. The man didn't know me at all. "I don't give a shit about material things. People should marry for love, not because their brother fucked up and is trying to avoid the consequences."

"People like us—"

"Stop," I interrupted. "There is no 'people like us.' You and I are different." I paced the length of the room, dragging a hand through my hair. "My future is my choice. It's not for you to decide. I won't be bullied into anything."

"Just think about it. I'll call Adrian back and let him know you're considering his offer."

"No, you won't." Anger heated my gut. "You're not hearing me. This. Is. Not. Happening. And by the way, he said to tell you that he'll be taking what he's owed another way."

"Yeah, out of my flesh," he snapped. "*Jesus*. Listen, Willow," he continued more quietly. "You wouldn't have to marry him forever. Just until I can find a way to pay him back and get control of the company again. Fortunately, I don't need your approval to sign over Lennox Securities, but for some goddamned reason, he wants you too. He won't settle for just the business."

"Here's what's going to happen." My knees shook, and I sank into a chair. "Ronan will pay your debts and you'll sign Lennox Securities over to him instead."

Tom laughed in disbelief. "You can't be serious."

"I am. You owe Petrov money, and you can't pay it, right? He'll wipe your debts in exchange for the company and me. Ronan will pay your debts in exchange for the company and nothing else. It seems like a no-brainer."

"I won't give our father's company to King," he insisted. "If Petrov has it, I might be able to get it back. If King takes it, he'll never let that happen. Do you really want Dad's legacy to leave the Lennox family?"

I sighed. "It's the best option we've got. Ronan is a good man. He'll run the company well. We've been hemorrhaging clients for years. It's time for us to accept that it would be better off in someone else's hands. Personally, I think Dad would approve."

Tom was quiet for a long moment, and I thought I'd gotten through to him, but then he said, "Ronan King will not get my company as long as I'm around to fight for it. Dad always liked him more than me. King was the protégé. The special one. Fuck that." His tone was bitter. "I see him for what he really is: the bastard son of a whore, who won't get the chance to lay a finger on my property." He hesitated. "I'm sorry, Willow. I never meant for things to end this way. I was trying to save us, but I've done my part; now it's your turn."

He hung up.

I handed Ronan the phone, feeling dead inside. Tom and I had never been close, but I hadn't realized his petty vendetta meant more to him than I did. Than honoring Dad's memory did. That realization made me feel less guilty for what was going to come next. Even if he didn't know it, Tom had already lost his fight.

———

Ronan

I kissed the top of Willow's head.

Her eyes had gone blank, and while I hadn't been able to hear Tom's side of the conversation, I got the gist of it from her responses. He'd turned her down. Damn him for making her feel as though she wasn't worth his pride.

I turned to Zeke. "Did we get a trace?"

He studied the screen. "He's at the Alton Motel. Not sure what room. You'll have to figure that out when you get there."

"Got it. Thanks, man." I held out a hand and pulled Willow to her feet. When she was upright, I planted a kiss on her mouth. "We'll fix this," I promised.

"Be safe." She stretched onto her tiptoes to kiss me again. "I need you to come back."

"I will." Reluctantly, I let her go. "Kade, you ready?"

"Fuck yeah." He was practically bristling for the chance to get Tom alone. Kade didn't like men who hurt women. Even if it wasn't physically.

He *really* didn't like them.

Twenty minutes later, we cruised up to the Alton Motel in one of the cars that Kade's team used for undercover work. I parked, and we locked it behind us. The motel was run-down. Based on the number of cars in the lot, it was mostly empty.

We headed to the reception area and found the desk unsupervised. I slipped behind it and flipped through the pages of the notebook beside the ancient computer. It seemed to be a log of which rooms were in use, along with *nom de plumes* for the occupants. I reached the newest page and saw that one Mr. Gatsby had checked in yesterday. I doubted this motel saw many high rollers, so the receptionist may as well have written "Tom Lennox is here."

I shut the notebook and ducked out from behind the desk. "Room eight."

Kade nodded, and we made our way down the corridor, moving carefully in case any of Tom's enemies had also tracked him down.

We reached the room, and I tested the door handle.

Locked.

I hadn't expected anything else. Tom was running for his life, so he wouldn't be careless.

I jerked my head toward the door and stepped back so Kade could do his thing. He shoulder-barged the wood. The flimsy lock snapped. He darted inside, gun raised. A bullet tore through the wall to my left, two inches from my shoulder, and I zeroed in on Tom, who was sheltering behind the bathroom door.

"Lennox," I barked, knowing he probably thought it was the men he owed, come to collect. "It's King."

Tom swore. "You traced the phone call."

I resisted the urge to roll my eyes. He'd have realized it sooner if he were thinking clearly. "Come out and put the weapon down."

The gun appeared around the edge of the bathroom door, and he lowered it to the floor. Kade strode forward and snatched it up, then Tom exited the bathroom with his hands held high.

I placed my gun back in its holster, and Kade set Tom's on the coffee table. We weren't genuinely worried about him making a move, but better safe than sorry.

"You love this, don't you?" Tom sneered. "Always the golden boy. It must be a dream come true to see me staying in this dump while you lounge about in your fucking penthouse."

I didn't respond. Under different circumstances, I'd have taken joy in the reversal of our positions, but now all I cared about was getting Willow out of a psycho's crosshairs.

"I'm not taking your deal." Tom sprawled insolently on the bed as though to emphasize the fact he wasn't afraid of us.

"Actually, you will." I watched him in disgust. The man wasn't worth the pricey shirt he wore. "If you don't, we'll turn in evidence of your illegal dealings to the police. This place is a palace compared to prison."

He paled. "You don't have anything on me."

I nodded to Kade. "Show him."

Kade brought a file up on the screen of his cell phone and held it in front of Tom. I couldn't see the details from here but I knew it displayed a list of off-book transactions Tom had made and clients who didn't exist according to the official Lennox Securities records. Kade scrolled down so Tom could see how far back our information went.

There were years of data he'd falsified. All of the remaining color leached from his face.

"We have more," Kade said. "That's only the beginning, and you can be sure that your buddy Petrov has people in prison who'll make sure you don't have a pleasant stay."

"Okay." Tom held his hands out, and they trembled. "You pay my debt and get rid of your evidence, and I'll give you the company." His expression was a combination of disappointment and respect. "I never expected you to play this dirty. I underestimated you. You're more like me than I thought."

I remained stone-faced, but his words struck hard. This wasn't my preferred way to do things, but sometimes the end justified the means.

"One more thing." I hesitated for a brief moment, wondering if I really wanted to do this. But if I was blackmailing my old nemesis to save his sister, I might as well go all in. "Leave the state and never contact Willow again."

Tom scoffed. "Are you kidding me? I'm not leaving Chicago. It's my home."

I raised a brow. "Yes, you will. Or everything we have goes to the cops."

Kade and I exchanged a glance. We didn't have quite as much dirt on Tom as we'd implied, although we definitely had enough to warrant a deeper investigation.

"Where the hell am I supposed to go?" Tom demanded.

"I don't care. As long as you leave Willow alone."

"What if I stay in Chicago but promise not to make contact?"

I mulled over the suggestion. I really wanted him gone, but we could set up safeguards to make sure he didn't get to her. "Fine. But one wrong step and you'll regret it."

He sighed. "Doesn't seem like I have much choice. You've got a deal."

We shook on it.

"For what it's worth," he added, "I don't think Petrov would have intentionally hurt Willow. He has a soft spot for her."

I shook my head. "What you think isn't worth shit. You're a crappy brother and she knows it. Now do her a favor and get out of her life."

Chapter Twenty-Seven

WILLOW

Zeke held up a hand to stop me as we arrived at Ronan's apartment. "Wait. Let Sean clear the place before we go in."

I nodded. When night fell and Ronan and Kade hadn't returned, Zeke and I decided to head back to the penthouse. They'd messaged to say they were working out the details, which I hoped meant they'd been more persuasive than I'd been.

Sean disappeared inside and returned a few minutes later. "It's clear. You can go in."

I tried to smile. "Thanks, Sean."

I liked Sean. We'd only spoken a few times, but he seemed like a good man.

Zeke and I left Sean in the foyer to stand watch and went to the kitchen. Zeke shadowed me, moving like a big cat, all soft footsteps and stealth. I couldn't help but wonder exactly what he'd done before joining King's Security. Imani had mentioned something about secret government departments, and that gelled with my perception of him. He was more than your average computer nerd.

While I made coffee, Zeke leaned against the counter, his legs crossed at the ankles.

"I'm curious," I said as I handed him a mug. "How did your partnership with Ronan and Kade begin?"

He tilted his head, studying me like a bug under a microscope. For a long moment, I thought he might not answer. "After your brother fired King, he got in contact with Kade, who'd recently left the military. They were in college together. I'm not sure whether you know this, but King got a full ride on an academic scholarship."

"I did." I nodded.

"Yes, well, Kade ended up leaving during their second year to enlist, but he and King kept in touch. King knew he'd be perfect for the personal security division."

"And you?" I asked. "How did you know them?"

"I didn't know Kade," he said, surprising me. I'd assumed all three of them went way back. He sipped his coffee and smirked as if my expression gave me away. "I met King in his former role, working for your father. We collaborated professionally. I'd been looking for a chance to leave my employer, and when he struck out on his own, it seemed like the perfect opportunity."

"So, you approached him rather than the other way around?"

He nodded. "I think Kade would have been happy to see the back of me, but fortunately, King talked him around."

A dozen questions leaped to my mind. What had he been working on to bring him into contact with Ronan when he'd been at Lennox Securities? Why had Zeke wanted to leave the organization he'd been in?

I drank my coffee while I ordered my thoughts.

"Who did you work for before?"

He stiffened for a second. "If I told you that, I'd have to kill you."

I frowned. "I can't tell if you're joking."

He winked. "That's the point, sweetheart."

I opened my mouth, uncertain about what I was planning to say, but the sound of voices stopped me. I put my mug down and hurried out, spying Ronan and Kade in the living room, shedding bulletproof vests.

"How did it go?" I asked, both hope and fear in my voice.

Ronan straightened, all business. "Tom has the money, and I have Lennox Securities. It's done. You don't have to worry anymore."

My breath whooshed out. "Thank God."

"Don't thank God," Zeke quipped. "Thank King. Without him, none of this would have happened."

How well I knew that. Without Ronan's interference, I'd never have dodged the kidnapping attempt. I liked to think I could have gotten myself out of it, but who knew?

I walked into Ronan's arms. "Thank you, you wonderful man."

He found my mouth in a searing kiss. We only pulled apart when we ran out of breath. His eyes were dark with desire, and he waved a hand at his partners. "Thanks for your help, both of you. I appreciate it. But I'd appreciate it even more if you left now."

Zeke grumbled, but Kade seemed grateful to go. The moment they were out the door, Ronan took my hand and led me to his bedroom.

"Is Tom okay?" I asked, trailing after him.

"He's better than he deserves to be." He turned to me. "Lucky for him, I'm in love with his sister."

"You...what? You love me?"

"I do." He kissed me again, this time slow and tender.

I pulled back, still stunned by his declaration.

I hadn't been able to put words to what I was feeling for him, but this fit. It should have scared me considering how fast things had moved, but it felt right. "I love you too. I didn't expect this to happen when I broke into your office, but I have no regrets. You're the most amazing man I've met, and I never want to lose you."

"You're sure you want me now that this is over?" He tucked a lock of hair behind my ear. "You weren't just drawn to me because I was there for you during a difficult time?"

I rolled my eyes, annoyed that he'd even have to ask, but then I caught sight of the vulnerability in his expression. "That's not what this is," I assured him. "I know my own feelings, and I've never felt about anyone the way I do about you."

He smiled hesitantly. "Sorry, I shouldn't have doubted."

Concern prickled at my gut. No, he shouldn't have, and the fact he did didn't bode well. But I'd just have to show him how very much I wanted Ronan the man, not the protector. I pressed closer and touched my lips to his. He returned the gentle pressure, groaning in the back of his throat.

"Clothes off," I ordered, stepping away so he could pull his shirt over his head.

While he did that, I worked his zipper down, careful not to snag anything important. The muscles of his abdomen rippled, and I sank to my knees and kissed them.

When I looked up, his pupils had blown.

"More," he demanded huskily.

I eased his briefs down, freeing the thick length of him. I'd never gone down on a man before, but based on the way he shivered as I caressed him and panted as I ran my tongue along his shaft, it didn't seem overly complicated.

I eased him into my mouth, tasting salt and desire.

"Fuck." He buried his hands in my hair. "Just like that."

I worked him slowly, using my hands to stroke the root of his cock because my mouth couldn't go that far. He urged me on with murmured praise, and heat pooled at my center.

I liked giving him pleasure. I loved his stuttered breaths and quiet moans.

Eventually, his fingers stiffened on my head, and he eased back.

"That's enough for now. Let me make you feel good."

I stood, almost dizzy with want. "It makes me feel good to make you feel good."

He just stared at me for a moment. "What did I do to deserve you?"

He took my mouth. The kiss was desperate. Carnal.

At some point, he lowered me to the bed, and his clever hands petted my sex. He rubbed my clit, making me gasp and arch my hips.

"I want inside you."

"Yes." I rolled out from under him and indicated for him to lie down. I wanted to try something new. He lay with his arms at his sides, giving me free rein to do as I pleased.

God, he was sexy.

I got a condom and eased it over him, then I straddled him and reached beneath myself to encircle his cock with my fingers. Inch by inch, I sank onto it. His jaw slackened, his mouth fell open, and he watched me with hungry eyes.

Finally, I couldn't take him any deeper.

I placed my hands on his chest and paused as I figured out how to ride him. He was patient while I experimented, and when I found a motion that worked, I ran with it. His cock reached deep inside me, stoking the blaze hotter. He grasped my hips, and when I needed something more, he sat up and kissed me with everything he had.

I flew over the edge. He thrust into me, each movement growing jerkier, until he came, gasping my name.

I collapsed onto his chest. "That was amazing."

He looped his arms around me. "You are amazing, Willow Lennox. Don't ever forget it."

***

Willow seemed somehow both more real and more angelic in sleep. Her features were beautiful in their serenity, but her smooshed cheek and the faint snuffle of her snores reminded me she was human.

I watched her for a while, then slipped from the bed and out of the room.

In the living area, I made a call to her supervisor to let them know she'd be at home recuperating today. She'd been through a lot in the past two weeks, and she needed some downtime.

Plus, I wanted her to myself for a few hours.

I made another call to Fiona and asked her to reschedule my meetings for the day. Then I went to the kitchen to prepare blueberry pancakes for breakfast. While they were cooking, I replayed yesterday's events in my mind. Everything had gone according to plan, but something niggled at me. I brewed coffee and poured it into mugs, then arranged the meal on a platter and carried it to the bedroom. I didn't know what exactly it was that bothered me, but I put it to the back of my mind because I had a gorgeous woman to spoil.

"Willow," I murmured as I placed the platter on the nightstand. "Wake up, sweetheart."

She made a soft sound, and her eyes fluttered open. They traveled sleepily around the room before settling on me.

"Hi." She smiled. "What time is it?"

"It's past eight," I said. "But I've called the office and told them neither of us will be in today."

"You did?" She looked disgruntled, and I wondered for a moment whether I'd overstepped, but then she noticed the platter and sniffed. "Mmm smells good."

"Coffee, and blueberry pancakes," I told her. "I wasn't sure what you liked. Hope that's okay."

"It's perfect." She patted the bed beside her. "Come join me."

I slid under the covers and accepted a mug of coffee when she passed it to me. I kissed her forehead, wondering what it meant that I'd finally obtained Lennox Securities but wasn't eager to stroll into their office first thing and let everyone know about it. I'd been planning to take the company from the day Tom had fired me, but now that the time had come, I'd have rather stayed cocooned with Willow.

"What's the plan?" she asked as she handed me a plate stacked with pancakes.

I set my coffee on the other nightstand to take it from her. I couldn't even remember the last time I'd stayed in bed after I'd woken up, let alone eaten breakfast here.

"Today, I'm all yours." Her smile was worth the hours I wouldn't be putting in at the office. "Tomorrow, I'll speak with the senior staff at Lennox Securities."

"You don't plan to restructure the company, do you?"

My heart constricted. I wanted her to trust me without having to wonder, but maybe that was asking a lot of someone who'd recently been let down by someone close to her. "Nobody will lose their job unless they absolutely deserve to, but they're going to have to pick up their game because Tom isn't the only reason things have been going downhill."

"They'll do that," she said. "They're good people."

"Then we won't have any problems." I touched a fingertip to her nose. "Now, can we spend the rest of today focused on us?"

She laughed. "I'd like that."

I cut a piece of pancake and offered it to her, thinking how much it felt like we were living in a dream.

But my instincts were telling me it was too good to be true.

Chapter Twenty-Eight

WILLOW

"Your door has been fixed."

I glanced at Ronan. "The apartment door?"

"Yes. I talked to the landlord and had someone repair it. They finished last night."

It was the morning following the most magical day of my life. I'd been midway through dressing when Ronan had walked into the spare bedroom—which I hadn't been using, except to store clothes—and made his announcement.

"Thank you." I wrapped my arms around his waist. "I hadn't even thought of that."

I'd been so wrapped up in Tom's drama and my newfound love life that I'd barely thought of the apartment at all. I supposed I should head back there soon. I couldn't continue to stay at Ronan's place indefinitely, however much I wanted to.

"A cleaning crew has been in, so it's looking as close to normal as possible," he added. "They've reported that a few things are broken, but the damage is reasonably limited."

"That's great."

Although I still didn't think I'd be able to live there. Sage would be flying into Chicago later this morning, and we could discuss our search for a new apartment when she arrived. We'd already agreed during a phone call that ours would never feel safe. We just needed to put this nastiness behind us and move on.

I pulled away from him, went to my suitcase, and started folding the items laid on the bed.

"What are you doing?" Something in his tone made me look up, and when I did, his brow was furrowed.

"Packing my things." I'd thought that was obvious.

"Why?"

I stopped to give him my full attention. "Because you've taken care of the mess at my place, and I'm safe now, so I should head home today."

He didn't seem pleased by that.

I put my hands on my hips, trying to figure out what was bothering him. He'd had the door fixed and the apartment cleaned, but didn't want me to go back there? Or was I reading him wrong?

"You could just stay here," he suggested. "I'd be happy to offset your portion of the rent to make sure it's still affordable for Sage."

My jaw dropped. "You what?" I fell back a step. "Are you asking me to move in with you?"

"I like having you here, and we don't know whether Petrov has completely backed off yet. It wouldn't hurt to wait until we know for sure."

I cocked my head, unsure how to feel about his offer. I liked the idea of him wanting me around, but things were moving very quickly considering we hadn't been together for more than a few days. "So, would this be temporary, or for the foreseeable future?"

He shrugged. "Whatever makes you more willing to say yes."

Part of me wanted to laugh and agree, but he couldn't just ask me to move in like that and expect me to go with the flow without telling me exactly what I'd be agreeing to.

"No," I said slowly. "I need an actual answer."

"The second option then."

"Oh, wow." I rubbed my temples. I was tempted to go along with his suggestion without questioning anything, but much as I wanted Ronan in my future, the past few days had been insane, and we both needed time to think. I finally had my feet firmly beneath me, and I needed to be sure that we both knew where our relationship was going. "Most people date for months before they move in together."

The furrow between his brows deepened. "There's no rule that says it has to be that way. We can do this however works for us. I want you close." He stepped closer and put his hands on my waist. "I love you."

My heart exploded with warmth. I'd never get used to hearing him say that. I also liked that he knew what he wanted. Nevertheless, part of me wondered if his desire for me to move in was a reaction to the danger I'd been in and if he'd regret it down the road. Without the events that had pushed us together, would he still want to move in so quickly? He was an inherently protective man, and I needed to be careful that his motivation to have me here was coming from the right place.

"I love you too." I stretched up to kiss him, then allowed my body to sink onto his, letting him support me. "You're amazing. But are you sure you aren't making different decisions than you usually would because you're worried about me?"

His facial muscles twitched, and he didn't seem to know how to react. For a long moment, he stayed quiet, and his silence told me what I needed to know. Perhaps concern for my safety wasn't the whole reason for his invitation to stay, but it was at least part of it, and I wouldn't be moving in until his sole motive was the desire to keep me close each and every day.

"You mentioned a couple of nights ago that I might see you as some savior," I reminded him. "You kind of are my savior, but that's not the only reason I love you. You're thoughtful, honorable, and you have a good heart. It might be a bit walled off, but it's generous and loving. The fact you even wondered about my reasons for being with you makes me think you need to be sure that I'm with you for who you are, not what you can give me, and I need to know that you're inviting me to stay for the right reasons. We're not at that place yet."

RONAN

This conversation was not going according to plan. I tried to think of a way to bring us back to the ease we'd shared earlier.

She was right though. Even if it had been brief, I'd worried about where her feelings might have been coming from. But I didn't want to lose her, and my chest tightened with panic at the memory of those men trying to grab her off the street.

I didn't know for certain she was safe yet. We needed to wait it out.

"I won't be able to think straight if you leave."

She kissed me chastely. "Then have someone keep an eye on me. I promise not to do anything risky. Sage and I will find a new place, and you and I can go on a proper date. See where things lead."

"There's no point in dating," I growled, my patience wearing thin. "I already know I want you."

"I want you too. But everything has been so topsy-turvy. It's not the right time to make a big decision like moving in together."

My heart sank. I wanted to argue, but I couldn't. She was right, and I didn't want to be another man trying to push her around. What if I got her here and she resented me for rushing things? Just because I was completely certain of what I felt for her didn't mean she was in the same emotional space. I was scared to let her go in case she didn't come back, but it was time to man up and trust her.

"Okay, that's fair." I stepped away from her. "If you need to leave, then go. But I'll be here. I'm not going anywhere."

She swiped at her eyes, which were shining with emotion.

"I love you," she whispered, and as she closed the distance between us to kiss me again, I felt something crack in my heart.

I knew this wasn't goodbye, but it sure as hell felt like it.

———

WILLOW

I managed to get through a day at work, although I spent way too much time replaying our conversation in my head. When I arrived back at our apartment and saw the new door Ronan had organized to have installed, my chest squeezed. It was a strange feeling, knowing he was looking out for me. I hated the thought I might have hurt him, but we both needed to know this relationship wasn't just a result of the situation we'd found ourselves in.

"Willow?" Sage asked as I let myself in and dropped my bag on the floor. She'd messaged a couple of hours ago to let me know she'd made it back safely. "Are you all right?"

The sight of her beloved face lifted my spirits, and I flew at her with open arms. She caught me in an embrace and hugged me tight.

"I'm sorry I got you involved in Tom's mess." It was my millionth apology to her.

"It wasn't your fault." She gestured to the sofa. "Come sit down. I want to hear everything. Then we can burn some of my namesake to clear out the lingering negative energy from the break-in."

She knelt in front of the coffee table and lit a pair of tall candles I hadn't previously noticed. They must have been new. She rubbed a white crystal positioned between them before sitting on the sofa.

I joined her and slipped my hand into hers.

"So, what happened?" Sage asked.

I word-vomited the whole story, ending with my conversation with Ronan this morning. "I haven't seen him since I left his place."

She cocked her head. "He didn't drop by to see you at work?"

"No." I sighed. "He's probably giving me space." I rested my head on her shoulder. "Do you think I'm being ridiculous? Is it crazy to ask questions when the universe has just dropped this perfect man in my lap?"

"No." She reached for the crystal and passed it to me. "Hold this. It will help." I took it, more to appease her than anything else. "You've been through a lot. It makes sense that your emotions are jumbled. His probably are, too. That doesn't mean you're not supposed to be together." She grinned. "You know how I feel about you two. But you're allowed to take as long as you need to work through your feelings and make sure that the choices you make are right for you. That's okay. If he really loves you, he'll be patient."

"I hope so."

I'd accused him of being motivated by the desire to protect me, and while I loved his protective side, I was scared that what I'd said might be the truth.

I really hoped it wasn't. This was real for me.

Please let it be real for him too.

"Okay." Sage nodded. "I'm here for whatever you need. Now, shall we burn the sage?"

"Let's do it."

———

WILLOW

The next morning, I woke alone. There was no Ronan to bring me breakfast or to snuggle in bed with. I ate by myself while Sage led a virtual yoga session in her room, and then locked the apartment when I left for work. I'd gone through the same routine hundreds of times before, but it had never felt so lonely.

I took the stairs to the ground floor and walked out into a gloomy Chicago day.

I'd barely made it twenty steps when I felt a sting in my shoulder. I glanced down and saw a dart sticking out of it.

My head spun.

Holy crap, was that a tranquilizer?

The world swam before my eyes, and the last thing I saw before I passed out was a white van.

Chapter Twenty-Nine

Ronan

I checked my phone for the third time in ten minutes.

Still no reply from Willow.

I'd called her this morning, hoping we could talk, and then sent a message when she hadn't answered. If I'd realized she was going to take this space thing so seriously, I'd have pushed harder yesterday. As it was, I'd spent an entire day barely able to accomplish anything because I was too distracted. I couldn't afford to be unproductive. My time was too precious.

If she didn't want to talk to me, perhaps I could use the security cameras to check she was safe. I clicked onto the feed and frowned. She wasn't at her desk. An image flashed into my mind of her huddled in her apartment, afraid. But the image didn't sit right. Willow was stronger than that.

I scrolled through contacts in my phone until I found her supervisor, Anja, and called.

"Hi, King," Anja said briskly. "What can I help you with?"

My mouth went dry. It wasn't exactly appropriate for

me to use my position to check up on the woman I was involved with. But given everything she'd been through, it was warranted. Somebody needed to look out for her.

"King?" Anja prompted.

I cleared my throat. "Is Willow Lennox in the office today?"

She fell quiet, and I assumed she was checking a calendar or roster. "Yes, I have her marked as present."

I stared at the empty desk on my camera feed. Perhaps she'd gone to get a coffee or a snack. But there was no jacket slung over her chair, and no bag perched on the desk.

It felt off.

"Thanks," I said. "Talk later."

I'd just have to go over there myself. With more eagerness than I'd have liked to admit, I left my office. Fiona glanced up as I passed but didn't comment. Perhaps she saw the concern on my face.

When I reached Willow's desk, she still wasn't there. Imani flashed me a quick smile but didn't say anything.

My eyes narrowed. I spent a lot of time reading people, and she was nervous.

"Have you seen Willow?" I asked.

She pursed her lips. "I'm sure she's around somewhere."

I strode to her desk. "But have you seen her?" She looked torn, and I continued more softly. "I don't want to get anyone in trouble, Imani. I'm worried about her."

"Oh." Finally, her eyes cleared. "She hasn't been in today. I covered for her because I thought she deserved the time off after what she's been through."

My stomach tightened. While Imani's behavior wasn't ideal, it wasn't something I'd usually make a big deal of. "Have you spoken to her?"

She shook her head. "I tried calling but she didn't answer."

"Damn. So did I. Thanks for your help." I left Imani at her desk and headed for Kade's office. He was speaking to Sean when I let myself in.

"King, what's up?" Kade asked.

"I need Sage Nichols's phone number."

Kade raised a brow. "You think I've got it?"

"Yes." I didn't have time for games. "You went with her to her grandparents' house, so of course you do."

I didn't mention the fact I'd seen him checking out the quirky brunette.

He sighed, scrolled through his phone, and scrawled a number on a Post-it note.

"Thanks."

I rushed back to my office, already entering the number into my mobile. I had a really bad feeling about this.

She answered after only a couple of rings.

"Sage, it's Ronan." My voice was terser than I'd intended, but I couldn't seem to do anything about it. "Are you with Willow?"

"No." She sounded confused. "Willow is at work."

"I can't find her."

She hummed in thought. "Maybe she's at lunch."

Maybe. But I didn't like the sense of dread creeping over me. "She left your apartment this morning to come here?"

"Yes. At the usual time."

"Thanks. That's all I need to know."

I hung up.

Something must have happened to Willow between leaving her apartment and arriving at the office.

And that tightness in my stomach? It was morphing into full-on fear.

Time to make another phone call.

I strode to the window so I could look out over Chicago. Somewhere out there, Willow might be in danger.

"Detective Lee."

"Joanna, I need your help. Willow Lennox is missing."

"How long?" she asked.

"She left her apartment this morning and never arrived at work."

I sensed her hesitation. "You know we can't consider her a missing person until she's been gone for forty-eight hours. She might have stopped for a coffee with a friend, or decided she'd rather spend the day shopping."

"She didn't."

Willow wasn't like that. A headache pinched at my temples. What if Tom had been too slow to pay his debts and someone thought they needed to make an example of the Lennoxes? I couldn't live with myself if anything happened to her.

"Given the problems she's been having, I'll get someone to canvas the area outside her apartment. See if anybody will let us view their security feeds. We don't have enough for a warrant to force them to allow access to their cameras though."

I nodded, trying to rein in my frustration. Rules existed for a reason, and they weren't her fault. "You do that. I'll do the same. If you find anything, please call me."

"I will." She paused before hanging up. "We'll do what we can to get your girl back, King."

"Thanks." I exhaled roughly. "I appreciate that."

I just hoped it would be enough.

———

WILLOW

Thick black fabric obscured my vision as my consciousness slowly returned. I could hear voices around me but could not decipher their meaning. All I knew was that they were unfamiliar and male.

I shifted in place, feeling woozy, but I remained upright. When I took a moment to mentally check my body parts, I realized I was tied to something. Rope looped my ankles to a chair, and my wrists were bound behind my back.

I tested the rope, but it held firm.

Panic began to rise within me, and my breathing grew shallow. I drew in a slow, deep breath. I was in a bad situation, but if I wanted to get out of it in one piece, I needed to stay calm and be smart.

"She's awake," a man barked.

"Good."

A shiver shot down my spine.

I knew that voice. Recognized it from a handful of unavoidable conversations over the years.

Someone touched the top of my head and I flinched.

Then the barrier between me and the room was torn off, and Adrian Petrov slowly came into view. I blinked against the brightness of the light and tried to say something, but my mouth was dry.

"Welcome, Willow." He captured my face between his hands and squinted at me as if to determine whether I was mentally present. "Nice of you to join us."

He released me, but not before my stomach heaved in revulsion because of his closeness. I gagged. When I recovered, I looked around, noting a number of men stationed like soldiers awaiting orders. Despite that, the room itself was nothing like a battlefield. We were in the living area of a luxurious apartment. Expensive art graced the walls, and the furniture looked custom-made.

"Why am I here?" I croaked. My throat felt as though I hadn't had water for days.

"So I can tell you how disappointed I am that you ruined everything."

I had? I frowned and tried to concentrate. He had his money. Shouldn't he be happy?

But perhaps he hadn't gotten paid after all. Was it possible that Tom had taken the money and run?

"The debt?" I rasped.

Petrov tsked and shook his head. "You're missing the point, you stupid girl. I never wanted the money. I wanted Frank's precious company and his beloved daughter."

My insides went cold.

He'd never wanted Tom to be able to pay the debt. He might even have manipulated Tom into a situation where Tom had no choice but to give Petrov what he wanted.

I remembered what Ronan had said about Orlov's last words. Orlov had tried to tell him.

My thoughts wandered back to Ronan.

How long had it been since we'd last spoken in his apartment? I glanced at the window, but the curtain was closed, so it was impossible to tell what time of day it was.

Surely Ronan would notice I was missing. Or if not him, then Sage would. Either way, someone would come for me. But until then, I couldn't sit here and wait to be rescued. I needed to save myself.

I tried to speak again but the words were unintelligible.

"Get her a drink," Petrov ordered.

A moment later, a glass of water was shoved under my nose. My dignity wanted to resist, but I was desperately thirsty, and being weak wouldn't get me out of the situation. I let the man tilt my head back and pour water into my mouth, enjoying the cool flow over my parched throat. The water kept coming, and I spluttered and closed my mouth, turning away so I could cough.

Then, panting, I faced Petrov again.

"What, exactly, did I ruin?" I asked.

He scowled. "I had everything set up. It was going to play out exactly as I wanted. If only you hadn't gotten that whoreson King involved."

He struck me across the face.

My head jerked to the side, and it took a moment for my brain to process the pain. I tasted blood from biting my tongue.

Petrov bent so that his face was an inch from mine. "You should never have fucked that interfering bastard or helped him take what should be mine."

My instinct was to cower, but something told me he would enjoy that, so I straightened my spine. "Ronan King is three times the man you'll ever be."

Smack!

His other hand clipped me around the face, and spots flashed before my eyes. Still, I didn't flinch. "What do you want with Dad's company?"

Petrov gripped my chin, his features twisted with anger. "We started our companies at the same time, but Frank married your bitch of a mother, which gave him connections to Chicago's elite. He took the clients I should have had. He never deserved his empire. I was more experienced. Willing to do whatever it took. But he got in the way time and time again."

"But you made your fortune," I protested. "You're a very rich man. Why do you care?"

"I did." He sounded smug. "No thanks to him. Now I can take away everything he worked for."

"But he's dead!"

He squeezed my face tighter. "And I am not."

I whimpered. He was crazy. I knew he and Dad hadn't had the friendly rivalry Dad had liked to pretend they'd had, but I couldn't understand why Petrov harbored so much bitterness.

"What do you want with me?"

His smile turned wolfish. "You were Frank's beautiful daughter. His pride and joy, as much as the company ever was. Making you mine would have been perfect." He released me, and my jaw throbbed where his fingers had been. "The juicy cherry on the top of my dessert, as you Americans like to say."

I felt sick.

"I see you're beginning to understand." He nodded appreciatively. "Good. Unfortunately, I've had to resort to other ways of getting what I want." His eyes traveled over my face. "You'd better hope your lover is willing to trade you for Frank's company."

My breath caught. That's how he was going to play this? Use me as a bargaining chip?

"He won't do it." I had no idea if I was telling the truth. I had a feeling Ronan would do nearly anything to protect me—far more than Tom ever would.

Petrov nodded to one of the men, and the fabric hood was dropped over my head again. "If not, then you and I will have plenty of time to get to know each other." He chuckled darkly. "Enjoy your stay. I'll be back soon."

Chapter Thirty

Ronan

"I've got bad news," Joanna said the second I answered her call.

"Damn."

Joanna was unflappable, which meant that if she said something was bad, it really was.

I flashed the screen to Kade and Zeke, who'd joined me in my office, to show them who was on the line, then put it on speaker.

"What is it?" I half expected her to mention Tom, but what actually came out of her mouth was so much worse.

"Traffic cameras near Willow's apartment building recorded her being dragged into a white van this morning."

My heart *ka-thunked* painfully, and I tried to corral my thoughts enough to focus on the important details. "Was she conscious?"

"No, but she appeared unharmed. Potentially drugged."

"Fuck." I rubbed my eyelids as Kade and Zeke

conferred in low voices. "Have you got a registration number for the van?"

"We do. I'm sending it to you now. I've put out a BOLO and we'll see if we can follow the van using the traffic cams, but the area is notoriously patchy."

"Do what you can, and I'll get Zeke on it too."

She sighed. "Just tell him to keep it legal."

"I will." But we both knew Zeke would do what it took. "Keep me posted. Got to go."

I hung up, and my screen flashed with Joanna's message containing the vehicle registration number. I forwarded it to Zeke.

"Find this van. I don't care how." All I cared about was Willow being recovered safely from whatever hellhole she'd been taken to. I pictured her locked in a warehouse, battering on the doors, unable to escape, and closed my eyes. I couldn't afford to dwell on that or it would cripple me. "I also want locations and anything else you can find on Tom Lennox and Adrian Petrov."

If Tom had anything to do with his sister's disappearance, I'd make sure he saw the inside of a jail cell.

"Got it, boss." Zeke leaped to his feet and left.

"What can I do?" Kade asked, scowling like he wanted to bust some heads.

"Get us prepared for a tactical operation. If Zeke finds Willow, I'm not waiting for the police. We're going in."

His expression was grim but purposeful. He clapped my shoulder. "Don't worry. He'll find her, and we'll get her back. I may not always like Zeke, but he's the best at what he does."

"I know."

I just hoped the best was good enough. Whoever abducted Willow had several hours of head start. By now, she could have been anywhere.

Kade left the office, and I started making calls. While I

might not have been as skilled in combat as Kade or as technologically savvy as Zeke, I had a network that was the envy of half of Chicago, and plenty of people owed me favors.

It was time to call them in.

I was halfway through my contact list when my phone buzzed with a text. It was from Willow's number.

I clicked on the message, and it opened, a photograph filling the screen.

My stomach dropped.

In the image, Willow sat tied to a chair, her head lolling back, unconscious.

Text popped up beneath it.

Willow: *Sign over Lennox Securities to Adrian Petrov by midnight tonight or she's dead.*

I shot to my feet. "Zeke! Get in here!" Seconds later, my partner arrived at the door. I passed him the phone. "It's Petrov. He's got her."

He scanned the message. "If it's possible to get a location from the phone, I will."

He left the room, and I immediately called Joanna, then Kade, and filled them in.

Joanna mentioned the van had been caught on camera earlier today, and I passed the information along to Zeke. Then, I called my lawyer and had him draw up papers for the transfer of the company. If that's what it took to get Willow back, I'd do it, no questions asked, but we had a little time before midnight, so we might be able to find her first. Willow was smart. She was capable. I needed to trust that she could keep herself alive until we came for her.

Each minute seemed to last an eon.

Finally, Zeke barreled through the door. "King."

I glanced up and stopped short. His complexion was waxy. "What is it?"

"Two things." He thrust a laptop at me. "We got access

to Petrov's secure cloud server. There's some messed-up shit there. I'm not sure he'll actually let her go, even if you sign over the company."

I scanned the screen and practically stopped breathing.

Petrov's cloud database housed hundreds of photos of Willow, taken when she wasn't looking. Going for a walk. Standing beside her brother at events. Arm in arm with Sage. Lying on her bed, blissfully unaware she was being spied on.

"He's sick." I raised my gaze from the screen. "You said two things. What's the other?"

"I was able to trace the text to a city block near where the van was sighted. Petrov owns an apartment building there. My money says that's where she is."

I stared at him. "Why didn't you lead with that news?" The cell phone buzzed in my hand, and the detective's name appeared. I shoved it at Zeke. "Tell her about the apartment building. Pass on whatever she says. Kade and I need to go."

He nodded, his jaw tight. "Kade already has the location. I sent it to him on the way here."

"Good." I rushed out, encountering Kade by the door.

"The truck is geared up and ready to go," he reported. "I've got three men to accompany us—all fully armed."

I hoped it wouldn't come to a shootout, but I'd be glad for the backup if it did. "Let's take this motherfucker down."

———

WILLOW

When I woke again, I was still bound to the chair, but the face covering had been removed.

Petrov and I were alone. He stood several feet away, watching me.

I shook my head, hoping to clear it so I could think fast enough to outwit him. That was my best chance of getting out of here alive. I needed to play the game. Make him think he had me where he wanted me.

"I'm sorry," I murmured, lowering my eyes submissively. It took every ounce of my self-control not to glare at him or betray my distaste some other way. Petrov wasn't stupid, but hopefully he'd buy the act. "I shouldn't have been so rude earlier."

"No, you shouldn't have," he agreed gruffly. I wished I could see his face so I knew what he was thinking, but I didn't dare risk it. "But you can make it up to me now."

Icy fear licked up my spine. "How?"

"By opening your legs for me the same way you did for King." I could hear the smirk in his voice. "I said I'd return you to him if he met my terms, but I never said what condition you'd be in."

Oh, God.

My eyes flew to his.

"That's more like it." He smiled cruelly, obviously enjoying my terror.

He wrapped a fist in my hair and yanked my head back, exposing my neck. He cupped his other hand around my throat and squeezed. Spots danced in front of my eyes. I tried to shake him off, but without my arms and legs, there wasn't much I could do.

After a moment, he let go, and I hauled in a breath. My throat burned, and my lungs ached as I refilled them.

Petrov drew his suit jacket open, revealing a gun holstered at his hip. "I'm going to cut your ropes because it's more fun if you fight. If you try to run, I will shoot you. If you make it outside the apartment, my men are waiting. There is no escape. Do you understand?"

My mind whirled, sifting through ideas, trying to figure out how I could use this to my advantage.

I clearly couldn't leave through the main door if he had men stationed there as he'd said, so I'd have to try something else.

I tried to look over my shoulder, but although the curtain was now open, I couldn't turn well enough to look out and guess what time of day it was. Based on the natural light filtering into the room, it might have been mid- or late afternoon.

Surely someone had noticed I was missing by now. Perhaps they'd be looking for me. They might even have figured out who'd taken me. Whether or not escape was possible, I could buy them a little time. Maybe it would be enough to save myself.

"I understand," I told him, holding myself rigid as he drew a Swiss Army knife from his pocket and freed one of my feet, then the other. I scarcely dared to breathe as he sliced through the ropes tying my wrists together. It seemed like a distinct possibility that he might cut me at any moment, simply because the urge arose.

"Get on your knees."

I did as he said, all senses on high alert for any chink in his armor. I heard the click of each individual tooth of the zip as he unbuttoned his fly.

I recalled what Kade had said during our self-defense session about aiming for weak points.

Eyes, nose, throat, groin.

Perhaps I could debilitate him for a few minutes.

He started to slip his hand into his pants, and I lunged forward, ramming my fist into his testicles. He grunted in pain and doubled over, the knife dropping from his hand. I snatched it off the floor and thrust it up, catching him in the midsection. The metallic scent of blood hit my nostrils.

"Bitch," Petrov hissed.

I stumbled to my feet.

He gripped the knife and yanked it from his body.

I took off, racing toward the hallway that led deeper into the apartment and flinging the door shut behind me. The place was as big as Ronan's, with rooms everywhere, and the corridor never seemed to end. I raced into a storeroom, spying a window, but when I looked outside, there was no balcony, and we were a good twenty stories up. I wouldn't survive the jump.

I spun around and raced deeper into the apartment.

At the end of the corridor, two rooms split off. One was a bedroom. The other an office.

I hurried into the bedroom and looked frantically for a place to hide or something I could use as a weapon. I wouldn't fit under the bed, and there was a closet, but that was the first place he'd look.

I started to turn, thinking I'd try the office instead, but a bench beneath the window caught my eye. It was the sort of reading nook that came built into a room.

The type I'd had growing up.

A kernel of hope grew inside me. I ran to it, grabbed the cushion, and lifted. Sure enough, the bench was hollow. I climbed into the space within, drawing my knees to my chest so I fit, and softly closed it.

Darkness engulfed me.

I shut my eyes and fought to control my breathing. If I panted too heavily, he'd be able to follow the sound straight to my hiding place. It took a few moments, but I managed to slow my inhales and exhales into a quiet, regular rhythm.

I listened for the sound of men coming after me, but my blood pounded so loudly in my ears that it was impossible to hear anything else.

All I knew was that I was stuck, and unless someone noticed I was gone and somehow managed to track me down, I'd have to try to fight my way out.

Chapter Thirty-One

RONAN

The apartment building wasn't much different from my own. Doormen questioned our identities as we entered, and as soon as we got through them, I headed straight to the front desk and slammed my palms down on it. The woman seated behind leaped off her chair, her eyes widening as she spotted Kade hulking beside me clad in full tactical gear.

"Tell me where to find Adrian Petrov," I said.

"I-I can't do that," she stammered. "Privacy law—"

"I don't care." I cut her off. "Get your manager. *Now.*"

She took a lingering look at Kade, then went to the door behind the desk and knocked. "Sir, someone is asking for you."

A small, bespectacled man stepped out of the office. His upper lip curled at the sight of us. "Can I help you, gentlemen?"

The way he said gentlemen left no doubt he thought that was the last thing we were.

"We need Adrian Petrov's apartment number, right the

fuck now," Kade barked, and the little man flinched, his hand fluttering to his chest.

"I'm afraid we can't give out those details unless you have a warrant."

I grabbed my phone from my pocket and opened a photo of Willow, then shoved it over the desk toward him. "This woman has been abducted, and the police are on their way as we speak. I may not have a warrant, but you can bet your ass they do. If you've seen her, and you know what's good for you, you'll tell me where to find her."

The manager grew alarmed. Kade stepped forward, scowling darkly, and the guy held his hands up and stammered a number. He directed the receptionist to give us a key.

"Thank you," I said crisply. "Let's go. We don't have time to waste."

One of Kade's men split off to find the emergency exit for Petrov's apartment while the rest of us took the elevator to the floor directly below Petrov's apartment, then the stairs to the top.

Kade entered the corridor first, and I took the rear.

Only one man stood guard, although several chairs were clustered nearby, giving the impression he'd recently had company. He dropped to the ground when Kade Tased him. Sean grabbed flexicuffs and secured the man's wrists and ankles, then withdrew tape from one of his pockets and tore a strip off to cover the man's mouth. Meanwhile, Kade removed the key from the guard's pocket and unlocked the apartment door. We entered in single file.

The place was ostentatious as hell.

We shifted through the foyer and into the living area, where we encountered another guard. Sean subdued him while the rest of us moved on. We found another man apparently searching a bedroom off the hall. I grabbed him from behind and clamped a hand over his mouth while Kade tied and gagged him. Then we shut the door to muffle any sounds. Sean rejoined us and took up the rear as we made our way along the corridor.

I glanced down and froze, noticing blood spots on the floor. I touched Kade's shoulder, gesturing at them. His lips pressed together, but he didn't say anything.

We followed the droplets until we reached the end of the hall.

Kade and Sean took the room to the left while I, and two other men, took the room to the right.

Petrov stood in the center, his back to us.

The air must have shifted, or perhaps we made a noise, because he spun wildly and raised a gun.

"I'll shoot," he cried.

I should have focused on the gun, but a patch of red above his waistband caught my eye. The front of his shirt was drenched with blood.

Holy shit.

Had Willow done that?

"There are three of us and one of you," I reminded him.

Where is Willow?

The fact Petrov was here led me to believe Willow wasn't far away. Hopefully, the blood from the hall belonged only to him.

"I'm the one with a gun aimed at your head," Petrov growled. "I've shot men before, and I'm not afraid to shoot you. In fact, I'll take pleasure in it."

"Do it, then." I noticed one of my support crew shifting silently to the right, so I opened my arms and egged Petrov on. "I don't think you can, old man."

His hands shook. He lined up a shot, but just as he was about to squeeze the trigger, a figure dived at him, hitting him in the waist and taking him to the ground.

I saw a flash of blonde hair as the shot went wild, hitting the roof.

Willow.

Plaster crumbled to the floor. I jumped out of the way.

Petrov grabbed Willow's hair and wrenched, but before he could do anything else, my man on the right hit him with the butt of a handgun. He let go, dazed, and I took advantage of the chance to wrestle the gun from his hand. Then, between the group of us, we managed to subdue him.

Seconds later, Kade and Sean appeared in the doorway.

"Everyone okay?" Kade asked. "We heard a shot."

"Didn't hit anyone," I replied.

"Thank God. The apartment is clear," Kade said. "It was just the three men we've already dealt with, plus our buddy on the floor."

"You're sure?" I asked.

He nodded.

"Good." I turned to Willow, who was standing over Petrov, wide-eyed. "Sweetheart. You're okay."

She flung herself at me. "I'm so glad to see you."

I wrapped my arms around her and inhaled her delicious vanilla scent. She trembled in my embrace.

"You didn't give him the company, did you?" she asked.

"No, but I would have." I peppered kisses all over her face, relief sinking deep into my bones. "I love you," I told her. "I was scared out of my fucking mind when I realized you'd been taken."

She gazed up at me with those glorious green eyes and opened her mouth to speak, but I pressed a finger to her lips. The room had fallen quiet, and I noticed the others had cleared out, taking Petrov with them.

"I need to say this. When I got snappy about you packing a bag, it wasn't only because I wanted to protect you. I did—I think I'll always worry—but the only reason I want you to live with me is because I'm crazy about you. I know it's fast, and I'm happy to wait as long as you need, but I want you to know that how I feel has nothing to do with the danger you've been in. I can't completely separate love from my protective instincts, because they'll always go hand in hand. I love you, so I'm protective of you. That's just the way it is. But it doesn't mean I love you less."

"I love you too, Ronan." She went onto her toes and kissed me. "I was just overwhelmed by everything that had happened." She framed my face between her hands. "Thank you for coming. I might not be able to count on Tom to have my back—he's really shown where his loyalty lies—but I knew you'd be here, I trusted myself to survive until you came, and I'm sorry for pushing you away."

———

WILLOW

"I'm sorry for making you feel like you had to," he replied, dipping his head to kiss me again.

I smiled up at him. "How about we just agree to move forward from here. I'm Willow, you're Ronan, and we love each other. That's all there is to it." I glanced around. "After all, this isn't exactly the best place for a heart-to-heart."

His lips curved gently. "Sounds perfect." Then he shook his head. "When I saw you fly across the room, you nearly gave me a heart attack."

"I couldn't let him hurt you."

"Well, he won't be hurting anyone from now on. At least, not outside of prison."

"Thank God." I couldn't believe it was actually over.

When I'd heard Petrov enter the room, I'd worried the sound of my heart battering against my rib cage would alert him to my presence, but before he'd had a chance to find me, Ronan had charged in like that white knight he'd told me he's not.

Kade stuck his head in the door. "Police are here."

Ronan met my eyes. "We'll talk more later. You're fine to answer their questions? I can buy you a little time to recover if you need it."

"No, I'll be fine. The sooner it's over, the better. I want to erase this from my mind."

"Fair enough." He offered me a hand, and I took it.

Together, we walked out to the living area, where Ronan's companions had gathered Petrov and his three men. They sat in the corner, bound, gagged, and glaring.

Detective Lee looked rather amused.

"Good job subduing them," she said. "Please tell me you didn't enter illegally."

"We had a key," Ronan replied evasively.

"Uh-huh." She didn't press, and for that, I was grateful. She directed one of the officers to read the men their rights, then approached me. She moved slowly, as if worried she might scare me. Her caution wasn't necessary, but I appreciated the thought. "I'm pleased you're okay, Miss Lennox."

"Willow." Miss Lennox sounded so formal.

"Willow," she amended. "We'll need to have you looked over by a paramedic, but in the meantime, how do you feel about answering some questions?"

I glanced at Petrov, whose hateful stare burned into me, and bit my lip. "Could we do it somewhere else? I don't want to be in the same room as that man."

She nodded. "We'll take you to the station and have a paramedic meet us there. Does that sound all right to you?"

I nodded.

Ronan curled an arm around my shoulders. "I'm coming, too."

"I'd expect nothing less." The detective checked her watch. "We'll go in a couple of minutes. Hold on." She strode over to the officers and spoke softly enough that I couldn't hear.

Ronan's fingers intertwined with mine, and our palms pressed together.

I raised my eyes to his and smiled, then winced at a flash of pain on the side of my face.

"I'll be with you every step of the way," he promised.

I squeezed his hand. "I know."

Even if he wasn't, I could handle it on my own. If I could fight off my kidnapper, I could do anything.

I cuddled into his chest while he spoke to Kade about transportation. They agreed that the King's Security men would take their vehicle to the office after giving statements to the police while Ronan and Kade would accompany me to the station. I tried to argue that they didn't both need to come, but they wouldn't hear of anything else.

Secretly, I liked that. It was nice to have people I could trust at my back.

Detective Lee returned from speaking to the officers and cocked her head. "It seems Petrov has an injury he refuses to speak about. You wouldn't know anything about that, would you?"

My cheeks heated, and I glanced sideways, noting that both Ronan and Kade were giving me their undivided attention. Since the stab wound was obvious, I assumed she was asking what else I'd done to him. "I punched his balls."

A booming laugh ripped from Kade's throat. "Good girl." His tone was approving. "Maybe you didn't need us to rush to the rescue after all."

Detective Lee smirked. "I like you," she said. "Come

on. Let's go take your statement. I'm sure you want to get home so Ronan can check you over and reassure himself you're not injured."

———

Ronan

When we were finally free to leave the police station and Willow had called Sage to let her know everything was okay, I took her back to my penthouse and we showered together. I soaped up her body, my hands lingering over the bruises on her wrists and tracing the marks on her face. Nobody would have the opportunity to hurt her again. I'd make sure of it. I gestured for her to turn, and when she did, I dropped kisses across the tops of her shoulders and lathered shampoo in her hair.

"I love you," I murmured, knowing I'd say it whenever I could for the rest of our lives.

"Love you too."

Despite my protests, she gave my body the same gentle and thorough treatment I'd given hers. Then I turned off the shower and we dried. I handed her a plush robe since her clothing was no longer here and pulled on jeans and a T-shirt.

"Sit down," I said when we reached the living area. "I'm going to make us a drink."

I fixed her a cup of hot cocoa with plenty of sugar because her adrenaline was bound to crash soon, and then she'd be exhausted. I made myself a coffee and carried both drinks to the table by the sofa, where I sat and drew her into my arms.

"You were amazing today. It was so brave of you to take on Petrov."

Foolish, perhaps, but definitely brave.

She snuggled closer. "Thanks for having my back. Again."

"I always will." I kissed the top of her head. "Even if you don't need me to."

She tilted her face up and smiled. "I might not always need you, but I'll always want you, and that's much better."

I held her close. "No more worrying about whether this is real or not, all right?"

"It's real." She rested her head on my shoulder and pressed a kiss to the side of my neck. "No matter how fast or unconventional, we are one hundred percent the real deal."

I nuzzled her, loving the fact she smelled of my soap. She belonged here, and we belonged together. "Stay with me tonight?" I wasn't ready to let her go yet.

She smiled, and it was so beautiful that my insides flipped over. "I'll stay every night with you, if you'll have me. But I'm keeping an apartment too. At least until you've taken me on our first date."

I chuckled. "You got it, sweetheart."

It didn't matter when she moved in. All that mattered was the fact she loved me and one day, I'd make her my wife.

But for now, we could take it as slow as she wanted. We had all the time in the world.

Epilogue

WILLOW

"Happy birthday, sweetheart." Ronan undid the blindfold so slowly I had to resist the urge to tear it off myself.

He'd insisted on keeping the destination of our date secret. I'd tried to guess where we were going based on how many turns the car took, but I wouldn't have put it past him to have intentionally taken a detour just to put me off. Impatient as I may have been, there was something sweet about that.

The fabric fell away from my eyes, and I gasped, my hand flying to my mouth.

We were in Dad's office, and it was like we'd stepped back in time. It was decorated exactly as it had been when he was alive, down to the row of vintage guns. I scanned them, recognizing each model. Remington, Winchester, Savage, Smith & Wesson.

Tears burned in my eyes. Ronan had replicated my father's office, and I could have sworn I felt his presence in the room with us.

"I can't believe you did this," I whispered. "It's perfect. But how did you remember everything?"

He tapped his head. "Good memory. This place meant as much to me as it did to you."

I went to the desk and ran a finger along it. I hadn't been into Lennox Securities for months. I'd known Ronan was keeping it as a satellite office, but after everything that had happened, I'd preferred to stay away and focus my energy on King's Security's social media presence and my own art. I'd started a side business selling my paintings. It was slow, but it kept me happy.

"This is where we talked for more than a few minutes for the first time," he said, curving a palm around my face and brushing his lips over mine. "I found you in here, crying about some stupid boy who didn't deserve you."

I blushed and looked away. "You were sweet that night, I had the world's biggest crush on you for years after. No one else could possibly live up to it."

"Good." He smiled, and I ached to kiss him again, but he pulled back. "You should have high expectations."

My cheeks grew even hotter. I was sure I looked like a tomato. "Do you think he'd approve of us?"

"I'm certain of it." He winked at me. "Two of his favorite people, together and happy. In fact, that's why I wanted to do this here."

He sank to one knee and reached into his jacket pocket.

"Oh my God."

He popped the lid open. The elegant diamond inside nearly dazzled me. It was modern and sophisticated but not showy. In other words, perfect.

"Frank isn't here for me to officially ask for his blessing, so I did the best I could to have him with us in spirit."

I swiped at moisture in the corners of my eyes.

"I swear that as long as I live, nobody will ever love you as much as I do. I will cherish you every day, protect you with my every breath, and adore you with my whole soul. Will you marry me?"

"Yes," I whispered, pressing my fingers to my mouth.

Nearly ten years ago, in this very room, I'd decided that Ronan King was the ideal man. Now, I knew him so much better. He wasn't some idealized hero on a pedestal. He was real and flawed, but he was mine. Perhaps Tom, my only remaining family, would never be supportive, but I knew that somewhere, Dad was looking down on us, and he approved.

"For richer or poorer, bad times and good, I'll be at your side."

One corner of his mouth hitched up. "I think you skipped ahead to the vows." His expression softened. "I'll be at yours too, Willow. Always."

A single beam of light shone through the window and illuminated the photograph on my father's desk. One of him with his arm around me as I smiled at the camera.

My heart leaped, and I met Ronan's eyes. It was almost as though Dad were giving his support.

Ronan nodded to show he'd seen it too, then offered me the ring. I slipped it onto my finger. He grabbed me around the waist and spun me. I laughed, feeling giddier than I could ever remember.

Nothing was perfect, but my twenty-sixth birthday came pretty damn close.

THE END

Fighter's Heart Excerpt

Lena

Eight words. That's all it takes to ruin my day.

"LaFontaine, I have a special assignment for you."

I recognize the voice without looking up from my desk. It's my prick of a boss, Adrian, and anything he's terming a "special assignment" will inevitably be a nightmare. That's all I get these days. The unfixable cases. The spoiled, self-entitled sports stars who screw up so badly, no one else wants them.

God, one massive win and I become the go-to public relations girl for the biggest jerks-with-abs in Vegas. Why can't I, just once, get a client who's a marginalized feminist with a cause? Sighing, I raise my head and meet Adrian's beady little eyes. This douchebag has my career in his hands, and he knows it.

"What's the case?"

His thin lips curl in a self-satisfied smile. It doesn't escape my notice that he's yet to close the door, which makes me wonder if he's keeping it open as an escape route.

"Jase Rawlins."

Oh. Hell. No.

"Nuh-uh," I say. "No freaking way."

Jase "The Wrangler" Rawlins is one of the bad boys of MMA. I don't even have to ask why he needs our services. Anyone who pays attention to the sports industry knows his ex-girlfriend has come forward with allegations of domestic abuse. I've seen photos of her bruised cheek and read the story in popular magazines. The guy is violent. But I suppose I shouldn't expect any different from a cage fighter.

I know the type. I've *dated* the type.

"There's no way I'm working with that asshole. Absolutely not. Find someone else. I'm not aiding and abetting a jackass who thinks he can get away with hitting women."

The door opens wider, and Jase Rawlins himself steps into my small, airy office, his gaze immediately drawn to the view out the window, which looks over the business district. I know him on sight, and I'm not even sorry he overheard my comment. He deserves all the condemnation he gets, and more. Fuck him.

Adrian's brows draw together, as if he didn't expect me to argue. "Everything is organized, Lena. The papers are signed. It's a done deal."

My teeth scrape together loud enough I'm surprised no one else hears them. I meet Jase's eyes, and a jolt runs through me. They're a strange color. Dark gray, or maybe green, it's hard to tell, and fringed with the thickest lashes I've ever seen. Pretty eyes. Out of place on a man known for choking his opponents into submission. He has high, arrogant cheekbones and plush lips, although the upper one is marred by a thin scar.

This is a face a woman could study forever—if she wasn't too caught up in his body. Because holy shit, he has a *body*. Broad shoulders, tapered hips, and strong legs with muscled calves showing beneath his shorts. Unfortunately, however panty-meltingly hot he is, he's also a brute, and I'm done with men like him. If I have anything to say about it, I'm not touching another MMA superstar—not with a ten-foot pole.

Time to shut this shit down.

"I'm *not* working with you," I tell him, and watch for a change in his expression, but his only reaction is a quick flick of his eyes to the right, where a man in an expensive suit has followed him into my office. "This is *not* a happening thing." I aim this comment at the suit, and he glowers. I don't care. There are some jobs even I won't take, and Adrian wants me to cross a moral line I'm not prepared to.

"Lena," Adrian says in a cautioning tone. "Hold on a moment."

Crossing my arms over my chest, I stare at him, wondering how far he's prepared to push. Considering Jase Rawlins is worth seven or eight figures, I'd hazard a guess that dollar signs are flashing in Adrian's eyes. Too bad. I don't operate that way. Money isn't my driver, and he knows it. So what approach will he take?

———

Jase

Sometimes, I wish it was legal to put someone in a chokehold outside of the cage. Like this uppity image specialist, for instance. Yeah, she may look like a school-boy's wet dream in an ass-hugging pencil skirt and V-necked blouse, but it's obvious from the second she opens her mouth that she's already judged me and found me wanting. Nothing I'm not used to, but it still stings.

Maybe it's the fact my dick has some really great ideas about what he'd like to do with those gorgeous red lips, which are currently set in a sulky pout, or maybe it's her instant dismissal, but I want to rile her. To ruffle up her silky feathers and find out just how mouthy she can get.

I step forward before her boss can intervene, and raise a hand. As expected, everyone falls silent, which only seems to piss the redhead off more. Fuck, we haven't even gotten as far as exchanging names before she's mentally convicted me. That's the shitty part of being in the public spotlight. Everyone thinks they know me. They believe every stupid lie anyone tells.

Well, guess what? This girl doesn't know a goddamn thing.

"Calm down, cutie pie." I love it when her eyes chill to an icy blue, silently threatening to cut my balls off. Yeah, I knew she'd hate the pet name. Considering what she thinks of me, I don't give a crap. "Turns out, I don't want to work with you either." I raise a brow at Nick, my manager, and ask, "Is this really the best you could do?"

The redhead gasps, and I want to check whether she's crossed her arms tighter over her chest, plumping her little tits up, but I resist the urge to look.

"We can go somewhere else," Nick says. "I was told these guys are the best for miracles, but I'm sure we can find someone else just as good."

"Now, wait a minute," the stuffed shirt interjects. I wasn't listening when he introduced himself so I didn't catch his name. "Lena is the best there is. You won't find anyone else."

Finally, I succumb to the desire to glance at her and see how she's taking this. I catch the tail end of an eye-roll, and it makes me soften toward her a little. She's not drinking up the flattery the way some might.

Lena. I try her name out. It suits her. Pretty, bordering on pretentious but not overstepping the mark.

"Whatever puppy dog stunts *Lena*"—I emphasize her

name now that I know it—"wants to pull, they aren't going to do jack." I address Nick. "I still don't get why we're here. Give it a couple of days; Erin will decide she doesn't want to act on her threats, and the hubbub will die down."

Lena's face twists into a sneer. "Die down?" she demands. "The only way this shit-nado is dying down is if someone gets proactive about putting out your fires, and fast. Also, have a little respect for your girlfriend."

"*Ex*-girlfriend."

"Whatever." She says it like the "ex" part doesn't matter. As if Erin and I didn't break up more than two months ago now. "She's not some problem that will disappear if you ignore her. Domestic violence is a serious crime, and you can't just hand-wave it away." Her nose crinkles like she smells something bad. "It disgusts me that you're callous enough to think otherwise."

Callous? Me?

I count to five in my head and remind myself she doesn't know me. Her perception of me is based on what she's seen in the news, and I have to admit, it's damning. It also isn't true, but I don't bother saying that because this woman isn't going to believe me. Stuffing my hands in my pockets, I decide the best way to deal with her is to call her bluff.

"Okay, so you say the problem isn't going away on its own. What did you have in mind to fix it?"

"I... I..." She flounders, and I can't stop the smile that tugs at my lips. She's all bluster and no bite.

"That's what I thought." I turn to leave, but her smarmy boss lays a hand on my arm. When I stare at it, he snaps it back like he's been stung, his cheeks going pale. This guy is even worse than Lena. At least she has the balls to say what she thinks to my face. He's the type who'll pretend to be on my side, but all the while he's secretly fucking terrified of me.

"Wait, wait, wait," he says. "Give me two minutes to speak to Lena in private and talk her around. I promise you won't regret it."

Lena looks like she wants to bash him over the head with a paperweight, and I don't blame her. He's a condescending little shit. "Adrian—" she says.

"My office." He snaps his fingers, like he's ordering a dog to heel. "Now."

They leave, her trailing behind, practically dragging her feet, and Nick gives a low laugh. "Good old Jase. Always charming the ladies."

I jerk a thumb at the door. "Can we go? I've had enough of this."

He sighs, his expression regretful. "I wish we could, but what she said is true. Whether you want to believe it or not, this situation has the potential to derail your career."

"How can it, when I have the championship bout so soon? I'll blow Karson out of the water, and everything will be fine."

Nick ums and ahs. "That's if you don't get arrested before the fight."

"Pfft." I shake my head. "Not gonna happen. Erin is full of hot air."

"She also has a taste for the spotlight, and she'll keep spouting this bullshit as long as the cameras are rolling." Damn, he's right, and he must sense he has the winning hand because he powers on. "Not to mention, you promised Seth you'd take this seriously and do whatever you could not to tarnish the reputation of Crown MMA gym."

Ouch. Low blow. Nick knows I'd go to war for Seth if he asked. My trainer gave me everything. He had faith in me, took a chance on me, and he had no way of knowing I'd pan out to be a good investment. I was just a kid from a poor neighborhood with a mother of a chip on my shoulder and a willingness to shed blood to escape.

"Fine," I concede, not surprising either of us. "I'll hear them out."

But I have a bad feeling about this, and my gut doesn't often lie to me.

Also By Alexa Rivers

Crown MMA Romance

Fighter's Heart

Fighter's Best Friend

Fighter's Secret

Fighter's Second Chance

Crown MMA Romance: The Outsiders

Fighter's Frenemy

Fighter's Fake Out

Fighter's Mercy

Fighter's Forever

King's Security

The King

The Veteran

Acknowledgments

This book was far from a solo effort. When I started writing it, I'd been playing around with the idea for ages. I've always loved romantic suspense, especially with bodyguards, and I was excited to write my own.

But it was *hard*. I mean, writing a book is never the easiest thing in the world, but sometimes it flows like magic, and in general, I don't get massively stuck. I'd written around 20 books when I stepped up to the plate to write *The King*, so I had a process and I was used to it working. Sure, some stories require more finessing than others, but getting the bare bones out has never been as much of a struggle as it was for this book. In fact, I got a few thousand words in and had to stop and take a few weeks writing short stories before I could get re-motivated and come back to it.

Because this book didn't come easily, I'm incredibly grateful to everyone who helped me get it into the world. In particular, Kate and Caroline, who read the earlier drafts and provided thoughtful feedback on the characters, the plot, and the fact I'd apparently repeated the same words and phrases a lot. Without you, this story wouldn't be what it is. Thank you from the bottom of my heart.

I'd also like to thank Maria, who designed a cover that's so on-point for what I wanted, and help guide my decision-making since I was stepping into a new subgenre of romance. You are amazing and I'm so glad to have you on my team.

Thank you to my husband, who had to listen to me

bemoan the fact I had writer's block for the first time in my life, and who has given me his complete support each and every day. Thank you to my friends and family. I really appreciate your goodwill and support.

Lastly, thank you to you, for taking a chance on a book that's a bit different from my usual ones. I hope you'll love the King's Security series because I plan for there to be many more to come!